THE FAELIN CHRONICLES

the Call of Eirian

C. AUBREY HALL

BOOK TWO

MARSHALL CAVENDISH

Website: www.marshallcavendish.us/kids

This book is a work of fiction. Names, characters, places, and incidents are products of the author's imagination and are used fictitiously. Any resemblance to actual events or locales or persons, living or dead, is entirely coincidental.

Other Marshall Cavendish Offices:
Marshall Cavendish International (Asia) Private Limited, 1 New Industrial Road, Singapore 536196 • Marshall Cavendish International (Thailand) Co Ltd. 253 Asoke, 12th Flr, Sukhumvit 21 Road, Klongtoey Nua, Wattana, Bangkok 10110, Thailand • Marshall Cavendish (Malaysia) Sdn Bhd, Times Subang, Lot 46, Subang Hi-Tech Industrial Park, Batu Tiga, 40000 Shah Alam, Selangor Darul Ehsan, Malaysia

Marshall Cavendish is a trademark of Times Publishing Limited

Library of Congress Cataloging-in-Publication Data
Hall, C. Aubrey.
The call of Eirian / C. Aubrey Hall. — 1st ed.
p. cm. — (The Faelin chronicles ; bk. 2)
Summary: Thirteen-year-old half-human Diello and his twin sister, Cynthe, embark on a perilous journey seeking the fabled land of the Fae, their mother's homeland, but Diello's budding magical abilities sometimes lead them astray.
ISBN 978-0-7614-6262-0 (hardcover) — ISBN 978-0-7614-6263-7 (ebook)
[1. Orphans—Fiction. 2. Twins—Fiction. 3. Brothers and sisters—Fiction. 4. Fantasy.] I. Title.
PZ7.H141137Cal 2012   [Fic]—dc23   2011042178

Book design by Alex Ferrari
Map by Megan McNinch
Editor: Robin Benjamin

Printed in China (E)
First edition
10 9 8 7 6 5 4 3 2 1
mc Marshall Cavendish

Cast of Characters

FAE

Clevn:
mage-chancellor of the Fae, Sheirae's brother, commander of wind and lightning

Dhrui:
Marshana's attendant

Ffoyd:
an aide to General Rhodri

Iones:
Owain's servant

Lwyneth:
mother to Diello and Cynthe (deceased)

Marshana:
a healer

Ninka:
a nursemaid who takes care of Amalina

Owain:
Diello's and Cynthe's uncle, Lwyneth's brother

Penrith:
Queen Sheirae's heir, Owain's daughter

General Rhodri:
commander of the Fae army

Sheirae:
queen of the Fae

FAELIN

Amalina:
younger sister to Diello and Cynthe

Cynthe:
Diello's twin sister, gifted magically

Diello:
a Faelin boy with crystal bones and other magic powers

GOBLINS

Brezog:
ruler of all the goblins

Scree:
a goblin-boy, befriended by Diello and Cynthe

HUMANS

Lord Malques:
the baron of Wodesley Castle

Stephel:
father to Diello and Cynthe (deceased),
a former Carnethie Knight

TESCORSIANS

Uruoc:
king of the eagle-folk

WOLVES

Canthroy:
a manservant now cursed to live as a wolf

Chorl:
a samal wolf, presently in service to Queen Sheirae

Shalla:
Vassou's mother (deceased), formerly in service to Lwyneth

Vassou:
a talking samal wolf pup

ANCESTORS, DEITIES, AND ORACLES

Afon Heyrn:
the Fae religious council

Agish:
a goblin deity

Ancient Harmonies:
elemental spirits

Ercoth:
father of Brezog

The Guardian:
the supreme Fae deity

The Knower:
an ancient oracle, appearing in tree form

Mobidryn:
the greatest warrior in Fae history, worshipped by Fae soldiers

Watchers:
twelve spirits that guard sacred Fae relics in the Cave of Mysteries

chapter one

diello clutched the heavy rucksack tighter to his chest and rounded a street corner, barely eluding the thick, grasping fingers of the man chasing him.

"You dratted thief!" the man shouted, making another lunge for Diello, who skipped out of reach. The man lost his footing in the mud, took a big step, and fell with a splat.

Awed by the sight of this well-dressed merchant now wallowing like a pig, Diello fought back a grin. It was supposed to be a quick and easy raid. With most of the townsfolk gathered by the road to watch the king's army ride by, the opportunity to steal food was too tempting to pass up. He hadn't expected this man to still be in his shop. And he hadn't expected a man this old and fat to give chase.

Beside Diello, his friend Scree danced a little jig and laughed gleefully.

"Shut up!" Diello warned him. Tugging at Scree's ragged sleeve, Diello spun him around and gave him a push while glancing over his shoulder.

It had been a mistake to laugh. The merchant, swearing

oaths, was levering himself out of the mud puddle. As he stood up, dripping, he roared, "I'll see you branded for this!"

Diello's twin sister, Cynthe, came running into sight behind the merchant and skidded to a stop. She carried a bundle of stolen clothing in her arms. Their wolf pup, Vassou, had a pair of mittens in his mouth. Cynthe smirked at Diello. He shot her a look of warning that she didn't need. Whirling around, she and Vassou fled without the merchant ever noticing them.

Scree snickered, clapping his hands over his mouth.

"Thieves!" the merchant was shouting. "Stop them! *Stop them!*"

Some of the townspeople at the far end of the street looked his way.

A young man in a blue tunic pointed at the boys. "Hey! That's a goblin." He and three of his friends came running. "Get 'em!"

Diello tightened his arms around the rucksack and looked for a way to escape. This section of street ran straight and narrow, bordered by rows of houses jammed together. The soaked merchant, shaking his fists, was advancing from one direction. Blue Tunic and his friends were coming from the other. It was impossible to reach the slim alley that Cynthe and Vassou had taken. There was no other way out.

Scree, who was half-goblin, shrank closer to Diello. "They will hurt us," he whispered. "They will hurt us very much. I do not want to be branded. I do not want to be beaten. If we give back the food—"

"Too late," Diello said, still eyeing the houses. "They'll have us for thievery either way."

Scree fumbled with his pouch's drawstring. "Then let us eat what we have stolen. Now."

Diello saw one of the doors swing open. A girl in a work-stained apron came out, setting down two pails—one holding sand and one sloshing water. Pulling out a scrub brush, she knelt and started scouring the stone step.

Diello tapped Scree's bony shoulder. "You follow me, no matter what. And don't you dare drop that pouch."

"But—"

"Come on!"

Diello ran for the open door. Tucking the rucksack in the crook of his arm, he jumped the step in one bound. Men were shouting. The startled maid threw her brush at Diello, thumping him on the head, then dashed her pail of water over Scree.

The goblin-boy wailed in shock. Sputtering, he staggered backward. The maid hit him with her empty bucket, knocking him to his knees.

"Sega, beware!" she shouted. She grabbed Scree by the arm. "I've caught a thief!"

Diello picked up the brush and threw it back at her, hitting her in the hip as Scree twisted in her grasp and bit her hand. She yelped, and Scree darted inside the house with Diello just as a large woman came out of the shadows.

"Scat!" she said, swinging a broom at them.

Diello ducked, but Scree was knocked off his feet. He crashed into a stool and turned over a table. The woman went after Scree, swatting him again and again with her broom while he scrambled to escape her.

Diello made his way through the dimly lit interior and found the cooking room at the back of the house. Delectable smells were wafting up from a bubbling cauldron of stew. Five fresh loaves of bread stood cooling on a well-scrubbed table, along with a meat pie.

He didn't hesitate. With the sounds of men's voices now in the other room, along with Scree's yelps and the women's shouts, Diello whisked a cloth off a hook and spread it over the table, tossing the warm loaves and the meat pie into the center before grabbing the corners of the cloth and twisting them into a knot. He gave the stew a regretful look and shouldered his way through the back door. He nearly tripped over a cat that was trying to get in, but kept his footing and raced out. All the while, his mind was buzzing with worry about Scree and how to rescue him.

"I'm coming!" Scree called. "I'm getting away from them. Do not fear for me!"

Diello smiled, but then he heard the merchant yell, "Got you!"

There was an awful crash and a terrible amount of swearing.

"My stew! Oh, Master Goodly, my stew!"

This time, Diello didn't dare look back. He just kept running down the alley with his loot and tried to think of where they'd gone wrong. If the merchant hadn't turned around just as Diello reached for that ham . . . Well, it was no good dwelling on old mistakes. He had to get back to camp with the food. Then he'd talk to the others about how to save Scree before he was branded with a T for thief.

My fault, Diello thought miserably. *I got Scree into this.*

At the end of the alley, he shot out into the main road and was almost trampled by an enormous war steed.

Breathless at the near miss, Diello pressed against a wall and watched the army go by. Drums were pounding beneath the blaring trumpets. The crowd kept cheering as company after company of mounted Shieldsmen rode by under the king's yellow-and-black banner. This was no time to pause and gawk, but Diello found himself unable to stop watching. They were not riding into combat—probably just shifting from one garrison to another—but these men were *real* warriors. The sun glinted off their steel helmets, and the jingling of their spurs, bridle bits, and saddle trophy bells rang out. Their massive horses wore long saddle cloths with strips of metal-studded leather to protect them in battle. The very ground seemed to shake from their progress, and it was impossible to count how many there were.

The last row of Shieldsmen went riding by. Behind them rolled the supply wagons, piled high with barrels and wooden chests, laboring through the churned mud of the roadway. Behind the wagons came the vanguard, the auxiliary foot soldiers and archers marching along, muddy to the knees, their faces splattered with grime.

Once, Diello had dreamed of joining their ranks, fighting under the king's banner, seeing the world. Now, he had other plans, and the main one at the moment was getting out of this town with the food he'd stolen. Scree sidled up next to him, startling Diello.

"By the Ancient Harmonies, how did you get away from them?"

Scree's brown-mottled face was swollen around one eye, and the corner of his mouth looked puffy and bruised. He was still clutching the bulging pouch that was his responsibility. He nodded, panting for breath. "I was clever. Very clever. You will be proud of me when you know everything that I—"

"Later," Diello said, patting his arm. Glancing around, he led Scree across the road through the slowly moving wagons. The footing was slippery, and Diello could feel the cold mud oozing through the holes in his moccasins, but they made it, ignoring the irate shouts of the drivers.

One swung his long whip, popping it right over Diello's head. "Fool! You'll get yourself run over, crossing the road among us."

Diello didn't answer. He flung himself down the riverbank on the opposite side of the road.

Weeds and rushes grew tall at the water's edge, providing good cover. Crouching low, Diello crept into them, taking his time. No matter how urgently he yearned to be across the river and safely in the woods, he didn't want the swaying weeds to give him away. He and Scree had accomplished the hardest part. Now, with the army between them and their pursuers, all they had to do was slip far enough downriver to cross the water without being seen.

I'll bet Cynthe's already made it across, he thought.

With Scree right behind him, Diello crawled beneath an old stone and timber bridge. There, they paused to catch their breath and share smiles of relief. Diello tied the cloth bundle more securely. He'd squeezed at least one of the loaves rather flat, and the fragrance of fresh bread tempted him to bite into the damaged one. He'd eaten nothing today, and last night's supper had been one scrawny rabbit roasted on the fire and shared by him, Cynthe, Scree, and Vassou.

I could eat the whole loaf and who would know? Only Scree, and Scree wouldn't betray him, but Diello couldn't do it. Stealing from strangers was bad enough. He wasn't going to start stealing from his friends, too.

Last week's frost had killed the remaining bushberries, leaving the few last clusters of fruit to hang withered and bitter on the vine. Game was scarce in this shire. There were too many towns, too many cultivated fields. The woods were over-hunted. Three times this week they'd stopped their journey to hunt, trap, and gather—without much luck.

Desperation had driven them into this town. The place looked prosperous, and it was less risky than sneaking into a farmstead, but Diello hated stealing. He was ashamed to think he was getting better at it. Still, the risks were enormous, and today had nearly proven disastrous.

There was so little time left now.

Winter was coming. Diello could smell it on the breeze, could see it in the shorter days ahead. Shivering through chilly nights around the dying campfire embers, with everyone huddled together for warmth . . . waking up at dawn with frost on his hair and clothes . . . Diello dreaded the turning season. Last winter, he and Cynthe were secure on the home farmstead, preparations for the family's survival completed to Pa's satisfaction, the cottage and barn secure against storm and snow. Now Diello and his twin were orphans and homeless, owning little save the rags on their backs, and they and their companions were unsure whether they would reach the end of their journey before the snows set in.

If we don't reach Embarthi before the first snowfall, we'll die.

He shook away the bleak thought. He was determined to reach the fabled realm of the Fae, their mother's homeland. Uncle Owain would take them in, once they found him. And with his help, they would find their little sister, Amalina, who'd been taken from them. Diello believed that her abductor was Clevn, the Fae mage-chancellor, who'd been an enemy of Diello's mother. *My enemy now.*

"Diello," Scree whispered, crouching closer beside him under the bridge. Overhead, more wagons and riders were crossing, and the creak of axles and plodding hooves of the horses echoed across the water. Scree tapped Diello's arm for his attention. "Here is stew."

"What?"

Scree dipped into his pocket and brought out a handful of meat, taties, and chunks of parsnip, the gravy dripping through his fingers. "Stew," he said, holding it out to Diello. "For eating. I am hungry, and I am certain you are hungry. Need to eat and not be weak."

Paying no heed to Scree's grubby hand, Diello cupped his palms together and took the offering. While Scree dipped into his pocket for his own share, Diello crammed the food into his mouth. The gravy dripped down his wrists, and he licked it off, wishing there were more. Finishing quickly,

Scree turned his pocket inside out and sucked at the gravy-soaked cloth before staring at Diello's bundle. His thin, pointed nose quivered.

"Is there bread for us?" he asked wistfully.

"No," Diello said firmly, shoving back temptation. "We must make that last, if we can. We've lost too many days around here already. We need to use our travel rations wisely."

"Better maybe to eat it now than get it wet."

Not bothering to answer, Diello tied the bundle of bread and meat pie to the strap of his rucksack, and then slipped it over his shoulder to leave his arms and legs free. "Ready?" he asked.

Scree nodded, and Diello climbed up into the bridge-work overhead. Although the bridge was supported on stone pylons, it was braced underneath with wooden trusses. Massive beams spanned the distance from one pylon to the next, with numerous crosspieces holding up the floor. The bridge featured a narrow stone apron on either side, hanging below the base of its railings, concealing most of the bracing. The apron could also conceal a boy, if he stayed flat atop a support beam and didn't let an arm or leg dangle. It was simple enough for Diello to pull himself onto one of the beams, moving slowly to avoid splinters, and stretch out full length on his stomach. Trouble was, the rucksack now proved to be awkward and bulky, making it almost impossible to crawl along.

Diello balanced his bundles in front of him. He kept one hand on them. To have them topple into the river below would be heartbreaking. It was difficult to squirm forward, push the bundles ahead of him, and then go forward again. His shoulders and arms were aching from the effort. Sweat dripped from his hairline and ran, stinging, into his eyes.

Squirm like a worm, he told himself. *Keep crawling, and don't think about anything else.*

It was a narrow river, and the bridge across it wasn't all that long, but what had been a quick crossing shortly after dawn this morning was slow and cumbersome this afternoon. Diello reached the first of the two pylons planted in the middle of the water. Where the beam topped the pylon, there was no headroom at all. His hair was brushing the bridge floor, and when someone walked across it, whistling, he almost jumped out of his skin.

Flushed and breathless, Diello lay there, listening, as the footsteps and jaunty tune faded into the distance. He slipped the rucksack over his shoulder and swung his body off the beam, catching his toe on a brace board and squeezing past the mighty crosspiece. His sweaty hands slipped a little on the weathered board, and his balance was hampered by the weight of the food, but then he was past and could flatten himself atop the support timber once more. He rested a little before crawling forward, pushing the bundles ahead of him.

The second pylon was in need of repair. Some of the stones on the inside had crumbled away, leaving useful niches for fingers and toes. Diello clambered through the bracing, sliding on his back at one point and nearly losing the rucksack. He grabbed it just in time, sweating and breathing hard. Then he pressed on. There was only one section left. Behind him, he could hear Scree's ragged breathing, but neither of them spoke.

Reaching the end of the bridge at last, Diello was wedging the rucksack safely into a corner brace and preparing to swing himself down to the bank when he heard a muffled cry, followed by a splash. Twisting around, Diello saw a few square stones falling off the damaged pylon into the river. Scree—arms flailing, mouth stretched wide in a silent cry— fell with them.

"No!" Diello shouted.

Scree hit the water, floundering in a panic before the river closed over his head. An instant later, he bobbed to the surface, waving one thin arm desperately, then he went limp and sank out of sight.

Diello scrambled over the beam, trying to gauge the speed of the current to see where Scree might come to the surface again.

But there was no sign of the goblin-boy at all.

chapter two

diello jumped off the bridge beam onto the muddy bank and slid into icy water. Swimming in his clothes was much harder than he expected, but it was too late now. Kicking strongly, he swam away from the bank until he could let the current catch him and carry him downstream.

Every few strokes, he raised his head in hopes of seeing Scree. This wasn't a fast-moving river, but Scree had looked unconscious the last time he went under.

Besides being numbingly cold, the water was filthy. It smelled like a swamp, and it was impossible to see anything below the murky surface.

Diello was a good swimmer, but the cold and the weight of his clothes quickly sapped his strength. He was afraid to call out Scree's name.

A faint shout came from behind him. Thinking he'd passed Scree, Diello turned around, treading water against the current. Instead of Scree, he saw Blue Tunic and some of the other villagers standing on the bridge. They were gesturing at him and shouting. Ignoring them, Diello stretched out his tired arms and swam on.

Ahead, the river took a sharp bend. The angle created a

backwater, and there—amid the sticks and floating trash—bobbed a small body.

"Scree," Diello whispered.

He kicked hard as he angled toward the bank. The current ran stronger here, foaming white as it rushed around the bend. Near the bank, he caught a knobby tree root and clung fast, panting, before he worked his way to the quiet, still pool where Scree floated.

Gripping the goblin-boy's tattered tunic, Diello heaved him up onto the bank, rolling him onto his back.

There was an ugly gash on Scree's forehead. His mottled face looked gray and pinched. He didn't open his eyes. Diello pushed on Scree's bony chest and abdomen, trying to force out the water.

"Come on," Diello muttered, teeth chattering. "Come *on*!"

Pa had taught him and Cynthe how to swim in the creek. Thinking of his father's instructions now, Diello dragged Scree over to a fallen log. Lifting the unconscious boy, Diello draped him, stomach down, over the log before thumping him between the shoulders. Nothing happened. Diello pounded on him again. Scree coughed. A gush of water spewed from his mouth, and he whimpered.

"Stop," Scree pleaded weakly. "I am hurting from this."

Gently Diello turned him right side up. Scree's eyes were closed, and he was gasping for air, but at least he was breathing. He opened his mouth in a wail that Diello swiftly muffled by clapping a hand over his mouth.

"Hush. You'll be all right, but don't make any noise."

"I am hurting," Scree said, coughing again.

Diello sat back on his heels and looked around. The weeds on this bank grew shorter than upstream. Although there were several trees, many of them were losing their leaves, providing thin cover. Blue Tunic had probably seen them climb out. The villagers would be coming.

Diello felt a familiar, clammy sensation come over him. This was no time for Sight! He tried to resist, but the sky, sun, and river vanished, leaving him in a place of gray mist. As he stared, the mist parted, revealing a swamp of brackish water and tall, skeletal trees hung with moss. He heard drums thumping and saw a shallow skiff being rowed across the dark-green water. Standing in the prow was the gorgoblin Brezog—the monster who had slain Diello's parents. Holding his skull-mace in the crook of his arm, the gorlord suddenly ordered his rowers to halt. He turned in Diello's direction. Then, with dreamlike speed, Brezog was coming at Diello. He leaped from the boat and crossed the water as though flying over its surface. His red eyes loomed larger and larger. Goblin-fire blazed from his talons as he reached out . . .

Shuddering, Diello flung off the vision and twisted away from Scree. He crouched low, doubling over and clutching his head. He felt sick to his stomach, freezing and yet hot.

For weeks, ever since they left the family farmstead near Wodesley, Brezog had been on their trail. The gorlord had destroyed their home in his search for the magical sword Eirian, a weapon of legendary powers that had been hidden—and guarded—by their Fae mother and human father for years. Although Diello and Cynthe still didn't know what their parents had been doing with Eirian, they had managed to flee with it. Now, they were trying to return it to its rightful place in Embarthi. At first, they thought they'd eluded Brezog, but within a matter of days, he'd come close to catching them again. That's because Cynthe and Diello had been practicing their flying. Well, not so much flying as rising into the air and trying to descend without falling. As Faelin children—mixed blood—they weren't supposed to have such powers, but they were discovering more Gifts all the time.

Their use of magic had apparently led Brezog to them, and the only way they'd escaped was by hiding beneath one of Vassou's *cymunffyl* spells that made them invisible. Now they were extra careful, constantly alert, always aware that at any moment Brezog might find them. Diello and Cynthe had taken to splitting up whenever they were doing something risky, like trying to steal supplies. The sword was designed to come apart, and Diello carried the hilt with him at all times while Cynthe was responsible for the blade. That way, if one of them was captured, the entire sword wouldn't fall into the enemy's hands.

Diello didn't know why Sight had given him a vision here, or what it meant. He didn't care. If Brezog caught them before they crossed the Embarthi border into safety, he would kill them and Eirian would be his. *That isn't going to happen*, Diello assured himself. *It's just a vision, coming to me because I'm worried and tired. It's not a foretelling of the future.*

Just the thought made Diello shudder again.

Sighing, he rubbed his face. He hated having Sight. Of all the possible Gifts that he could have manifested, it had to be the worst. Still, he wasn't about to disregard its warning.

"Can you move?" he asked Scree. "We mustn't stay here."

Scree grimaced, his eyes still closed. Diello checked his belt to make sure he had his knife and the pouch containing Eirian's hilt. Fortunately it didn't weigh as much as a normal sword hilt, or it would have anchored him to the bottom of the river.

Slinging his dripping hair away from his eyes, Diello stripped off his tunic to wring it dry and pulled it on again. He gave Scree a shake.

"You can't sleep. We have to go."

Scree didn't rouse.

Worried, Diello put his lips to Scree's grubby ear. "Brezog," he murmured.

The dreaded name had no effect.

He debated whether to run to camp for help. But what if Cynthe hadn't reached it yet? Diello didn't think it was a good idea to leave Scree here.

Teaming with the goblin-boy usually resulted in mistakes and mishaps. Scree meant well, and he was always willing to attempt anything Diello asked of him, but he wasn't Cynthe. The pouch Scree had been carrying was now lost in the river, and Diello's rucksack and bundle had been left under the bridge.

Worst of all, Scree was hurt.

Diello pulled Scree to a sitting position and draped him over his shoulder. The goblin-boy was small and scrawny, but standing up with his added weight proved to be almost beyond Diello's strength. Diello staggered up the bank, fighting to keep his balance on the muddy slope. There was no cover at the top. Downstream, past the kink in the river, he saw a dam of sorts made of stones and stout timbers stretching perhaps three-quarters of the way across. It forced the water to rush through a narrow channel and turn a large waterwheel attached to the side of a ramshackle building.

A mill, Diello thought. *If Scree hadn't been caught in the backwater, we'd have both gone into the wheel paddles.*

Ahead of him lay an enormous field with woods beyond it, but reaching them involved crossing the open expanse for anyone to see. He was no longer concerned about pursuit from the townspeople. But if goblins were lurking in the area, they might be watching him right now.

Gray fingers of cloud closed around the sun, and the air felt chillier than ever. To the west, more clouds were piling up along the horizon. They would shorten the amount of daylight left. He still had to figure out a way to recover the ham, meat pie, and bread he'd abandoned under the bridge. If only there were bushes and trees near the structure to provide some cover. But the bridge stood in the open.

Tall shocks of grain sheaves dotted the harvested field between the river and the woods. Over to Diello's right, at the end of the field closest to the town, women and children were straggling back to work now that the passing army had marched out of sight. Carrying gleaning baskets, the workers gathered whatever stray grain heads had fallen on the ground during harvest. A wagon drawn by horses was angling across the middle of the field while serfs loaded it with sheaves.

So far, no one was looking his way or shouting at him. The busy people seemed intent on their tasks.

Maybe, Diello thought, *I'd pass as a gleaner if anyone glanced in my direction.* Except the unconscious Scree didn't look like a bundle of grain.

Take the risk! Diello told himself, trying not to stumble as his feet sank into the soft soil. It was light and crumbly, the perfect tilth for crops, but difficult to walk in. He was very tired from the swim, and Scree weighed more with every step. How Diello wished he could work a *cymunffyl* spell to render himself invisible. The wolf pup had tried to teach him and Cynthe, but so far Diello and his sister had shown no knack for it. Besides, to practice magic was to leave a trail for the goblins to follow.

His head was pounding, keeping time with each step.

When he was halfway across the field, he halted a moment to catch his breath. Scree felt like a boulder, and Diello's legs burned.

He caught himself closing his eyes and snapped them open. It had been a mistake to pause. He had to keep going.

Behind him, he could hear distant talking as the gleaners worked. No one was paying him any attention. His luck, it seemed, was holding . . . except that it was so difficult to move.

Go!

Diello forced himself to take a step, but it was like struggling through sludge. His feet dragged, and he gulped in air. Another step. Another.

He couldn't keep going. He felt tethered in place. The more he struggled, the more exhausted he became.

When Diello tried to wipe the sweat from his face and found that he could barely move his hand, he realized that he *was* being held in place.

He battled down a surge of panic. As soon as he stopped fighting to take another step, the mysterious force holding him eased slightly. He felt an overwhelming compulsion to change direction and walk toward the opposite end of the field, away from their camp. Resisting, he looked but saw no one at the edge of the woods.

The magic pushed at him again, so hard he took a step before he managed to halt, shaking with fear. He realized why his legs felt on fire. It wasn't from fatigue. Diello possessed crystal bones—a term used by the Fae to describe someone able to strengthen the magical powers of others. Crystal bones also made Diello especially sensitive to dark magic. Someone was using it now, employing a spell designed to lure him into a trap.

Goblins?

He heard a sound. Someone was coming toward him.

Abruptly the spell holding him fell away. Diello spun around just as a heavy net landed on top of him and Scree, knocking them down. Diello hit the ground on his side.

He kicked and struggled to break free, but he was too entangled in the net and Scree was in his way. A tall figure in black twisted the ends of the net deftly. The net was woven coarsely enough for Diello to run his arm through the gaps, but it held him just the same. Trussed like wild game, Diello turned his head, trying to get a better look at his captor.

It wasn't Brezog.

This man was stocky. His head and face were shaved smooth, and his skin was unnaturally white, the color of a goose egg. His deepset eyes were dark, like those of so many people in the eastern shires.

"Well, thieves," he said. His accent was soft and slurred. His gaze held no compassion. "Let's see if you are indeed the goblins that Master Goodly claims you to be."

Drawing a dagger, he poked it through the net and used the sharp tip to push Diello's shaggy, dark-gold hair back from his ears.

"No," he murmured, letting the dagger tip trace lightly along Diello's jaw and throat. Then he tapped the pointed end of Scree's nose. "Yes."

"He's half-goblin," Diello said. "Surely you know what that means."

"Did I ask you, thief? Be silent!"

Diello had no choice but to obey. His bronze knife was examined before being thrust through the captor's belt. When the man reached in to finger the pouch containing Eirian's hilt, Diello steeled himself not to twitch in protest. *Don't give away how important it is.*

Yet the man's hand stopped. His black eyes narrowed at Diello. "You are trying too hard, Faelin," he said. "What matters so much to you, eh?"

Diello closed his eyes as the man opened the pouch and drew out the hilt, pulling it free of the net. When the man said nothing, Diello opened his eyes.

He saw his captor turning the hilt over and over as though puzzled. The hilt looked old and battered, a worthless piece broken off a sword. Its pommel jewel was crusted with the mud that Diello had rubbed over it, but he feared this man would see through such a simple disguise. He might even be one of Brezog's spies looking for it.

The bald man turned his gaze back on Diello. "How came you by this?" he asked. "Did you steal it, as well as Master Goodly's ham?"

"It's mine," Diello said. "I found it. My father let me keep it. I—I want to be a Shieldsman some day. A—a Shieldsman auxiliary, and I—"

"No, I think not." The man wrapped his fingers around the hilt and held it aloft. "Hmm."

Just then, an arrow pierced the man's hand. A shrill war-cry came from the woods. "Let them go!"

It was Cynthe!

The man dropped the hilt. He yanked Diello and Scree upright, wrapped together in the net, using their bodies to block him from further attack. Blood from his right hand dripped onto Diello as he held the boys close. His left hand pressed the dagger to Diello's throat.

"How many more of you thieves are there?" he whispered in Diello's ear. "Well, no matter. I'll set you as bait to catch the rest."

chapter three

iello gasped, writhing in disgust.

"Be still," the man said as he studied the trees. After binding his wounded hand, he lifted his nose to the wind and flared his nostrils like a hound after a scent.

"Danger!" Diello shouted to Cynthe. "Run!"

"Be quiet, or I'll cut your throat."

Diello resumed struggling. With a grunt, his captor swung him off his feet and carried him and Scree away.

Jounced along, with Scree's weight squashing him, Diello prayed that Cynthe would get the hilt before some gleaner stumbled across it. The only good thing about this mess was that the man had seemed more interested in Diello than the sword.

Diello and Scree were carried over the bridge and back into the town, where curious gawkers followed after the pale man and his burden. The rough handling hadn't revived Scree, and Diello grew more worried.

Master Goodly was waiting in the town square, his hands planted on his hips. He hadn't bothered to clean off the mud streaking his clothing. His jowls were red with anger. When Diello and Scree were dumped on the cobbles at his feet, scattered chuckles ran through the gathering crowd.

"Thank you, Loye," Master Goodly said. "I was certain you'd be able to catch them."

Saying nothing, the bald man extended his hand.

Master Goodly untied a purse from his belt and dropped it into Loye's palm with a clink of coinage. "Well done," he said.

"That's a heavy price to pay," announced a young man. Struggling to sit up under the net, Diello saw that the speaker was Blue Tunic. "And where's your ham, Master Goodly?" he called with amusement. "Isn't that what this is about?"

"The thieves will tell me that," Master Goodly replied.

"Lost in the river, most likely," Blue Tunic said.

"And who asked you, sir?" Master Goodly retorted. He gestured at Loye. "Bring these boys along. They can answer to the magistrate."

Diello had enough of magistrates when Lord Malques stole his family's farm. Now he envisioned another series of questions that would end only in injustice. Besides, he *had* stolen the ham. The fact that he and his companions were starving while Master Goodly possessed an abundant larder wouldn't matter in an Antrasin court of law. It would end with Diello and Scree both branded, to live forever with that mark of shame.

"Where's the shire's reeve?" Diello asked. If the reeve had to be summoned from another town, the delay might offer him a chance to escape. "I demand to be brought before him."

Laughter broke out on all sides, and even Master Goodly managed a snort before pointing a fat finger at Loye.

"And so you are, thief," he said. "Loye is reeve of this shire, and a fine keeper of law and order."

The mocking laughter went on. Diello couldn't meet their eyes.

"This Faelin boy should be branded at once," Master Goodly said. "We'll take him to the smithy and have it done. And that goblin should be killed."

Diello began struggling again. Blue Tunic planted a foot on him to hold him still.

"Here now," he said. "They're only children. Starving, by the look of them. I say we run them out of town with a warning never to return."

"And would you encourage theft and beggary," Master Goodly demanded, "allowing any vagrant to pillage among us?"

Blue Tunic bent closer to Diello. "Give up the ham, you little fool," he said. "It's not worth the penalty. Or have you truly dropped it in the river?"

"It's under the bridge," Diello confessed.

"There! You heard the lad. It can be recovered and you've lost nothing, Master Goodly, except your time and"—Blue Tunic gestured at the mud-encrusted merchant—"a small portion of your dignity."

The chuckles in the crowd were kinder this time. Diello sent Blue Tunic a look of gratitude.

Master Goodly bustled away, pushing through the onlookers. He muttered, "You, Orl, and you, Sims, come along and help me recover my ham at once."

Blue Tunic nodded. "Master Goodly is satisfied, Reeve Loye. Will you be?"

"What about my missing cloak, mittens, and blanket?" a woman demanded, stepping forward. "Yes, and my husband's best wool tunic hung to air on the clothesline? All of it gone!"

The murmurs turned angry again.

"These boys must be punished," Loye said.

"Not branded," an elderly voice protested. "Not when they're so young, and if the ham and clothing are recovered—"

"What about my bread and meat pie?" asked the woman called Sega, who'd swatted Scree with her broom. "And my fine stew knocked half out of its pot? What's to be done?"

A man in the back of the crowd laughed. "That's right, Reeve Loye! Judge the value of Sega's stew, but better taste it first."

More mirth and catcalls broke out. Diello looked at their faces. He didn't see anything funny about this, not now.

Loye held up his hand to quiet the onlookers. "We all know a ham is worth more than a loaf of bread."

"To Master Goodly perhaps," Sega said, "but not to me!"

"What about my blanket?" the other woman insisted.

"The boys will be punished publicly to set a proper example for others." The reeve stepped back. "Hang them."

"No!" Diello cried out. "Please!"

Shrugging, Blue Tunic moved aside. Eager hands lifted Diello and Scree. Diello twisted around to plead with

Blue Tunic, but the young man was walking away with his friends. He had no more help to offer.

One of the reeve's men doffed his cap to Loye. "Do we hang 'em separately or together, sir?"

"Together will do."

Diello jabbed Scree with his elbow, but still the goblin-boy did not rouse. *Maybe he's better off this way*, Diello thought.

He found Loye's dark eyes watching him. "You know how to stop this," the reeve said. "How many others are out there?"

Diello's fists curled. He said nothing.

"There are no loyal thieves," Loye murmured. "Your friends have abandoned you by now. They're well away down the road, leaving you to take all the punishment."

"No!" Diello protested hotly, then bit his lip, angry at himself for speaking.

"So you hope for rescue. If it comes, I'll catch you all." Turning away, Loye gestured at two of his men. "Get it done before sunset."

chapter four

twilight closed in early. Shadows pooled around the stone and brick buildings, filling the streets. Diello and a still-unconscious Scree were carried along.

"Thieves!" shouted the men. "Come and see the thieves, about to be hanged for their misdeeds. Thieves! Here be thieves!"

Some giggling little boys raced after them, pelting them with dung. One of the men swung around fast, nearly dropping Diello.

"You stop that!" he said, shaking his fist. "Time enough to throw stones and rubbish once they're swingin'. But you don't throw nuthink at me, Tibby Evans, you hear?"

Why don't they get it over with? Diello thought. *Why do they have to torture us like this?*

He'd never witnessed a hanging because his parents didn't believe in attending public executions, but last year he'd seen a road bandit's body swinging from a tree branch by King's Road. It was dried up by the hot sun and pecked to bits by the ravens—mostly a dark leathery *thing* held together by weathered bone and tatters of clothing. The gruesome sight had haunted his dreams for weeks afterward. Now, he could imagine the scratchy noose around his neck and that abrupt, terrifying yank that would snap his neck quickly if done properly. If the job were botched, it would be slow, agonizing strangulation.

I'm sorry, Guardian! he prayed to the supreme deity of the Fae. *We were so hungry. Forgive me and grant me the mercy of swift death.*

As darkness gathered, the men reached a low, squat building at the edge of town. It was built solid and square, its windows no wider than arrow slits.

The jail. Diello stared at it. He thought he heard a wail of agony coming from inside. Again his imagination ran wild, conjuring up images of torture while Loye bent over some poor victim, demanding confession.

At least I'll be spared that. Diello was glad that he'd told where he'd left the ham. He prayed that Cynthe and Vassou had run away, but he knew his sister too well to believe she had.

"Wake up, Scree," Diello whispered, shaking the goblin-boy's shoulder. "You should be awake when you die."

"No, no, no," Scree replied. "It is better not to see, not to know."

Has he been pretending to be unconscious all this time instead of helping me escape? "Thanks a lot, Scree."

"Here we go," one of the men muttered. "Ready?"

They shrugged their burden off their shoulders, shifting Diello and Scree like a sack of taties.

"No, you fool," said the other. "Got 'em upside down. This way."

"Don't see that it matters."

"Got to keep the ends of the net together, don't we?"

And then, with collective grunts, they lifted the boys and caught the net on a stout iron hook fixed to a gallows frame of weathered timbers. Leaving the boys swinging in the net, they walked away, wiping their brows and chatting about their dinner.

At first Diello didn't understand—until the men looked back at him and Scree and laughed, slapping each other on the shoulder.

"See his face?" one said. "As pale as cheese, he is."

"Serves him right, the little greedy guts. Hey, boy! You'll think twice before you steal what don't belong to you, eh!"

"It'll be a long, cold night for you two, hanging in the breeze."

Hanged? Diello thought furiously. *What a dirty trick.*

As soon as the men strolled out of sight, Diello squirmed around inside the net, pushing and wiggling until Scree was beneath him instead of on top of him. Having steeled himself for death, Diello felt hollow and foolish, almost disappointed in a peculiar way. Most of all, he wished he could run the reeve through.

But seething over cruel games wasn't going to solve his current problem.

"Is it safe now to talk if I am very quiet?" Scree whispered.

Diello swallowed several things he wanted to say. "How long have you been awake?" he asked.

"Since before we were caught in the field."

"So if you'd been on your feet we could have made a run for it. Very helpful of you."

"You're welcome." As usual, the goblin-boy seemed unaware of Diello's sarcasm. "I would have run straight to the goblin trap. It *was* a goblin trap luring us, wasn't it? Before the reeve caught us?"

"Yes."

"I thought so. I could not have stopped myself from going to it. But I knew you would be strong enough to resist such magic. Now we have escaped the goblins, but we are most unlucky to have fallen into a human trap instead. I am sorry that we are here in this cold wind, among these unkind people, with no food for sharing with—"

"Hush," Diello said fiercely. "No names. Not here."

Scree nodded. "I will not tell. Even if I am branded, I will not betray Cyn—"

Diello clapped a hand over his mouth. "Shut up. Don't you understand? The reeve's set a new trap here, and we're the bait to lure her in."

Scree's breath tickled hot and moist against Diello's palm. When Diello dropped his hand, the goblin-boy said simply, "I will do as you command."

"We've got to get out of here," Diello said. He worried that Loye had a spy hidden and watching them, ready to follow them back to camp. Still, he couldn't just wait for Cynthe to come and free them. He was certain that if she entered the town, Loye would catch her. On the other hand, she might run afoul of whatever had tried to lure him and Scree to the woods. That worried him even more than Loye.

"As soon as we're free," Diello murmured, "we might be followed. Understand?"

Scree started to speak, but Diello silenced him.

"Listen to me," he whispered. "Whatever the risk, we can't lead them to the others."

"But if we don't return to camp, how do we—"

"Whatever I do next, don't squeal."

Diello looked in all directions before he flicked fire.

Little flames burned through the netting, which smoked and charred, letting them tumble to the ground. Somehow, although he'd been at the bottom of the net, Scree landed on top, knocking the wind from Diello.

He shoved off the goblin-boy and scrambled to his feet. Diello ran for the cover of shadows, his moccasins silent on the cobblestones. Scree followed at his heels. As they eased around the corner of the building and looked across the road toward the dark ribbon of river, Diello could hear a furtive scrape of leather against stone behind them.

The spy.

Diello gathered a fold of Scree's damp tunic in his fist. They were going to have to return to the river, letting it take them downstream and through the dangerous weir by the mill. If they could get past that point, they might have a chance to swim past the fields to the forest. Never mind that their camp was upstream. If they could lose the spy, there would be time later to circle back.

Diello was already chilled to the bone, and at night the water would be extremely cold. How he could stand it, much less keep Scree afloat, was the problem. *I have to do it*, he told himself.

Giving Scree a tug, he ran across the road and plunged down the bank into the tall reeds. Just as they reached the water's edge, Scree seemed to realize what they were about to do and halted. Diello yanked him into the water, throwing his arms around the struggling goblin-boy.

Thanks to Scree's thrashing, Diello went completely under. The icy shock of immersion overwhelmed him. He felt Scree pummeling him wildly and fought to hang onto his friend as he reached for the surface.

Diello's head broke through, giving him the chance to suck in a lungful of air before Scree's flailing dragged him under again. The muddy bottom dropped away, and he felt the current grab him. Scree got free from him, and Diello angrily shot to the surface before turning around to look for the goblin-boy.

A light shone in his face. On the bank, he could see the silhouettes of men. Some of them, mere shadows in the dusk, were jogging down the road, keeping pace with him. A shout from ahead made him look toward the bridge. More men were gathered there, unrolling something over the railing toward the water.

Another net.

There was a splash, and to his left he saw Scree swimming clumsily toward the bank.

Diello kicked after him. He caught Scree's foot, hanging on. Then he grabbed Scree's belt and yanked hard, dragging him beneath the water.

Scree didn't fight him as he had before. Diello managed to turn Scree away from the bank and aim him deeper into the channel. They surfaced once, twice, for air. Now the bridge was coming up. Diello could hear the excited murmurs of the men holding the net. He saw it hanging down beneath the support pillars, its fibrous grid backlit by the rising moons, one waxing full and the other waning. Some of the net spread over the river, waiting to enfold him and Scree.

Diello hoped none of it was underwater. He and Cynthe had—in better days—woven nets and weighted them with small stones before stretching them across the creek just under the surface. The smallest fish could swim through, but sometimes they caught huge silver mullins, wide-mouthed and fat, flopping as the twins twisted the net around them and lifted them out.

Slowing his stroke, Diello tightened his arm around Scree. The goblin-boy was still sporadically moving his arms and kicking, although clearly he was exhausted. His head lolled against Diello's shoulder.

Diello knew Scree was an inexperienced swimmer, and he didn't want his friend to panic again. He put his lips to Scree's ear. "We're going deep," Diello warned him. "Hold your breath and, by the Ancient Harmonies, try not to drown this time."

Then Diello felt the edge of the net. With a quick gasp, he plunged down into the dark water, dragging Scree with him, and kicked with all the strength left in his aching legs. Deeper and deeper he went, his chest already bursting from the need for air, the cold so intense that he felt numb.

He was blind down here. The current was very strong,

knocking him into the base of a bridge pylon before snatching him onward. His left shoulder ached from supporting Scree's weight. It was tempting to let his fingers loosen, to bob up to the surface, to survive at any cost.

No!

Diello stayed down, clinging to Scree by instinct more than choice. They swept past another pylon, and Diello's body slammed against a second net. This one was hanging under the water's surface. Now he understood how clever Loye's men had been. They had hung one net on the west side of the bridge, knowing he would see it and dive. But they had hung a second net on the east side and weighted it deep so it would catch him.

I'm going to drown, he realized.

But then he felt anger, an anger so extreme that it seemed to ignite inside of him. And despite part of his mind insisting that he couldn't flick fire underwater—that it was impossible, that he was *dead*—he swept his free hand across the net with a blaze of orange flame, cutting a hole.

Flicking fire was an ordinary Faelin skill, a minor bit of magic that anyone with a drop of Fae blood could do. At home, Diello had used it to light his bedroom candle. But he'd never generated this much power before. *Has desperation brought me a new Gift?*

The current sucked him and Scree through the hole, and they were free of the trap. The water flowed much faster now, thanks to the weir ahead. Diello knew he had to swim for the bank. The water was churning, and it pushed him to the surface just in time for his desperate lungs to drag in air. He swallowed water and choked, floundering. Suddenly his anger faded, and with it his strength. His arms were lead, his shoulders locked up, his legs cramping.

Scree's head bumped his chin, and he remembered that he still held the goblin-boy. Scree floated limply. But how could they stay afloat when Diello could barely keep his head above water?

There was a roaring sound, and Diello saw the weir's gates looming above him, moments before he was slammed brutally into one of the panels. He lost consciousness briefly, dropping his hold on Scree. He was vaguely aware of the water swirling him around before shoving him through the narrow passage. He knocked against a sharp edge, thumped over what felt like a series of steps, and tumbled in midair before landing in a sort of whirlpool.

The great wooden wheel turned, its paddles rising above him with cascades of water. Diello kicked, just missing being scooped up. Then he was safely past the danger, with the roar of the weir and the groaning wheel gradually fading behind him. He had no idea what had become of Scree.

The current grew sluggish once more, and at last—forcing his arms into one sloppy stroke after another—Diello was able to angle toward the bank. His knees dragged into the mud, and he sobbed with relief as he reached out for the reeds. His frozen hands could not grasp them, and he slipped back. Something bumped into his leg, and he would have shouted with fright if he'd had the strength.

It was Scree, bobbing in the water, eyes closed.

Diello grabbed at him and half-pulled, half-pushed Scree up the bank. Crawling beside him, Diello collapsed, face down, in the mud. His plan had been to run for the cover of the woods, but he couldn't move yet.

A shout in the distance brought him back from his stupor. Men were coming, searching the riverbank methodically. Their lantern beams swung back and forth.

We must hide in the water, Diello thought, but knew he couldn't do it. The idea of sinking into that numbing cold again was too much for him.

He heard them coming closer.

The reeds are too thin. They'll see us, even in the dark.

Scree whimpered, and Diello gripped his thin shoulder in warning.

As the men drew near, Loye's voice called out, "You can't hide forever, thieves. I saw you leave the river, but you'll never make the woods. Better surrender yourselves now, and let's be done."

A shrill whistle came from the left, and Cynthe's voice jeered, "Can't catch *me*! Too slow!"

The men shouted, and some of them ran in her direction.

Her laughter mocked them from the right. "Wrong! Try again!"

Diello was grateful for the diversion, but he couldn't take advantage of it with Loye and two others standing at the top of the bank, almost directly over him and Scree. It would take only the right angle of lantern light, and they'd be visible.

Then a faint tingle of magic spread through Diello's half-frozen body. *Vassou's magic!* A *cymunffyl* spread over Diello and Scree like a soft blanket, making them invisible to their

THE CALL OF EIRIAN

pursuers. Although he was not yet fully grown, Vassou had been serving Diello and Cynthe since the day his mother had died saving their lives. Samal wolves were found only in Embarthi, and by legend they had been the first inhabitants there, known as the Far-Seeing People in a time beyond antiquity. So far, Vassou had proven himself invaluable to the twins, particularly with his ability to perform magic like this.

Diello pushed himself to his knees and tugged at Scree. The goblin-boy roused slowly, still in no shape to run.

"Hey!" Cynthe's voice called. "What's wrong? Can't find me?"

Loye swore. "Anyone see her?"

"No! There's magic afoot here," one of the others replied.

"Touch your crumixes and say your warding prayers," Loye ordered. "But don't stop searching."

A man began moving among the reeds, holding a lantern aloft in one hand while he stabbed among the plants with a pitchfork. Scree twitched in fright, and Diello pulled him to his feet. Supporting each other, they tiptoed past Loye, taking care not to make the reeds sway. At the top of the bank Diello halted, aware that if they headed for the open field, the men would be able to see their tracks in the soil.

Another man joined the reeve, walking within inches of Diello and Scree. "No sign of 'em, sir. Appears they've gone."

"Impossible!" Loye said. "I know I saw them reach the bank here."

"Could have been farther down, sir. Shadows can play tricks in the dark. Or, perhaps they made it into the woods? We'll not find 'em tonight if they did."

Loye grunted. "Set fire to the reeds. We'll flush them out that way."

Scree tried to bolt, only to be grabbed from behind and held by Diello. Both boys sank down. Afraid Scree's struggles were going to dissipate the *cymunffyl*, Diello gave his ear a yank.

"Stop it!" Diello breathed, and Scree subsided.

In the distance a wolf howled. Several men called out in alarm. The lanterns swung back and forth.

"We ain't had wolves in these parts since my granddad's day," someone said. "I told you there's magic afoot."

"Bad things, sir," said another, sounding breathless as though he'd been running. "That voice we keep hearing. Ain't no girl, sir. That there's a will o' the wisp calling out to us. We could chase it until we die and never catch it."

"Then go home to your hearths," Loye said in frustration and tossed his lantern down the bank.

Flaming oil spilled onto the ground, and the dry reeds whooshed into blazing torches. The fire spread fast, crackling and sending up billows of smoke that drove Loye and his men back. Vassou howled again, and they broke away, heading for the village.

Scree popped up, wild-eyed. Before Diello could catch him, he ran, suddenly visible as he left the *cymunffyl* and angled away from the fire. Sparks and bits of burning stalk swirled in the air, spreading the flames to the field, where the stubble began to blaze. Diello found himself surrounded by fire.

"Diello!" Cynthe cried. "Run!"

Coughing from the smoke, he turned this way and that, seeking a way through the flames.

He could feel Vassou's magic encircling him, changing the *cymunffyl* into something else. The wolf pup was trying to put a *cloigwylie*—a protection spell—around him. Only it wasn't strong enough.

The heat from the fire made Diello gasp for breath. His skin seemed to be shrinking like jerky on a drying rack. He crouched low in an effort to breathe, barely able to hear Cynthe over the roaring flames.

I have to help Vassou save me, he thought. Closing his eyes, he concentrated on the wolf pup, imagining his keen blue eyes and white fur with the golden tinge. Diello felt his crystal bones grow warm as they strengthened the wolf's powers.

The weak *cloigwylie* grew stronger, holding back the flames so they didn't touch Diello.

"Get up!" Cynthe urged him. "You can do it! Come to me!"

He pushed to his feet, still finding it hard to breathe the hot, smoky air. The orange flames dazzled him, but he didn't burn.

Cynthe called again, and he followed her voice, running out of the fire. Then the blaze was behind him, and the air felt cool and clean.

Ahead of him, he saw Cynthe appear, shedding her *cymunffyl*. She gripped his arms, her coppery-green eyes wide and shiny with tears, before she hugged him tight.

"You're safe," she cried. "I didn't think Vassou was going to manage it in time."

Diello tried to grin at her, to say something that would ease the fright in her face, but he couldn't fight his exhaustion.

"Diello? Are you hurt? What's wrong?"

He tried one last time, but it was no good. He fainted.

chapter five

the touch of something cold and wet on his cheek woke Diello. He sat up, looking around. He was next to a small campfire with Vassou beside him.

Vassou nuzzled Diello's face and gave him a swift lick before settling back on his haunches.

"Stay alert," Vassou growled. "There is still danger."

Diello rubbed his forehead, trying to clear his head. He wasn't sure how long he'd been asleep, but someone—Cynthe, maybe with Scree's help—had carried him back to camp. He looked at the trees surrounding him and Vassou. Their dark mass reassured him, and he was glad to be well away from the village.

Still, from Vassou's warning it seemed they weren't free of trouble. *Why did we ever come to this awful village?* Diello wondered. His quarterstaff and their collection of bundles lay against a fallen log as though in readiness to break camp. His wet, muddy tunic had been exchanged for one that was much too big but warm, and he'd been wrapped in a thick blanket, but he still wore his damp leggings. Shivering, he scooted closer to the meager fire, although its hissing and crackling brought back memories of his narrow escape. He could feel tracings of magic in the air and knew that Vassou was holding a *cymunffyl* around the camp, to keep anyone from seeing the fire.

That made him feel guilty. He figured that Vassou must be getting tired from expending so much magic. Now, thanks to his passing out, Vassou was having to work even more. They should have moved camp by now. They'd taken enough risks for one day.

"Where are Cynthe and Scree?" Diello asked. "And what kind of danger?"

Vassou was gazing at the woods with his ears pricked. One of his front paws lifted off the ground, but he wasn't growling. Diello stared in that direction, too.

"What kind of danger?" he repeated. "Are the reeve and his men still hunting us?"

"No. There is goblin scent on the south wind."

"Goblins!"

"Faint scent," Vassou said, tipping his head to look at Diello. "They are not close. Not yet."

Far from reassured, Diello touched his old tunic that was hanging from a low branch to dry. The cloth was still wet, so he hadn't been unconscious long.

Then he noticed the rucksack among the bundles. Opening it, he inhaled the fragrance of ham and laughed. Cynthe must have taken it from beneath the bridge while Diello and Scree were under arrest.

He pulled off a piece of meat and chewed hungrily. "Cynthe, you're wonderful," he whispered. "So where's my sister, Vassou? Where's Scree?"

"Scree is well. He is with her."

"Then what is she up to? We need to get away from here."

"Agreed, but not without the hilt of Eirian."

A flush of shame made Diello fasten the rucksack flap firmly. He noticed that Vassou had one paw planted on something long and narrow, wrapped in leather.

"She left the blade behind!"

"No one can be caught in possession of both pieces," Vassou said.

I'm at fault, Diello told himself. *I should be out there hunting for the hilt, not her.*

"She'll never find it in the dark," he muttered. "I should help her."

"You will stay," Vassou said sternly. "I can protect her and I can protect this camp. More, I cannot do."

Diello understood. He paced around the fire, staying inside the *cymunffyl's* protection. How was Cynthe going to find something as small as the hilt in that large field? Scree would be no help to her.

"Rest," Vassou said.

"I'm not sick."

"You have been too much in the cold river and you have used magic. Regain your strength."

Sitting down, Diello shut his eyes, but not to sleep. Sight immediately filled his mind with a vision of the hilt. It was glowing like a beacon. Cynthe—tall and slim in her usual boy's clothes—crouched to pick it up, but just as her fingers closed on it, a dark shape loomed above her.

"Cynthe!" Diello murmured.

He reached for the knife he no longer had. Wanting to

run to her aid, he struggled to break free of the vision. But Sight held him prisoner. He couldn't stop watching as his sister dodged the goblin. She swung the hilt as a weapon, slamming the pommel guard into the creature's face before she twisted away and ran. The goblin chased her. At first she outdistanced him, then she stopped, whirling around to face her pursuer. Before he could reach her, she lifted her free hand high and ascended into the air, rising fast with a skill that made Diello gasp in relief.

The vision disappeared. Diello grunted and pitched forward, catching himself on his palms. He opened his eyes, panting as though he'd been fighting alongside her.

"She's coming," he said to Vassou. "I didn't see Scree at all. She's flying, but I don't know how long she can keep it up. And there's a goblin. Just one, I think. It nearly got her."

"Brezog's scout, perhaps." Vassou whined in concentration. "The creature is moving this way, following her."

"If she has to descend, he'll get her," Diello said. "I thought you were protecting her. Why isn't she hidden under your *cymunffyl* spell?"

"It is too weak to fool a goblin," Vassou admitted. "I—I am tiring."

Diello touched his back. "Take strength from me as you did earlier."

"It is not me you should help now, but her," Vassou said.

Diello rose to his feet, staring at the glittering stars above the treetops. He tried to ignore his fatigue. But the *cymunffyl* around the campfire felt heavy. It seemed to smother him.

As soon as he stepped outside its protection, he was aware of how much colder the air felt. The campfire and Vassou vanished, although if Diello squinted he could detect the faintest glimmer.

Diello had never been able to touch Cynthe's thoughts directly with his own, but he'd always possessed an innate sense of where his twin was. Slowly, his body turned in her direction. A tingle ran through his limbs. Encouraged, he tried harder, wishing he knew what he was doing, wishing Mamee could've taught him how to use his abilities, but she would never know how many Gifts he and Cynthe had begun to manifest.

There! He found Cynthe, felt the rhythm of her magic as she flew toward the woods. But he also felt her struggling, tiring. She'd never flown this fast or long before. Trying to keep light contact without distracting her, Diello spread his hands and released a flow of warmth toward his twin. His legs began to itch and tingle. His body felt weightless, as though he might float into the air. It was working! He grinned.

Then some invisible force grabbed him.

"No!"

"Have you forgotten me, little Faelin morsel?"

Brezog had control of him now. Memories of the last time the goblin gorlord had taken over his thoughts and violated his mind brought fear surging through Diello.

He twisted and turned, trying to break the gorlord's hold on him. Diello had channeled potent magic before, most recently when he broke the spell guarding Eirian's hiding place on the farmstead. That had been frightening, but also exhilarating. This was far different—a cruel and selfish force feeding off him.

The more Diello fought, the stronger the gorlord grew. Diello felt as though his bones were about to shatter. He screamed.

There was a rumbling growl. The wolf nipped his hand. That sharp, stinging bite snapped the connection between Diello and Brezog.

Diello collapsed in a heap. Vassou whined and licked his face. The autumn night air felt blissfully cool as the magic died down inside Diello's body.

Cynthe came flying down from the sky, dropping to the ground with a muffled grunt. She tucked her knees and rolled over until she crashed into the log. She lay there for a moment before bouncing to her feet with the hilt held high.

"Got it! Guess what was out there, trying to stop me? I was too quick for him, though, and my ascension was *perfect*, the best I've done yet. No zigzagging this time. I—uh, Diello?"

She knelt beside him. He could only lie there shuddering, dimly aware that she was back and unharmed. *Brezog's found us*, he thought. *He'll never stop.*

She gripped Diello's hand, and he tried weakly to curl his fingers around hers.

"What's wrong?" she asked.

"Glad . . . you're . . . safe" was all he could manage.

"What's happened?" Cynthe demanded. "Vassou, tell me! He wasn't this bad when I left."

"He tried to help you," the wolf replied.

"Oh, Diello," she said. "Haven't you learned by now that I can take care of myself? At first, I thought I was going to fall, but then I picked up speed." She laughed, hooking her chin-length hair behind her pointed ears. "The wind's so cold up there. It's like you're one with the stars."

Lying there, listening to her brag, Diello thought, *If she knew I helped her, she'd be so disappointed in herself.*

Her skin was glowing with silver sparkles. "If I could just practice more, I'd be *good.*"

Diello felt a little finger of magic seeking him out.

"Not safe," he mumbled. "Must . . . get up."

She held him down. "Don't be daft. You need to rest. Your hair's still wet, and you're as clammy as a dead fish."

Scree came running from the woods and dropped a handful of grubs so he could pat Diello's cheek. "I have been hunting food. Are you feeling better? Remember the day we caught fish and did not cook them long enough? You look like you have eaten raw fish."

"Lift his shoulders," Cynthe said. "Let's carry him back to the fire."

Diello pushed their hands away and struggled to get up. "Help get me to my feet. We need to break camp now."

"Why? That goblin couldn't have followed me here."

Vassou slipped between them. "Is the gorlord coming?"

"Yes," Diello said.

"Meeting up with one goblin doesn't mean the entire horde is here," Cynthe said. "Are you worrying again about Brezog finding us? Just because I flew a little? Well, not just me. We've all used magic today."

"I did not," Scree announced.

She patted the goblin-boy's back absently, her gaze still on Diello. "You're really scared, aren't you? What's happened?"

Diello looked down and saw that his hands were trembling. He curled them into fists.

"Then we'll break camp," Cynthe said without further argument. "But first let's carve some of the ham to eat as we go."

"No! Forget the food. We need to go now."

"We can't keep going if we don't eat. You're already ill—"

"I'll eat sapling bark if I have to," Diello said. "Brezog knows exactly where we are."

"Because of one scout?" she scoffed. "Besides, I got away."

"You were lucky."

"And maybe we're safe enough here in the woods until dawn. We agreed we wouldn't travel in the dark. We're all tired, you especially, and we need to eat something."

"I am hungry for ham," Scree said. "And there is bread, too. All good things should be eaten now."

Cynthe nodded. "Scree's right. Since I flew, I left no tracks for the scout to follow. Besides, we've got Vassou to protect us."

"Vassou's tired," Diello said. "Do you really expect him to keep both a *cymunffyl* and a *cloigwylie* around us all night? And have you already forgotten that the goblin saw through your protection?"

"The important thing is not to panic," she replied. "You're too tired. You're not thinking clearly."

"Brezog knows where we are," Diello insisted.

"But he's not here yet, and by the time he arrives, we'll be long gone. Let's eat and rest. Let me handle things. You'll be able to think straight once you've had some sleep."

Diello imagined lying helplessly while Brezog's horde prowled nearer. "It's no good. He's been in my thoughts tonight, Cynthe."

Cynthe hugged him, pressing her forehead to his. "So that's it. He's made you sick, hasn't he? I'm sorry."

Diello felt the questing sweep of the gorlord's senses. They seemed stronger, closer. He felt something inside him trying to respond, as though Brezog's magic was calling to him. Diello wondered how much longer he could withstand it. Twisting away from Cynthe, he paced in a circle.

"Diello?" Cynthe said hesitantly.

"He's hunting me now. We can't hide here."

"Do you agree with him, Vassou?" Cynthe asked.

"Yes," the wolf said. "The risks here are too strong."

"Scree?"

The goblin-boy grinned. He never seemed to get over the delight of having a vote.

"I am very tired and my head hurts," he said, lifting his brown-tipped fingers to the cut on his brow. "And my friend Diello, who was brave to keep me from drowning, he is—"

"Scree," Cynthe broke in. "Just say yes or no."

"Brezog will do more harm to my friend Diello. We should go. Let us go!"

She sighed, tucking the sword hilt back in Diello's belt pouch before she picked up the leather-wrapped blade and slid it into her quiver with her arrows. Scree gathered the bundles stacked by the log and fetched Diello's wet tunic, rolling it up and tucking it under his arm. The goblin-boy's clothes were just as wet, but he was squelching around as though the cold didn't affect him. The fire and its ashes were carefully smothered with dirt. Cynthe and Vassou went back and forth, rubbing out their tracks and kicking fallen leaves over them.

The night closed in. High above the treetops all the stars looked dim. An owl hooted far away, and in the quiet, Diello could hear the distant river rushing over the weir. His bones tingled ever so slightly, and he tensed.

Cynthe cut four chunks off the ham and broke apart a loaf before sharing out the pieces with everyone. "At least we have enough food," she said, slinging the rucksack over her shoulder. "Now we won't be heading into the Westering Hills without supplies."

Diello clutched his supper, unable to eat. His fear was clawing at him. Every instinct was screaming at him to *flee*. "I don't know what Brezog will do to you if he catches us, Cynthe. But I know what he'll do to me. I—I can't bear it."

She made a shushing sound the way Mamee used to do when he was little and cried from a bad dream. "As soon as you grow tired, tell me, and we'll stop."

But as they set out, Diello vowed that he would walk until his feet bled.

His stomach was hurting, both from emptiness and fear. His legs wobbled under him for the first few steps, causing him to use his quarterstaff for support. Then he set his jaw and forced himself to take longer strides. After a while, he managed to choke down his food and felt slightly better.

I won't be used by Brezog. I won't be his slave, Diello promised himself.

"You know," Cynthe said to him, "in the dark I can't see to use my bow. If sprites attack us—"

"We've worse things to worry about than sprites," Diello replied. "Hurry."

chapter six

the night wore on while they trudged stealthily through
choked undergrowth. Vassou led the way, for his night
vision was the best. Cynthe followed at the pup's heels,
with Diello behind her, holding onto her belt. Scree came
last, gripping Diello's belt. No one spoke. The only sounds
they made were the scuffing of their weary feet through
the fallen leaves, an occasional snapped twig that seemed
to echo through the silent trees, and their ragged breathing. Now and then, the trees opened onto a clearing where
woodcutters had sawn logs, and the tall, ragged stumps cast
shadows like headstones.

They skirted the first two clearings. At the third, they
saw a pile of bones picked over by scavengers and scoured
clean by the weather.

Scree pressed against Diello's back. "Goblin bones," he
whispered.

"How can you tell?" Cynthe asked.

But Scree only moaned, mumbling something they
couldn't understand.

"Quickly," Vassou said. "We must not linger here. There
are spell traps and wards."

"Death place!" Scree said shrilly. "Death—"

Diello twisted around. "Quiet," he breathed. "Come on."

Vassou trotted a few steps, then paused with one paw raised before veering to the right. Again he paused, then veered to the left.

Traps, Diello thought. *And if we're caught in one . . .* He watched his sister following each slight change of direction, and Diello mimicked her, trying to step exactly where she'd placed her feet. He was hampered by Scree, still clinging to the back of his tunic and sometimes treading on his heels. Normally he would have shaken off the goblin-boy, but now he put up with it. He couldn't blame Scree for being terrified, not when he was close to panic himself.

Diello's shoulder brushed a mossy tree trunk, and from the corner of his eye he caught the glint of metal. When the breeze shifted the branches overhead, moonlight showed him a palm-sized emblem nailed to the tree at head height. Diello felt a strange compulsion to touch it, to trace his fingers over the embossed design.

"Danger!" Vassou said sharply, and Diello snatched his fingers back.

"Are you witless?" Cynthe hissed. "You know better than to touch a spell trap. Come on!"

Breathing hard, his face hot with embarrassment, Diello wrenched himself away. He'd never come across one of these ancient groves before, but from the time he and Cynthe were old enough to play alone in the woods around the farmstead, Pa had warned them to stay away from any carvings or plaques they might find, never to touch anything lest they be trapped and turned to stone. Pa told them that he'd once seen such a man, kneeling on the ground with vines growing over his shoulders, frozen there for all eternity.

"The groves are dangerous," Pa had said. "No one knows who created them or what they were originally for, and no one alive today knows how to undo a spell trap."

Just thinking about how close he'd come to disaster made Diello sweat.

Not until the clearing was well behind them did Vassou stop to rest. Diello leaned against a tree, fighting to keep his gritty eyes open. Scree and Cynthe sprawled on the ground at his feet.

"Any water left in the skin?" Diello asked Cynthe.

She pulled it from one of their bundles and tossed it to him. It was full and heavy. He drank deeply of the tepid contents before handing it back to her. She took several swallows then filled her cupped hand for Vassou to lap. When the pup was satisfied, they passed the waterskin to Scree.

The goblin-boy rejected it. "I do not want water," he complained. "I am too sleepy."

"You're foolish," Vassou said. "You should always drink on the trail."

"Let him be, Vassou," Cynthe said. "Scree knows if he's thirsty or not."

Diello sighed. From the beginning, Vassou and Scree hadn't gotten along. At best, they tolerated each other. Vassou tended to ignore the goblin-boy's existence unless he was being critical—like right now—and Scree usually avoided the wolf pup's company. It didn't help that Scree seemed jealous of the twins' affection for Vassou and liked to tag after Diello for his attention.

They aren't equal, Diello thought. *It's hard to treat them that way.*

Something large swooped silently over Diello's head, and he ducked. He glimpsed pale outstretched wings and heard the squeak of a mouse before the owl lifted, flying away through the trees with its prey. He heard a rustle, and the bird hooted plaintively.

Diello exchanged a look with Cynthe. She punched him lightly on the shoulder, and, with a smile, he punched her back.

The owl hooted again, and Diello understood the creature as though it spoke to his mind in Antrasin: "*Who are you, large beings, that disturb my hunting grounds with your noise? I rule the night. I have fed, but I am not yet filled. How can I hunt again if you frighten my prey?*"

Astonished by this new, unexpected Gift, Diello tried to order his thoughts enough to reply. In his mind, he said, "*Forgive us, Owl. We didn't mean to interfere with your hunting.*"

"Come." Vassou started forward once more.

They fell into line behind him, but before they took more than a few steps, Diello felt a peculiar sensation. He stopped.

Cynthe turned to him. "What?"

"Quiet," Vassou said. "Listen!"

"It sounds like someone's moving through the brush," Cynthe whispered. "I think—Diello, what are you doing?"

He'd dropped his quarterstaff and had his arms wrapped

around his waist, fighting the urge to turn and retrace their steps.

"Diello!" she said in his ear and pinched him hard.

He twisted her sleeve in his fist. "Brezog's found me. Don't let him turn me against you."

She held his arms. "Scree, take the blade from my quiver. We'll assemble Eirian and use the sword to fight."

"No," Diello said. Brezog's power pushed at him. He tried to resist it. "Take . . . hilt . . . *run!*"

"We aren't leaving you behind," she argued.

Diello felt the gorlord's touch crawling through his thoughts. "*Come,*" a voice whispered. "*Come to me now.*"

His bones began to tingle. "No!" Diello moaned, struggling in Cynthe's hold.

"Vassou!" she cried.

The wolf whined, wrapping his cool magic around them. "You must fight him, Diello."

"How?" Diello felt the burn spreading through his limbs. His heart was racing, and he couldn't get enough air. The only time he'd ever been able to fight Brezog successfully had been through channeling the magic of Clevn, mage-chancellor of the Fae. And Clevn wasn't here. "Brezog's too strong."

He kicked Cynthe, making her yelp, and broke free, running back the way they'd come. She tackled him from behind, knocking him down, and sat on top of him. Diello pushed her off and scrambled away from her. Again, she caught him, and this time she wrenched his arms behind his back and pinned him despite his struggles, pressing his face into the soil and leaves until he was nearly smothered.

"You're smarter than some stinky goblin," she said as he squirmed and kicked. "Think, Diello!"

But Diello couldn't think. The panic was raw in his mind. Vassou's magic dissolved. He heard a yip of agony from the pup. Then Brezog's voice was back in his thoughts: "*Bring the sword to me.*"

"No," Diello cried. "No!"

"Hurry, Scree," Cynthe said. "Help me. Get the hilt from Diello's belt and hand it to me."

"I must not touch it," Scree said. "It will kill me!"

"Do it!"

Diello squirmed, unable to throw off Cynthe's weight. He felt Scree's arm snaking around his waist. The goblin-boy fumbled with the pouch.

"Don't," Diello said, gasping. "Scree, no!"

But Scree pulled the pouch off his belt and handed it to Cynthe. Diello could hear her swift intake of breath as she held both pieces of the sword. A pale light shone around them, growing steadily brighter as she fitted blade and hilt together with a loud click. Cynthe grunted in satisfaction.

"Done," she said.

Brezog struck at Diello's mind. "*The sword is mine. Bring it to me!*"

Diello cried out in pain.

Cynthe scrambled away, freeing Diello. He rose, swaying, to his feet. The agony was splitting his head.

"*Obey me!*" Brezog commanded.

"Diello, look at me!" Cynthe said.

He saw his twin holding the shining sword high. She

was staring at an orb of sickly green light suspended in front of her.

"What is this thing?" she asked. "Help me."

The orb was growing larger. Diello hurried toward her.

"Get away from it," he said, but too late.

The orb shimmered into the shape of a hunched creature with crooked shoulders and a face from Diello's nightmares. Whether it was real or a magical image, Diello didn't care. Despite all their efforts, Brezog had found them.

The gorlord's red eyes peered at Cynthe. "So it's you, Faelin girl, who obeys me." Brezog stretched his hand toward her. "Give me the sword."

She stood transfixed, her eyes wide.

"Leave her alone!" Diello shouted.

He tugged Cynthe to one side, causing Brezog to miss as he reached for the sword.

Growling, Vassou attacked Brezog. The gorlord swung a mace—made from a skull attached to a shaft of polished bone—and knocked the wolf pup back. Diello heard a yelp before a flash of light dazzled him. Blinking hard, Diello saw Vassou lying motionless on the ground. The skull-mace struck Diello's shoulder, spinning him away from Cynthe with such force he lost his footing. As he fell, he saw Scree cowering behind a bush.

Diello almost called to the goblin-boy for help, but he knew Scree was too afraid to take action after the beating Brezog had given him back at the farmstead.

I have to use Eirian, Diello thought. *It's our only chance to drive Brezog away.*

Diello straightened, trying to ignore the numbness spreading from his shoulder down his arm. He seemed to be moving slowly, and he stumbled as he gained his feet. Meanwhile, Brezog was advancing on Cynthe, who hadn't budged from where she stood.

She still held Eirian high, and Diello could see her arms trembling from the strain. She was panting, her eyes frantic. She appeared unable to move on her own.

"Hit him with the sword!" Diello shouted. "Move, Cynthe! You can do it."

She uttered an inarticulate, enraged sound.

Brezog's choking her, Diello thought. He found his quarterstaff on the ground and lifted it.

"All you have to do, Faelin girl," Brezog said, "is obey my command. Give me the sword. I cannot take it by force from the hand that holds it. You must surrender it. Do so now."

Her arms jerked, lowering the weapon.

Diello struck the gorlord from behind. Brezog didn't even stagger from the blow.

He twisted to face Diello, batting away Diello's second strike. The quarterstaff caught on fire, blazing momentarily before it crumbled to ashes. As Diello dropped it, Brezog sprang at Cynthe. His talons grabbed Eirian.

The sword blade shot sparks that drove Brezog back, howling. The green light shining around the gorlord went out like a snuffed candle, and Eirian's radiance spread across the clearing. Brezog shielded his face with his cloak.

"See if you can loosen your fingers," Diello said to Cynthe.

Cynthe's hand trembled, but she managed to open her grasp slightly.

"Eirian," Diello said, "I take you with her permission."

Holding his breath, Diello plucked the sword from Cynthe. The sword did not resist him as it had Brezog. Grinning, Diello lifted it. The weapon shone even brighter. Its magic thrummed through Diello's wrists and arms as Eirian's power flowed into him. Diello was aware of the burning in his bones, but in that moment, he truly felt like a man. He thought of his strong, stubborn father, who'd once been a Carnethie Knight—an order of elite warriors in the king's service. Diello's Fae mother had been just as brave and determined. Both of them had been killed by this creature. *Now, Gorlord,* Diello thought, *it's your turn.*

Bracing his feet, he swung the sword at Brezog, putting his whole body behind the blow. The shining blade passed through the gorlord. His projected image flickered and vanished. Only the acrid smell of scorched air remained.

Diello slowly lowered the sword. But Eirian's blade was still throwing off sparks. Warily, Diello turned around. He saw no sign of danger. Then Sight filled him, showing him an image of Brezog. The gorlord was striking something.

One of the nearby trees split down the middle with a loud crack.

"Diello!" Scree shouted.

The tree came crashing down, smashing bushes and lesser saplings beneath it. Diello pushed his sister aside just in time for them to avoid being crushed by a heavy branch.

Then, there was only silence and the hot smell of charred

wood and dust fogging the air. The forest was unnaturally still. The gap made by the fallen tree allowed the twin moons to shine down. With Sight, Diello saw Brezog's face floating high above him, glaring.

I'll use no more magic for him to follow. Diello twisted Eirian's blade and hilt, pulling the weapon apart, and laid the pieces on the grass. Eirian's clear, pale light faded rapidly, leaving them in darkness. Diello's vision of the gorlord dissolved, too, and he no longer felt Brezog's presence.

With a gasp, Cynthe crumpled. Diello caught her and lowered her to the ground. Her skin was glowing faintly, sparkling the way Mamee's used to at night. He touched Cynthe's cheek. Her flesh felt cold.

"It's over," he said, reassuring himself as much as her. "Easy now. It's over."

She sat up and clutched his tunic, pressing her forehead to his shoulder.

"He hurt you," Diello said. "I'm sorry."

"He was in my head. I couldn't block him out. It was horrible!"

Diello's throat grew dry. "Is he still in your thoughts? Spying?"

"I—I don't think so." She pulled back. "So that's what he did to you back at the farmstead when he wanted us to tell him where Eirian was hidden."

There was nothing Diello could say.

"I wanted to strike him," Cynthe continued, "but the sword wouldn't obey me." She stared at Diello, her eyes widening. "It wanted *you*."

His mouth tightened. He was all too aware of what the

sword wanted, but he felt reluctant to admit how strongly it stirred him. His hands were still throbbing from holding the weapon. If he should ever carry it for any length of time, would it possess his mind and soul?

"Let's put the pieces away," he said.

"What if Brezog comes back?" Cynthe asked. "For real the next time?"

"We've got to keep moving."

"It's no use. We can't get away from him, ever."

That didn't sound like his twin. Diello hated hearing the defeat in her voice.

"You can't think like that," he said. "We've been careless, but we're still ahead of him."

"Not far enough."

I tried to tell you before, he thought. *Stubborn Cynthe. Now you understand.* But he was sorry she'd been forced to learn such a lesson.

"So we'll move on now, while we have the chance," he said.

"Then you should carry the sword for protection," she insisted.

"Not tonight. That's not really what it's for."

"It worked," she said, but then she shrugged.

Diello wrapped up the blade, then put the hilt back in his belt pouch, taking care to handle the grip and crosspiece as little as possible. He hadn't forgotten the very first time he held the weapon, when his fingers locked and wouldn't release it. Even now, the bones in his hands were tingling, and part of him would always yearn to claim the sword for his own.

Easing out a shaky breath, he heard Scree sidle up to him.

"I'm sorry I did not help you," Scree said quietly. "I was scared. I am ashamed."

"You couldn't help it. We were all scared."

"But you tried to fight." Scree turned to Cynthe. "I watched you stand up to the gorlord. You are the bravest girl in all the realms."

"Not really," she said, but she sounded pleased. "Hey, where's Vassou?"

Diello remembered the pup being struck down, and his heart lurched. "Over here."

They clustered around Vassou, who lay limp where he'd fallen, hardly more than a white blur in the shadows.

Cynthe dropped to her knees beside the wolf. "No!"

Diello was afraid to speak. "Is he—"

"Help him."

Diello realized she was crying. He crouched next to her and touched Vassou's wiry fur, digging his fingers into the pup's soft undercoat. The young wolf was alive, but barely breathing. Holding one of his paws, Diello tried to send some of his strength into Vassou, but the effort made him so dizzy he had to stop.

Cynthe tapped his shoulder. "I'm sorry. I'm sorry. I didn't mean for you to hurt yourself more."

"I'm all right," he said. "It's just—I'll rest a moment and try again."

"I will fetch our food," Scree offered. "I will get the bundles, and we will eat. I will fetch water for Vassou."

Diello nodded at the goblin-boy. "Thank you."

As Scree scurried off, Cynthe stroked Vassou's neck. "What else can we do for him?"

"His bones aren't broken. I think he's just stunned."

"But shouldn't he have woken by now?"

"I don't know, Cynthe. Brezog hit him awfully hard."

"But how could he do that? He wasn't really here, was he?"

Diello poked at his sore shoulder. "It felt like it when he hit me."

"It's my fault," she said after a short silence. "I wouldn't break camp fast enough. I was trying to hold us back, trying to help you when you looked so tired."

"Don't," Diello said. "It's as much my fault as yours. If I only knew how to block that monster from my thoughts!"

"Did you help me fly faster tonight?"

Diello didn't want to answer, but Cynthe was staring at him.

"Yes," he said.

Her hand slipped into his and gripped it hard. "I don't mind, you know. I'm glad you helped me."

Scree came hurrying up to the twins, dropping their bundles on the ground and handing the waterskin to Diello. Cynthe cupped her palms, and Diello carefully poured a measure into them before lifting Vassou's head.

She held the water to the pup's muzzle. Vassou roused only enough to lick feebly before he fell limp again.

Diello shared out the bread among the rest of them. The loaves were squashed, but they still tasted delicious.

"It would be better to eat ham," Scree suggested.

"In the morning," Diello said. "Let's go."

Cynthe got to her feet. "If you can lift Vassou onto my shoulder, I'll carry him."

"He's too big for you. I'll do it."

"No."

"Cynthe," Diello said firmly, "you've got to lead us to the hills. And you need to be able to use your bow in case of more trouble."

"I don't think I can handle another attack by—by—anyone."

He hugged her. "Yes, you can."

Diello held her for a moment. He could feel his own weariness creeping through his body, and he fought off the desperate need for sleep.

"We have to get as far from the woods as we can before we camp. Once we reach the hills, I'll feel easier," he said.

"I won't feel easy until we're safely in Embarthi." She pulled away from him, sniffing, and scrubbed her face with her sleeve. "If you think you can travel farther, then I can. But as soon as Vassou grows too heavy, tell me and we'll switch. Or camp."

"Agreed."

"Diello." She clasped his wrist. "Don't be stupid and try to do it all. Tell me. Promise?"

He bent over, trying to pick up Vassou gently. Cynthe helped him lift the pup across his uninjured shoulder. Vassou weighed a lot more than Diello expected. He took a cautious step, then another, and nodded to Cynthe.

"I can do this," he said. "For a while. Where's Scree?"

The goblin-boy had curled up, using the rucksack for a pillow. While Cynthe coaxed Scree to his feet, Diello started walking. Behind him he could hear Scree protesting.

"My head hurts. I am sleepy. The danger is gone now. I will sleep here with joy in my heart."

"And what will you do," Cynthe asked, "when the sprites come to feast on your bones?"

"I am coming," Scree said quickly. "I will carry the bed-rolls and food."

Diello heard their steps hurrying to catch up with his. A moment later, Cynthe took the lead, and Scree edged his scrawny body next to Diello.

"I know you are very tired," Scree said. "I will help you. I am glad to help you because you are my best friend. You saved my life today. And now you have driven the gorlord away. I am proud of you."

"Thanks," Diello mumbled. He wanted no credit for taking on Brezog. He and Cynthe had made too many mistakes today, taken too many risks.

From now on they'd have to be more careful to keep Brezog from finding them again.

It's a race, Diello thought. *Can we reach Embarthi and safety before Brezog stops us?*

He no longer felt sure of it.

chapter seven

a week later, they reached the rugged border country between the settled part of Antrasia and the wilds of Embarthi. They avoided any farmstead; even sighting a remote curl of hearth-smoke was enough for them to veer away. And all the while, the ground was rising, until they were climbing steep goat tracks and woodcutter trails that wound precariously up the hillsides. Some mornings they awoke to find a light dusting of snow on their blankets.

Vassou had recovered and led them once more. They spent an entire day climbing one hill. It was dense with forest in vivid hues of yellow, copper, crimson, and burgundy. Fallen leaves carpeted the rocky ground, and countless tiny springs seeped water from stone ledges. There was game, too. Sightings of rabbits, deer, gamecock, and boar had Cynthe keen for hunting, her eyes taking note of every track, every rubbed sapling, every trampled mud hole. Rainy mist fell on them, beading on leaves and mossy stone outcroppings and bringing out the mingled fragrances of soil, bark, cedar, and rotting wood.

By late afternoon they reached the summit and stood gazing out at the vista. The hills seemed to run all the way to the horizon. Foggy cloud had settled in, filling the narrow valleys so that only the hilltops—shaggy with trees and brush—poked through. Twilight threw long purple shadows, and rain began to fall in earnest.

Diello pointed at the smoke-colored hills. "Look at it. That's Embarthi!"

Cynthe's dirty face lit up. "At last!"

Vassou came over and sat between them. "No," he said. "Those are the Westering Hills."

"But haven't we been crossing them already?" Cynthe asked.

"No."

"It looks very far," Scree said.

"Do we have to get through all of them?" Diello asked. "It will take a year to walk up and down those slopes."

Vassou grinned, displaying very sharp teeth. "Yes, *if* we went up and down, but we will take the pass instead."

"Look over there." Cynthe poked at Diello and pointed. "See where there's a break in the clouds? Mountains! Far away. They have snow on their tops. Is that Embarthi?"

"You see the mountains of Tescorsa, land of the giant eagles," Vassou said. He swung around, pointing with his muzzle. "Look this way."

Beneath a black rain cloud, the hills to the southwest appeared rounder, shorter, and dense with trees. Thanks to the clouds and rain, visibility was poor. Diello frowned with frustration.

"How close are we?" he asked.

"Maybe two weeks more, if we keep up the pace," said Vassou.

"Two weeks!" Cynthe said. "I was hoping you'd say two days."

His sister's disappointment was as strong as Diello's own. Still, the end of this journey was getting closer all the time.

"Well, then," Cynthe said with a nod. She turned up one of her feet to look at the bottom of her moccasin. "I've got holes worn through the leather again. We'd better make a good camp and stay here tomorrow so I can hunt and patch my footgear."

"Mine need patching, too," Diello said, feeling cold mud oozing under his heel.

They all set to work. Vassou went off into the trees on some purpose of his own. Scree gathered a large pile of fragrant cedar boughs. Diello found long sticks and propped them against a stone outcropping to form a lean-to, then helped Scree lay the boughs over the framework to create a shelter that would keep out the rain. Usually they piled leaves over themselves at night, but it was too wet for that. Diello unrolled his blanket to take out the few pieces of kindling he'd gathered at the first drop of rain that morning. They were nice and dry. He laid them inside the ring of stones that Scree built. Everyone knew their job. They worked efficiently and quietly as a team, too tired to chatter.

Cynthe started to snap her fingers to flick fire, but Diello stopped her with a shake of his head and brought out his tinderbox. Made by his father for Diello's thirteenth birthday, the flint and steel had served him well on this journey. The protective wax coating the steel had worn off, however, and—because he was part Fae—Diello couldn't handle the metal without his fingers turning red and itching. He pulled the ragged edge of his sleeve over his hand, shielding his skin from the metal before he struck a spark.

The kindling and fluff of dried grass caught fire. Diello breathed on the tiny flame lightly, feeding it one stick, then another, until the blaze strenthened. Cynthe added dry wood chips from her own supplies.

"Not too much," Diello warned her as the fire leaped and crackled. "We don't want to set our roof on fire."

They crowded into the shelter. Cynthe had made their stolen food last all week, but it was nearly gone. She was just dividing the final scrap of ham when Vassou returned, shaking rain off his pelt. He laid a plump hare on the ground. Cynthe skinned and dressed it while Diello whittled a spit. Soon the meat was browning over the fire, its fat and drippings hissing in the flames. Diello took their battered pot and ventured out into the rain to fill it with spring water. When he returned, the supper was ready. Cynthe divided the meat equally among them. The portions were small, but they'd grown used to that. This juicy, flavorful meat seemed like a feast. Diello chewed with pleasure, grateful for what he had. He tried not to think about the large platters of chicken, ham, or goose with roasted taties and bubbling root squash baked with cream and butter that Mamee used to serve on chilly autumn nights.

He'd been lucky to find a long, straight stick about the same length as his old quarterstaff. With his knife he peeled off the thin bark, the shavings curling over his knuckles.

"You are skilled with wood," Scree said, watching Diello work. "I wish I were clever like you."

Diello smiled. "Pa was the skilled one, but he taught me what little I know." Pausing, Diello held out his knife and the staff to the goblin-boy. "Care to try?"

Delight and apprehension mingled on Scree's face. He started to take the staff then shook his head. "No. I would ruin your work and make you angry."

"If you make a mistake, I'll find another stick," Diello told him. "Try."

"Go ahead," Cynthe chimed in. "Cut the bark with long, even strokes of the blade. Don't gouge the wood."

Scree's grubby fingers closed on the stick. He took Diello's knife in his other hand and scraped tentatively at the remaining bark. The knife slipped, and only Diello's quick grab kept it from cutting Scree's leg.

"Careful!"

Scree cringed. "I am sorry! I warned you I would not do it right."

"You can't improve if you don't keep trying," Diello said. This time, he kept his hand around Scree's, guiding the knife in a steady cut. "Like that. See?"

"Yes. I can do it," Scree said excitedly. "Cynthe! Vassou! I am carving wood."

"Good job," Cynthe said.

"It is wise for you to gain new skills," Vassou added.

Vassou's praise surprised Diello. It was unusual for the wolf to show Scree kindness.

Diello sat back and let Scree finish scraping the bark by himself.

Scree looked up with shining eyes as he handed knife and staff back to Diello. "Is it enough?"

Nodding, Diello finished smoothing the wood. "If you find a good stick tomorrow, I'll help you make a staff of your own."

"I would like that very much," Scree said. "But I would rather have a spear. A spear with a pointed end. Then I would have a weapon for stabbing instead of hitting. I think that I would like that more."

"Then we'll make you a spear," Diello said.

Cynthe started talking about her plans for tomorrow's hunt. If she brought down a deer, they could dry enough strips of meat to supply them for the rest of the journey. And the hide could be worked into pliant leather for clothing. Scree was already nodding off. Vassou yawned hugely, showing all his teeth, before he curled himself up tightly with his bushy tail over his nose. Diello banked the fire while Cynthe rolled herself in her blanket and snuggled against him.

Soon she was snoring, her head heavy on his leg. Scree's back pressed against Diello, and he spread his blanket over himself and the goblin-boy. Warm and fed, Diello slept well, but then woke abruptly. He wasn't sure what had disturbed his slumber. He listened for any indication of danger before realizing that the steady patter of rain had stopped. That seemed to be all. He gradually relaxed. But he was very cold, for Scree had taken more than his share of the blanket. The fire had long since died.

Through the opening of their lean-to, Diello could see the gray tinge of dawn. The world seemed to be holding its breath, caught between the death of night and the birth of day.

The stars were fading into the twilight. Diello stared at them, wondering if Mamee watched over her children now as one of those bits of light. He missed her and Pa with an ache that had become a part of him. He and Cynthe no longer talked about them much. This journey was about survival; there wasn't much point in grieving.

But it had become his custom each night to pray to the Guardian for his little sister's safety. After their parents were killed, the wife of Lord Malques, the local baron, had wanted to adopt Amalina, but the little girl had vanished mysteriously from Wodesley Castle. Was the three-year-old cared for by her abductor? Was kindness shown to her? Was Amalina fed enough and warm? Where was she? Would Diello and Cynthe ever see her again?

Two more weeks to reach Embarthi. Not so long, yet it seemed an eternity. Besides, that was just the border. They still had to locate Uncle Owain, wherever he was. He wasn't going to be standing at the gateway of that fabled land, bidding them welcome. He didn't even know they were coming. They had never met—he was just a name that Mamee had mentioned sometimes. Diello hoped his uncle would help them solve their dilemma. Mage-chancellor Clevn had said the sword would be Amalina's ransom, yet Diello had promised Pa that he would return Eirian to its rightful place. Diello knew he had to put Amalina's safety first. But it was important to restore Pa's honor.

This wasn't the first time Diello had awakened early and worried. He kept hoping that some morning he'd open his eyes with a perfect solution to his problems. But he never did.

Diello must have fallen back asleep because he awoke to sunshine on his face. Someone had piled the extra blanket over him, and the bundles were stacked against his back to add their meager protection. Sitting up, Diello rubbed his eyes and gazed around. The others were gone, but a flat, palm-sized stone with three twigs crossed on top of it left him a message from Cynthe: Everyone was hunting.

He also found two leather ovals waiting for him, cut to the size of his feet. He pulled off his moccasins and fitted the leather pieces inside.

Crawling out of the lean-to, Diello stood in the sunshine and stretched before stamping his feet and rubbing his hands across his face and ears to warm them. The sun might be shining, but there was scant warmth in it yet. His breath fogged white as he set about fetching fresh water from the nearby spring. He didn't know water could be that cold without freezing. It made his teeth ache, but he drank anyway, feeling it chill him from the inside out.

Eager to find some breakfast for himself, he took his bearings, picked up his new quarterstaff, and set off cheerfully.

Studying the tracks in the rain-softened ground, Diello made sure he took a direction no one else had followed and headed downhill, going at an angle so the footing was less steep. He enjoyed the challenge of scrambling along. Soon the exercise warmed him, although his stomach rumbled insistently. A whistle caught his attention. He saw an eagle sailing the wind currents, lazily circling. The fog between the hills had mostly burned off, and the view was stunning.

His spirits rose even more. Their luck had turned. He was sure of it.

He came to a ravine. Brush and brambles choked the bottom. Diello spotted a treasure load of bushberries hanging in ripe clusters, the swollen purple fruit bright and tempting in the sunshine. Frost had not yet withered it in this protected spot.

There was nothing more delicious than sun-ripened bushberries, but the vines were bristling with thorns, and the fruit was hanging in the center of the thicket. The outer canes had already been stripped of their bounty, probably by birds, and the remaining berries were tucked under a spray of newer growth arching over them like a cage. He wouldn't have noticed them if the sun hadn't been shining at this angle, making them glow.

There was no easy way to climb down into the ravine. The sides were steep, almost sheer, with lots of loose rock that made footing even more unstable. He could probably get down into the thicket, but he wasn't sure whether he could climb out.

Fly! he told himself, and laughed. Cynthe's skill might be improving, but his was nothing to brag about. And it was no good moaning about the lack of practice. Until they entered Embarthi, it would be stupid to use magic except when truly necessary. Not even for breakfast.

He moved back from the edge and slithered farther down the slope until he found a way into the ravine that would also allow him an exit.

Be patient. Be steady. Be sure.

Pa's voice seemed to whisper in his ear. Diello checked all around him, sniffing the air. From this angle, the brush-tangled ravine looked like the perfect site for a trog den. He didn't smell the rank musk, however, and he wasn't sure if the beasts ventured into mountainous country. Even so, he took the time to search for scat or the distinctive claw marks where trogs marked their territory.

Nothing.

Satisfied, Diello pushed his way into the thicket. Soon brambles were catching his tunic and leggings. Using his staff to push them aside, he advanced gingerly, pausing now and then to free himself. A thorn raked his palm, leaving a stinging weal of blood. He sucked at it and struggled forward.

He could see the fruit now. The berries were smaller than he'd thought, but so heavily clustered it was a wonder they hadn't snapped the canes supporting them. The closer he got, the longer the protective barbs seemed to be, grabbing at his clothing and skin. The brambles were like a wall against his legs. Wincing, he strained to reach, and by wriggling his fingers, managed to brush the fruit with his fingertips. Several berries fell into his hand while others dropped to the ground.

He grimaced at the loss. Some lucky mouse would find them. With great care, he withdrew his hand and popped the berries into his mouth. Rich, flavorful juice squirted between his teeth. He swallowed in delight. They were even better than he'd imagined. He could barely wait to pick the rest of them. There was enough for him to eat his fill and still have plenty to share with the others.

But, no matter how far he stretched, he couldn't quite touch the next cluster. A briar sawed across his arm. His feet shuffled for better purchase on the muddy ground, but the stiff new leather kept him from digging in his toes.

One more try, Diello thought, and lunged.

The ground crumbled beneath him, and he plunged straight down into a hole.

He landed hard on his backside with his new quarterstaff thumping down on his head. He sat there, a bit stunned.

He'd fallen to the bottom of a narrow shaft, about the depth and circumference of an old dry well. In front of him yawned a crudely dug tunnel that looked very dark. It smelled of dank soil and crawly things.

This *was* a trog den. Only a trog possessed the strength to tunnel through soil this stony. The man-sized creatures were dangerous at the best of times and quite lethal when defending their territory. It didn't matter that he couldn't smell trog scent. Maybe the den was abandoned, or maybe it was just an older section of a large den still in use.

He had to get out of here.

Scrambling to his feet, he looked up. The top of the hole was beyond his reach, even if he jumped. He took a try at it anyway, his fingers slapping the tunnel wall far short of the top. He slid down, raking his palms on sharp bits of flint. Clay mud streaked his tunic front.

Undeterred, Diello found a thin rock with a pointed edge and started digging toeholds. It was awkward work, but he chipped away until he'd scraped shallow indentations as high as he could. Dropping his rock, he braced his feet on either side of the tunnel and started climbing, jamming fingers and toes into the holds.

When he finally curled his fingers over the top edge, he strained to scramble up, only to feel the ground giving under his weight. Down he went again, his hand snagging painfully on a berry cane. He landed on his stomach under a pile of dirt.

Winded and coughing, Diello worked his way out of the landslide. He picked several thorns out of his palm as he gave his situation some thought.

The bottom of the ravine must be riddled with old tunnels that were collapsing. He wasn't going to get out by jumping or climbing. That left one more thing to try.

Lifting his arms, he tried to "grab air," as Cynthe called it. *Up!* he thought, but nothing happened. His body felt as heavy as a mountain. He concentrated even harder.

Up!

His body grew lighter. His heels rose off the ground, then his toes. Diello grinned, looking skyward.

Thump! The magic failed him and down he went.

He was going to have to crawl along the tunnel to find another way out. It was insanely risky, but what else could he do? Sit helplessly and hope his twin eventually found him?

If he met up with a trog, that would be the end of him. His bronze knife couldn't pierce trog hide, and his quarterstaff was useless in these tight quarters. Eirian's hilt hung in his belt pouch, but what good was it?

"Scared?" Diello said aloud softly, taunting himself.

Maybe the den really was abandoned. He'd feel foolish

if he didn't take the risk. The quicker he began, the quicker he'd escape. But what if he found himself lost, or buried alive?

Tucking his quarterstaff through his belt, Diello took one last look at the sky before crawling into the darkness.

chapter eight

At the first bend in the tunnel, Diello lost the light from the open shaft. He tried to remember everything he'd ever heard about trogs. They grew sluggish in winter, but didn't hibernate. Most were solitary.

He drew several deep breaths for courage and flicked a little fire ahead of him. There was nothing in front of him but more tunnel. He crawled forward a ways and flicked fire again.

Listening to his own ragged breathing, he thought, *I can do this. Just keep my head and take things slowly.* The ground beneath him angled upward now, giving him hope that he would soon find the exit.

He felt a puff of fresh air in his face and strained to see ahead of him.

His outstretched hand touched nothing, and he pitched forward. He hit the ground with a jolt.

When he sat up, he could see—thanks to light filtering dimly through a hole choked with brush. There were old scents here, a faint but pungent mingling of snake, trog, and bitterweed. He sneezed from the haze of dust he'd stirred up and scrambled for the exit.

Diello blundered over something mounded beneath the dirt and heard a faint clink of metal. He jumped sideways and slammed his back against the wall. It took him a moment to realize nothing was in here with him, nothing had attacked him.

He ventured back to the mound. Curious, he thrust his fingers into the soil and touched little squares of metal buried there.

Coins!

He uncurled his fingers to peer at the dirt-crusted pieces. When he rubbed one of them, it glinted. He bit it, and his tooth dented the soft metal. He hefted the money in his hand.

It was gold, all right, even if it didn't look like the money minted nowadays. The design stamped on the pieces felt worn but was difficult to make out in the gloom. It hardly mattered. He'd stumbled upon a trog's treasure!

With a burst of glee, he dug with both hands, scooping out more of the coins. He filled his pockets. After a moment's thought, he extracted Eirian's hilt from its pouch, tied a spare bit of cord to it, and hung it around his neck before filling the pouch with the rest of the coins. The money was dragging at his belt and weighing him down, but he didn't care. This was a fortune.

We're rich! he thought. *I'll use this to ransom Amalina. Cynthe can have half of it, and there'll still be enough to buy myself a horse and armor. I'll be a warrior yet.*

Now he just needed to escape.

He peered out through the hole before sticking his quarterstaff through the opening and using it to move the brush aside. He eased his shoulders through, wriggling against the tight fit. Once his arms were out, it should have been simple to pull himself the rest of the way, except he was laden with the money.

He finally made it and sat resting, taking in breaths of fresh air. All he had to do was figure out how to leave the ravine.

He studied the steep sides. To his left, the ravine ended in a cleft of stone that rose to a sheer cliff towering above his head. Water was trickling down the rock face, and Diello washed the worst of the grime from his hands before cupping them and drinking. The rest of the ravine held that choked mess of brambles, with the unstable ground ready to collapse. If he crept along the edge, pressed as close to the side as possible, he might be able to squeeze past. The ground was less likely to crumble under him there.

With the money clinking in his pockets and the pouch bumping against his leg, Diello struggled along, pushing past the briars. The bushberries still looked as enticing as ever, but he had found a better treasure. His head buzzed with plans as he fought his way free and clambered onto the hillside.

He paused to catch his breath. The slope leading back to the campsite looked very steep indeed, especially with his burden.

A yip came from higher uphill. Grinning, Diello waved at Vassou.

The mid-morning breeze shifted slightly, ruffling his hair and bringing with it a scent of something rank and musty—*trog*.

Diello had just enough time to whirl around and raise his quarterstaff before the animal was on him. He swung his weapon hard across the trog's snout. Yelping, the beast veered away, giving Diello the chance to see that it was small and young, with shaggy dark-gray fur and yellowish eyes that looked bewildered. Whimpering and snuffling, it rubbed its injured muzzle on the ground.

Diello started up the hill, only to falter as a second young trog came at him from the right. A shrill howl made him look back, and there was a third, rising on its hind legs as it set up a fearsome racket.

They were all roughly the same size. Littermates, he supposed, and about half-grown. Come next spring, they would scatter as solitary adults, establish their separate dens, and start their gold hoards gleaned from bits of ore dug from the hills or by robbing wayfarers; for now, they were hunting together as a pack. No one knew why gold attracted trogs. One legend claimed that trogs were descended from a long-ago group of bandits foolish enough to pillage the treasury of the most ancient of gods. They'd been caught, and as punishment they were turned into animals forever cursed to hunt for their prize. Maybe these cubs had come prowling around the old den today in search of its treasure. But Diello had become their prey.

They attacked. He managed to hit two in the snout, driving them back, but the third batted at him clumsily, nearly knocking him down.

The trio circled him, growling. Diello turned with them, trying to protect his back. Their inexperience was all that had saved him so far. He only hoped there was no parent trog close by.

One of the cubs leaped at him. Diello yelled loudly and whacked it in the head, making it howl with fright. The other two should have rushed him, but they rose on their hind legs instead, snarling and displaying their large yellow teeth. None of them had started to grow tusks yet. If he was going to escape, he'd better do it now before they figured out how to work together.

Two closed in, trying to trap him between them, but he dodged. He went only a few steps, though, before the third blocked his path, trying to rake him with its long claws. Diello twisted away from the swipe, but was butted hard from behind.

If he stayed down he was finished. Scrambling awkwardly to his feet, Diello felt another paw swipe his shoulder. It spun him around, and he used the momentum to power his blow. He jabbed the blunt end of his staff at a shaggy throat.

All three cubs retreated. Again they circled him, sniffing and growling.

About twenty-five paces away stood a walner tree, substantial enough to support his weight in its upper branches—if he could reach it. Trogs were poor climbers.

Taking a coin from his pocket, he held it up and let their small eyes focus on it. "Smell it?" he asked, waving it around to excite them. "See it? Want it?"

One of the cubs tried to roar. The others bounced and jostled each other, making a chittering noise. He tossed the coin, and all three lunged for it.

Diello ran for the tree while a furious fight broke out behind him.

He jumped for the low fork in the trunk . . . and didn't make it. Without the gold, he could've been scrambling into its lower branches.

The cubs caught up with him. Putting his back to the trunk, Diello swung his quarterstaff, but they'd learned its dangers. Now, they took turns pouncing at him and retreating, making a game of it. One mistake, and this game would turn lethal for him.

If only he could fly. One short ascension was all he needed to reach the lowest branch. Tightening his grip on his weapon, Diello thought, *Up!*

No good. Little gray spots danced in front of his eyes. His ears roared, and he stumbled.

The trogs rushed him.

Diello swung, but one creature caught him from the side. He went down, the quarterstaff flying from his hand. The snarling beast was on top of him, its breath hot in his face as it went for his throat. He punched its bony face, and the pain in his hand was horrible. Then its sharp teeth closed on his forearm, and that agony was worse. He felt another cub biting at his foot, tugging at his moccasin. The third tore open the money pouch. The coins spilled everywhere in a shining stream as the cub shook the pouch like a dog killing a rat.

The cubs released him, going for the treasure with more chittering and snarling. Two of them rolled together in a brawl while the third began sniffing the money avidly, scooping up the coins in its jaws and tucking them away in its belly fur.

Diello sat up. *This is my chance*, he thought. He limped to the tree and managed to boost himself into its fork just as the roar of a full-grown trog shook the air. The cubs stopped fighting and bounced with excited shrieks as an enormous female trog came shambling out of the woods on all fours. She crouched at the sight of Diello and snuffled the air. Her pale mane of coarse hair bristled upright along her spine as she reared, waving long claws.

"Mama trog," Diello whispered.

The youngsters surrounded her, grunting. Diello climbed higher, reaching a stout branch and perching there.

"Take the gold," he muttered, watching her. "Take it all!"

She ignored the spilled treasure and approached his tree. Her movements were slow yet aggressive. Baring her teeth, she shook the tree trunk.

Diello clung to the bark, determined not to fall.

She struck the tree, balancing on her hind feet and stretching to her full height so that she could almost reach him. When she roared, he could see down her gullet.

His own throat was closing up, making it hard to breathe. He climbed higher, aiming for a broad limb. But just as he braced his feet and grabbed it, she rocked the tree again.

He lost his hold and fell. And she was right beneath him, ready to tear him to pieces.

Instinctively, he spread his arms wide and his hands caught the air. Suddenly he was no longer falling, but rising instead, his body as light as the breeze itself. He turned his body vertically, lifting his arms like a swimmer preparing to dive.

Only he kept rising, gaining speed now. His hair blew back from his brow. Laughter bubbled up inside him. He spread out his arms once more, throwing back his head to yell in triumph.

In his excitement, he forgot to watch where he was going. He flew into a branch, and a wad of leaves smacked him in the mouth, filling it with a leathery, cold taste.

And then he was falling, even faster than he'd risen.

chapter nine

Plummeting, Diello knew better than to reach out and grab the passing branches. That was a good way to break his arm. But with the trog family still crouched below him, he had to do *something* or he'd find himself right in their jaws. He slapped at leaves and twigs to slow his fall.

Up! he thought. *Up! Up!*

"Diello!" It was his sister's voice, sounding both amused and alarmed. "Stop flapping your arms like that. Let the air hold you."

"I can't! I'm heavy. I—"

Now she was flying beside him, controlled and relaxed. Her hand caught one of his flailing ones and held it.

"Don't fight," she said. "Float, like you're in the creek."

His whole body was tense. His head was aching, and he could feel his bones tingling. *No!* screamed a tiny voice in the back of his skull.

But Cynthe would never harm him. He forced the knots from his muscles and let his body go limp.

At once, his descent slowed. He grew lighter and more buoyant.

"That's right," Cynthe coached. "Now, stay that way. Just float."

"I'm so tired!"

"Let the air hold you. You don't have to make this happen. Stop controlling it."

"The magic's going to fail."

"It won't, unless you keep forcing it. Just *be*."

He lay there on his back, hanging in midair, and realized she was right. He wasn't doing anything now. The ache in his head faded, and he eased out his breath.

"See?" Cynthe said calmly, floating beside him. "Now turn over if you like."

When he did, he saw that he was no higher off the ground than his upstairs window back home. The trog family was sitting beneath him, staring up.

"You're fine," Cynthe said. "I'm going to tow you."

"You can't," he gasped, and felt himself dip.

"Do what I tell you." It was like hearing Pa give an order.

Diello obeyed, knowing he trusted no one more than his twin. She let go of his hand, and he nearly panicked again, but then she came up on his other side and curled her fingers around his.

She smiled at him. "You won't fall," she promised.

He let himself believe her. And as he relaxed, he felt lighter and happier than he'd been in a long time. It was like being part of the very air. The breeze seemed to be whispering secrets in his ears. He kicked, but Cynthe's grip tightened.

"Don't do anything," she said. "Leave this to me."

They moved away from the tree, and then they were aloft in the open sky. The sunlight was dazzling. He squinted, catching glimpses of blue mingled with puffy cloud, the wind tickling his hair and billowing his clothing. The air was sharp with cold, but he didn't care. It seemed to sing through his body.

She's right. It's exactly like swimming. Why didn't I figure this out before?

"Stop thinking," Cynthe said. "I brought down a deer for us."

He saw the pride in his twin's face. "Well done! We'll eat like royalty tonight."

"If I can get the meat dressed."

"I'll help you," Diello said, his mouth watering at the thought of venison steak. Then he glimpsed the trogs on the move, heads up and watching, following him and Cynthe. "Are Scree and Vassou at the camp?"

"Scree should be. He helped me carry the buck. Why? Do you want them to see you flying?"

"The mama trog's following us there."

Cynthe twisted to look, the wind whipping her hair across her face. "No, she's stopped. What are they grubbing for, there on the ground?"

Diello reluctantly told his sister about the treasure he'd found and lost. "All I have left are a few coins in my pockets."

"That's the most witless thing you've done yet," she said.

"And I suppose you would have left it there?"

"I wouldn't have crawled into a trog's den in the first place."

He opened his mouth to argue, but they were slowing, angling downward now to the camp. Vassou was standing next to the deer carcass, staring up at them. Scree emerged from the lean-to, saw Diello and Cynthe, and called to them in excitement, clapping his hands.

Together, the twins landed. As soon as his feet were back on the ground, Diello whooped. Grinning at his sister, he gave her a hug and swung her around. "Wasn't it great? Thank you, Cynthe! I'd probably have broken my neck if you hadn't come in time."

She pushed him away, but with a smile. "You'd be trog fodder."

"Absolutely." He nodded. "Thank you."

"We'd better take care of your arm."

"No time." Diello glanced at the others. "Let's break camp. The trogs will be coming up the hill for us—"

"Do not worry," Scree said. "The wolf is doing a protection spell."

Diello felt a *cloigwylie* shimmer around the camp. "Vassou," he warned, "she can come through that."

"Throw those coins away," Cynthe insisted. "And let me bind your arm so the blood won't draw her."

"That's not enough to discourage her."

"And I'm not leaving our meat for her, either," Cynthe said.

A wolf howled nearby. Diello heard a second howl, then a third.

"Watch," Vassou said.

Five gray wolves appeared at the edge of the trees halfway down the hill. As soon as they broke cover, they headed for the trogs.

"What are they doing?" Diello asked. "Are they samal wolves, too?"

"Not samal. But kindred to us. In ancient times we shared a common ancestry, until the Guardian offered us magic. Those that accepted it became samal. Those that did not remained as animals in the wild. We call them cousin, though we do not mingle our packs now. They will drive away the trogs."

"But a cub drew Diello's blood," Cynthe protested. "They'll come after him."

Vassou sniffed Diello's wound while a clamor of snarls arose from downhill. "This bite is not deep." He gave it a gentle lick, cleaning it for Diello. "The young ones lack good hunting instincts. Watch! The mother is now distracted by my cousins."

Downhill, the fight began. Circling, the wolves attacked the adult trog, nipping quickly before dodging back. Roaring, the trog swiped with her powerful claws, but she wasn't fast enough. Her cubs huddled beside her, getting in her way. She dropped to all fours and broke into a shuffling lope, her cubs following her. The wolves chased them out of sight.

Diello sank to the ground.

Cynthe busied herself digging out the tiny jar of Mamee's healing salve and binding up his arm. He sucked in his breath a couple of times, refusing to yelp.

"You won't have a scar," she pronounced. "Nothing like mine."

He cradled his sore arm against his stomach. "I'd just as soon not compete with you for getting the biggest trog scar."

She lifted the hilt hanging around his neck before letting it drop on his chest with a thump. "What about this? I suppose you lost the pouch because you filled it with money and they got it."

He nodded, feeling his face grow hot.

"You could've lost the hilt, carrying it this way. And where's your new quarterstaff?"

"I dropped it by the tree when I was fighting. I'll recover it as soon as we're sure they're really gone."

"Fine, but you can't carry the hilt like that for anyone to see."

He smiled up at her, tilting his head to one side. "Make me another pouch? Please?"

She dug her hand deep in his pocket and pulled out a few square coins. "So you can fill it with these?"

"I promise I'll put only the hilt in it. Please, Cynthe?"

"Very well." She tossed the coins on the ground instead of handing them back. "This money's too dangerous to have."

Scree crouched and began picking the coins out of the grass, while Vassou paced, still holding the *cloigwylie* in place while he watched the woods and open hillside.

"I wanted ransom for Amalina," Diello said. "I told you that."

Cynthe's gaze softened. "We've already got the means

to ransom her. The sword isn't yours to keep and never will be."

"It's about honoring my promise to Pa to return the sword where it belongs. If we use it for ransom, then what will become of it?"

"We can't be responsible for everything," Cynthe said. "And our sister comes first."

"I know that." Diello had also promised Pa that he would take care of his sisters. But he hadn't expected to face so many difficult choices. Dusting off his hands, he looked downhill. "I'm going for my quarterstaff."

Scree held out the money he'd picked up. "This is goblin gold," he said happily. "Very old. I cannot read what is stamped on it, for it is in the ancient words, but I know these are symbols of the gorlord-*agish*."

"Brezog?" Cynthe asked.

Scree shook his head. "No, the *agish* is more. It is the Great One of the Ancient Times, before Ercoth, father of Brezog. The *agish* is the force behind all goblin magic. It is—"

Vassou growled, and Scree's voice faltered. His big eyes stared up at Diello, then shifted to Cynthe's suspicious gaze. Vassou's ears were flattened, and he bared his fangs at Scree.

"Hush, Vassou," Cynthe said softly.

"How do you know all this?" Diello asked Scree. "I thought you were raised in Wodesley and your human mother died while birthing you."

"I—I—"

"Who taught you this?" Cynthe demanded. "How do you know goblin lore? And goblin symbols?"

Scree's thin shoulders hunched as though he expected a beating. He appealed to Diello. "Please! You are my friends," he whispered, dropping the money. "Do not become my enemies. Do not look at me in this way of hatred. I know what I am, unfit to live. Please remember that I am always your friend."

"Then answer Cynthe's questions," Diello said.

The goblin-boy pressed his grubby hands to his face and sobbed. "I was not always at Wodesley. Before, I—I was among the . . ." He glanced up. "It is true that I grew up motherless. Her people did not want me and gave me to a band of hobgoblins. They are the least cruel, but there was a hard winter and food was scarce. No one wished to feed me. They cast me out to starve, to die in the snow. But I did not die. A raiding party of goblins made a slave of me. They treated me harshly. So I ran away and found traveling beggar folk, Antrasins. They would not take me in, saying I was hideous and bad luck. But they let me sleep beneath their wagon and eat the scraps they threw away. I watched them at their work in the villages, and I learned their trade."

"You were a cutpurse?" Diello asked.

"No, no, no. I was never a thief," Scree assured him, sniffing. "I begged. I had a little cup with a broken bottom that I took from the refuse pile. I had to hold my hand beneath it so the coins wouldn't fall out. Then the warden of Wodesley Castle caught me, and I was put among the boys to be apprenticed."

Diello remembered that group of misfit boys that no one wanted. He and Cynthe had met Scree when they were all jammed together in the labor peddler's wagon, on their way to be bound to apprenticeships . . . or sold into a worse situation. Together, they'd escaped.

Scree flung himself at Diello's feet. "I am not a false friend to you! I cannot help if I lived among the goblin-kind and learned some of their ways. I am not a spy. I am grateful for your kindness to me. It has been so different since you called me friend. Please don't cast me out now. I—I have nothing else but your—"

"Stop it," Diello said. "Please. No one's saying you have to go."

"No, Scree," Cynthe said, pulling him upright. "We were just asking questions because you tell us different stories."

Scree faced her, hiccuping a little. "Do you distrust me now? Because I recognized a goblin coin?" He turned back to Diello. "Are you going to always wonder if I am lying? What must I do?"

Vassou nudged Scree's hand. "Tell us the truth. You must trust *us* if we are to trust you."

"He means," Cynthe broke in, "that you shouldn't panic when we ask you questions. Now please stop crying. You can keep the coins if you like. Why don't you go with Diello to fetch his staff? Be sure he stays out of trouble."

"That's right," Diello said, making a face at his twin, who smirked back. "I need guarding today."

A wide grin spread across Scree's face. He rubbed his hands, bowing to Cynthe. "Thank you, Cynthe. Thank you! I will help Diello for he looks very tired. I wish I could fly as you do. I wish I could know all the things that you both know. I will help you, Cynthe, and bury the offal for you and scrape the hide if you wish me to do those tasks. I do not mind."

Diello, aware that Scree would babble on forever if unchecked, held up his hand. "Scree," he said, "the best way you could help right now is to bring back my quarterstaff. I don't feel up to walking down there and back. Any coins you come across are yours to keep."

"But I will be rich! Oh, thank you—"

Diello waved him off. "Don't take too long."

Vassou lowered the *cloigwylie*, and Scree pattered away, rubbing his hands and mumbling to himself in delight.

"Did you believe all that?" Cynthe asked, when he was out of earshot.

"Maybe." Diello sighed. "I don't think he's a spy. He could have betrayed us a long time ago."

Vassou wandered away in silence.

"Vassou doesn't agree with you," Cynthe said thoughtfully. "He has never fully trusted Scree."

"Goblins and wolves don't mix," Diello replied. "At least not usually." He hesitated. "I don't think you and I should split up anymore."

"Why? Because I had to come save you today?"

Diello saw the teasing glint in her eye.

"We rely on each other," he said. "We're a team, and staying apart isn't working. Not for me anyway."

Cynthe nodded. "You know, Vassou keeps reminding us that the pieces of Eirian have to be kept apart for its safety, but I think it's time we worried about *our* safety. If you and I had been the pair stealing food back in that last town, things wouldn't have gone so wrong."

"Agreed."

"And maybe Brezog wouldn't have caught up with us."

"We don't know that," Diello said. "We've used too much magic today. He could find us again."

"But wasn't it glorious? We were flying together!" She pointed at the sky. "How I wish we could race into the clouds right now and fly the rest of the way to Embarthi. No more trogs and goblins to worry about. No more trudging along. No more being cold and wet."

Diello heard the worry under her words and gave her an encouraging nudge with his elbow. "We'll make it," he said. "Now let's get busy so we can eat well tonight."

She stiffened, moving closer to him.

"Diello," she whispered.

He followed her gaze and saw a pack of wolves emerging from the woods behind their campsite.

chapter ten

the twins faced the wolves. It was a pack of twenty animals or more. Most were mottled gray with brown markings, their eyes intense and predatory. Cynthe held her bow. Without his quarterstaff, Diello felt very vulnerable. He knew enough to stay calm. Pa always said that was the way to command a dog or any animal.

Vassou returned, joining them. His bushy tail stood out straight behind him. He kept his gaze focused on the pack leader: a tall, rangy wolf with a dark muzzle.

Hearing a faint noise behind him, Diello turned just as Scree tossed him the quarterstaff. The goblin-boy scuttled away to climb atop the stone outcropping supporting their lean-to. As he went, he nervously gathered handfuls of rocks.

The wolves ignored Scree. The pack leader lowered his head and rubbed his muzzle on his front leg.

Vassou advanced a short distance. The two of them exchanged sniffs before the pack leader dropped to his belly. Vassou sat down before him, and they began to yip, mutter, and growl to each other.

"Have you ever seen anything like that?" Cynthe whispered to Diello.

"No," he murmured back. "At least, not the talking part."

"Talking!"

"Hush. I want to listen."

Her brows knotted, but she stayed quiet. Diello concentrated, and after a moment the wolf sounds began to make sense.

"*Thank you for coming to our aid, my cousins,*" Vassou was saying. "*Those of you who drove away the trogs did well. We must keep these Faelin children safe.*"

"*You serve them?*"

"*My dam, Shalla, served their mother. So do I serve them.*"

"*Shalla,*" the pack leader said with respect. "*A mighty warrior. And their dam's name?*"

"*Lwyneth of the Fae.*"

The pack leader stood up and stared hard at Diello, uttering a low whine.

"What's going on?" Cynthe said. "Can you understand them? How long have you been able to do that? When did you plan to tell me?"

Diello put up his hand in warning. He wasn't sure whether the pack leader could understand what they were saying, but he didn't want to take chances.

When the pack leader and Vassou resumed talking, Diello turned to his sister. "I think I'm manifesting a new Gift. I've only understood like this once before—the owl that night in the woods when Brezog attacked us."

"You never talked about it."

"I wasn't sure—at first, I thought it might be a Gift. Then, when it didn't happen again, I decided it was a trick of Brezog's. But now . . . I guess it wasn't."

She looked excited. "Another Gift. What are they saying?"

"They're talking about Mamee and Vassou's mother," Diello murmured. "You know how the folk in Wodesley always greeted a stranger to the shire by asking about his kin? That kind of thing."

"So they're friends?" she asked. "They don't act like it."

"Don't forget they got rid of the trogs for us. Vassou's thanked them for that."

"What else are they saying?"

Diello felt a peculiar sensation. It wasn't magic, exactly. He turned his head toward a wolf standing at the outer edge of the pack. Unlike the others, this one had a red pelt, and there was something odd about his eyes.

"What's wrong?" Cynthe whispered.

Diello shook his head. He tried to use Sight on the wolf. For an instant, the air shimmered between them. Diello glimpsed a different shape—man-sized and crouching—before he felt an invisible blow between his eyes.

He staggered back, blinking. The vision vanished.

"Diello?" Cynthe asked.

Before Diello could gather his breath, Vassou rejoined the twins. "This pack comes to us in friendship," the pup said. "They are migrating to the border lands for the winter. They have smelled your kill, Cynthe."

She stiffened. "They can hunt their own game."

"The snows will begin soon. The pack is half its usual size, and many of its members are old or crippled from injuries." Vassou paused. "They have been at war with goblins. They are moving their territory, and they wish to do so quickly. If you will share your kill, they will escort us into the border lands."

"No," Diello said quickly.

The pack leader lifted his head. Diello refused to glance at the red wolf.

"You do not trust them?" Vassou asked. "Humans are taught to fear wolves, but they are not enemies to us."

"Think of it, Diello," Cynthe said. "If we don't have to worry about trogs or even sprites, we can go faster."

"I know samal wolves ally themselves with people," Diello said, "but—"

"With Fae," Vassou corrected him. "And not just any Fae."

"But these," Diello went on, "are regular wolves?"

"Commons," Vassou said. "Of the wild."

"Isn't it strange that they would approach us like this? Did you summon them in some way?"

"We needed help with the trogs, and I sensed they were nearby." Vassou hesitated, flicking back his ears. "But you are right in thinking it's strange for them to ask to travel with us. I think it's because I am with you. Now that they know who you are, they understand—in their own way— what your journey means."

"But—"

"I say we accept their offer," Cynthe interrupted. "We can use the protection. And if snow is coming, we've got to hurry."

"What about the goblins following them?" Diello asked.

"Not following," Vassou said. "They were driven from their territory." He tilted his head. "At least, that is what I gathered. There are . . . limitations to what they can express."

"Do they understand human speech?" Diello asked. "Do they know what we're saying?"

"Not by your words. By your scent and tone of voice."

"Could they be under a disguising spell?"

Vassou pricked his ears. "What have you seen?"

"The one with red fur," Diello murmured very low, aware of the pack leader watching them. The stares of all the wolves were beginning to make him nervous. "Like a man, but not exactly—"

A growl rumbled in Vassou's throat. He turned and advanced toward the red wolf.

Diello moved to stop him, but Cynthe intervened.

"Stay out of this," she said.

"But he's challenging the—"

She gave Diello's arm a light punch and nodded in the pack leader's direction. The leader was watching Vassou without any sign of aggression. The wolves closest to the red one backed away, leaving him to face Vassou alone. After a moment, the red one dropped to the ground and stretched on his side, exposing his throat and belly. Bristling, Vassou sniffed him from nose to tail.

"What are they saying now?" Cynthe asked.

"Nothing."

"They have to be talking. You can't tell?"

"There's only snarling." Diello shrugged, unable to explain it.

Vassou stalked back to the twins.

"What did you learn?" Cynthe asked the pup.

"I do not have the word in your language. Once he was a man, but now he is cursed into animal form."

"A *nonseen*," Diello said in astonishment.

"Those are just old stories," Cynthe said. "They don't really exist . . . but, well, I guess maybe they do. Can he be trusted?"

Vassou looked at the pack leader, and he responded by trotting over to the red wolf, still lying on the ground. The leader placed his paw on the red wolf's throat.

"He will kill the accursed one if you command it," Vassou said.

"What do you think is best?" Diello asked.

"I serve you," Vassou answered.

Cynthe plucked Diello's sleeve. "Come over here," she said, leading him a short distance away. "You don't like any of this, do you?"

He shook his head. "It's too strange. Too confusing."

"You mean that even these wild animals knew of our mother?"

"That. And their wanting to stay with us. I'm grateful for what they did with the trogs, but it's odd." Diello touched Eirian's hilt around his neck. "I don't trust that *nonseen* at all. He stopped my Sight."

"So he can do magic? Do you think the pack leader is bluffing about killing him for us?"

"Probably. I couldn't give an order like that," Diello admitted. "Could you?"

She shook her head.

"What if this creature is one of Brezog's spies?" Diello asked. "He's awfully good at disguising spells."

"But you usually sense those. He's never been able to trick you before."

"We can't count on that."

"And we can't stay frightened of everything. We'll paralyze ourselves until we can't act at all." She turned her gaze toward the hills leading to Embarthi. It was barely midday and already clouds were building up from that direction, their dark bellies carrying rain . . . or possibly snow. "Are you hearing any of the animals speak now?"

"No." Diello frowned. "Maybe they're blocking it. Maybe it's a fluke instead of a Gift."

"Don't be silly," Cynthe said. "Of course it's a Gift. You'll get better at it. Well, we've got to trust someone sometime. Especially if they can protect us from the trogs."

"It still seems too good to be true."

She wrinkled her nose. "I know. But Vassou doesn't seem worried."

"He's just missing his own kind."

"No, he feels very superior to the 'common wolves.' Haven't you noticed how he's enjoying dominating them?"

"So you're in favor of this," Diello said. "Even with a—a *nonseen* around."

"Are they supposed to be dangerous? All the stories I've ever heard were kind of sad."

Any compassion Diello might have dredged up for the creature had been vanquished by that unseen blow he'd taken. If the red wolf could block Sight, what else might he do? Still, he could have hurt Diello by now, and he hadn't.

"All right," Diello said.

Cynthe nodded briskly. "Let's go cut up the venison. Vassou," she called out, "are they going to share our camp?"

"No. They are allies now, but never forget they are of the wild."

The twins rejoined the wolves.

"Let the *nonseen* live," Diello said.

Vassou and the pack leader touched muzzles while the red wolf regained his feet and shook grass from his coat. Moments later, the whole pack retreated into the woods as though they'd never been there.

"Old and injured, my eye," Diello muttered. "I didn't see a single wolf limping."

Cynthe drew her knife and knelt by the deer carcass. "I did. Come on and help me."

Diello took the rope of braided leather that she'd made weeks ago from the skins of other kills, tied it around the deer's hind feet, and—with Cynthe's help—ran the rope over a tree limb before pulling the carcass into the air. Then he worked with Cynthe to dress out the deer. It was a filthy job and made a sticky mess on the ground that was bound to draw more than wolves. They should've done this job well away from their campsite, but it was all too likely that something would've stolen the meat in the night.

Cynthe was generous, cutting less than half the venison into thin strips for their portion—with a thick steak reserved for tonight's supper—and leaving the majority of the carcass for the wolves. Meanwhile, Diello built a tall A-frame from sticks lashed together with lengths of sedge grass and numerous crosspieces. Scree, having been coaxed down from the boulder, helped Diello gather cedar boughs for the fire under the meat. A great deal of smoke wafted up, and Scree was given the job of adding more boughs and as much green wood as he could find to keep smoking the meat.

They were rushing a job that normally required several days of slow, steady drying, salting, and smoking. But it couldn't be helped. The sunshine had been swallowed by the clouds, and the air felt damp with the kind of cold that sank deep.

Cynthe untied the carcass and let it fall to the ground. Together, she and Scree dragged the wolves' share to the edge of the woods and left it there. Then Cynthe stretched out the hide and started scraping it clean with a piece of sharp-edged flint. Diello scraped with her, taking care not to nick any holes. With proper handling, the deer skin could be tanned into soft, luxurious leather.

By nightfall, the little group gathered around their fire under the snug lean-to, while a chunk of venison cooked on its spit. The deer hide had been rolled up and added to Cynthe's bundle for further work. She sat cross-legged, with two rabbit skins lying fur-side-down on a flat stone, and was meticulously poking small holes along the edges with the tip of her knife.

It was Diello's job to keep turning the meat so it cooked evenly. He was getting sleepy, his stomach growling in anticipation of their supper. Their one pot, filled with water and a mess of greens picked from a wild patch growing on the creek bank, was balanced on a tripod of stones at the fire's edge, boiling merrily.

Outside the lean-to, the sound of the wolves feasting on the deer was punctuated with growls and snarls. Vassou sat near the entrance, his muzzle tipped up as he drew in scents. Scree had wedged himself against the stone outcropping at their backs. He'd had little to say since the wolves arrived. He started at every sound. Every so often, he untied a dirty rag pulled from his pocket and carefully counted the square coins he'd gathered from the hillside. Each coin had been washed and gleamed dull gold in the firelight.

Looking at the strange symbols on the coins made Diello uneasy. Now that he knew they were goblin coins, he wished that he'd never found them. Even more, he wished that Scree would stop fiddling with them. But having granted Scree permission to keep them, he couldn't say anything now.

Scree bent over his hoard, his brown nails clicking on each coin. "One," he breathed. "Two. Three. Eight. Six. Mine."

"Our sister Amalina can count better than that," Cynthe said, threading string through the holes she'd made and lacing the two rabbit skins together. "You've got seven coins, Scree."

Scree covered them with his hand, then pulled back and frowned at the little pile. "Seven? Is that more than eight?"

"Less than eight. More than six."

"No, I do not think that can be right, Cynthe." He turned to Diello. "How can this seven be more than six? Six is a great many."

"Seven *is* greater than six," Diello replied, nearly scorching his fingers as he tried to move the pot of greens away from the fire.

"Greater than six?" Scree echoed, fingering each coin again. "That is good."

"Yes, it's wonderful," Diello said patiently. He'd taught Amalina to count without difficulty, but Scree didn't seem to be catching on as fast.

Scree crammed the bundle into his pocket again. "Perhaps in the morning I can look for more."

"We're leaving at daybreak," Cynthe said, tossing her handicraft at Diello. "There! A new pouch for the hilt."

He held it up, admiring it from all angles before sliding the hilt inside and folding down the flap. The rabbit fur felt soft and warm against his fingers. He secured it to his belt. "Thanks!"

"Try not to lose this one. Let's eat!"

The venison was a bit tough but delicious. The greens made a good accompaniment, although they had a bitter aftertaste. With the wolves snarling and moving around nearby, it was hard to find anything to talk about and still harder to fall asleep as they stretched themselves out on more cedar boughs. Cynthe had a smear of dried blood on her cheek that she'd failed to wash off, and her hair smelled of smoke. Diello watched the firelight slowly burn itself out, listening to his companions snore and aware of every wolf-shape that moved past their fragile lean-to in the night.

It was a dream of shadows and strange bursts of light and sound. Diello was wandering in a cave, his shoulders brushing walls of damp stone. More light glowed from somewhere in front of him. It was probably firelight, for it cast unsteady shadows on the ceiling of the cave. He hurried forward, eager to find the fire's warmth.

A dark shape blocked his path. He couldn't see its face, but it stood upright on two legs, about his height yet wider through the shoulders.

Diello tried to retreat, but his feet seemed frozen. He listened to the other figure's hoarse breathing.

"What do you want?" Diello asked.

"You see me," a voice replied. It was deep and guttural, with a note of desperation. "You see me, so I still exist. I am not entirely gone."

Diello knew then that this was no ordinary dream. "You're the *nonseen*," he whispered.

"But you *see* me. I exist."

And you're crazy, Diello thought. His feet still wouldn't move. It was as if he were pinned by one of Brezog's spells.

"It's risky to approach you this way, but I had to take the chance. I owe you my gratitude. Thank you for your mercy, my lord," the *nonseen* said, almost sobbing the words. "Thank you for my life. Miserable though I am in this accursed limbo, I'm not yet ready for death. My hopes—all our hopes—lie in you."

"W-What?"

"Break the curse that holds me. For the sake of your dear mother, for the memory of her, set us free."

"I can't undo a curse."

The shape extended its shadowy hand. "You can. You carry Eirian and with its power—"

"No," Diello said. "That's not true."

"You carry Eirian."

"The sword is broken."

"Not broken. Separated," the shape whispered fervently.

The sword whispered to Diello, as it had once before: *Make me whole.*

He brushed the temptation away.

"I can't do it," he said firmly. "Sorry, but it's not possible."

The shape wavered, ghostlike, and seemed about to vanish, but then it loomed even closer. "Perhaps, if I could touch some piece of it . . ."

"No!" Diello clamped a hand on the pouch that held the hilt. He managed to wrench one foot free and stepped back.

The *nonseen* cried out and knelt before him. "Don't leave me, my lord. Don't be angry with me for daring to ask so great a favor. Please forgive me. Have mercy on me."

It was like listening to Scree beg. "I really can't help you," Diello said. "Let me go."

"There is another chance. Soon, you will see the queen. You can beseech her to release us from this bondage."

"Who's us?"

The *nonseen* gasped. "You show interest in our plight. My lord is great!"

"I'm no lord, so stop groveling," Diello said. "Who are you talking about? Who are you?"

"Once, I was called Canthroy. I served as steward in your mother's household."

"A steward! Mamee had *servants* in Embarthi?"

"Of course. When she left, when the Dark Times came, a curse was placed on all who had served her. I don't complain, my lord! I was honored to be in her service."

Diello frowned, trying to understand. "You mean you're Fae?"

"I was once."

The sorrow in that answer touched Diello. "And now you're all wolves?" he asked.

"Not all. We were changed into many animals and scattered, so that we couldn't band together for your mother's cause. Some of the others have perished by now. This has been a difficult time. These wolves permit me to live among them, but the pack doesn't truly accept me. They'll kill me one day, if I ever make a mistake among them."

"Why did you stop my Sight?" Diello asked.

The *nonseen* did not answer.

"Well? Why don't you tell me? If you could stop that, you should be able to find a way to break your curse."

"I have no powers, my lord. I didn't act against you."

"Don't lie to me. I felt it."

The shape shrank back. "You are watched, my lord. Forgive me! I should never have endangered you this way."

"Who's watching me?" Diello asked. "Tell me!"

"Quiet, my lord. If it becomes known that we've spoken, I'll surely be destroyed."

Diello realized he was starting to believe Canthroy despite his suspicions. The *nonseen's* fear was real enough.

"You and your sister have returned to us. You will find a way to soften the queen's heart, and when you do, please, my lord, beg her to release us from this punishment."

"Why should I meet the queen?" Diello asked. "We're in search of our uncle—"

There was a scream and a blinding flash. Canthroy's shape vanished. Diello felt something strike him, knocking him flat, and then he was being smothered. It felt like an invisible pillow pressing over his face. He gasped and fought, waking up with a strangled yell.

"Diello, hush!"

Cynthe was holding him by the shoulders as he flailed. Diello struggled to distinguish the terror of the dream from the reality of the smoky lean-to. He could hear a faint rattling sound, like something scratching at their shelter. The wolves were howling in an eerie chorus.

"Diello, you're all right. It's all right. You've been dreaming." Cynthe fumbled in the darkness and handed him the waterskin.

His fingers curled around it, but he didn't drink. *Dream or real?* He wasn't sure, but the feeling of being watched didn't go away.

"What's that sound?" he asked. Diello knew by Scree's breathing that he was awake and pretending to sleep. Vassou was a pale shape on the opposite side of the lean-to, his head up as he listened to the wolves howling. "Not the wolves' racket," Diello added, "but that rattling noise. Is it sleet?"

"Yes," Cynthe said reluctantly. She hitched the worn blanket higher around his shoulders. "We could be iced in by morning. If we're trapped in these hills for the winter, I'm not sure we'll survive."

"We're not going to be trapped," he said. "Don't be scared."

"Why not? You are."

He thought of what Canthroy had told him, piecing it

with the rest of his knowledge. His mother had lost most of her magic after she was exiled from Embarthi for stealing the sword. Even her death dust was not allowed to return. Now he'd learned her servants had been cursed, and it was probably Clevn—mage and adviser to the Fae queen—who'd done that, too.

His fingers, icy cold, found Cynthe's in the dark. "Uncle Owain will tell us the truth," he said.

"What truth? What are you talking about?"

"Lies and secrets," he murmured, shivering.

"Go back to sleep," she said, pushing him down. "You're not making sense."

But Diello was afraid to close his eyes, afraid of what else might speak to him in his dreams.

chapter eleven

hey walked for days, shadowed by the wolf pack. Cold winds buffeted them, and sleet sometimes pelted their faces. The fog was the worst, for it came over the hills without warning, seeping through the forest and filling the ravines. At times, it was so thick they lost the trail and had to huddle around a fire and wait. Diello's fingers and toes were constantly chilled, and although he now wore his blanket swathed around his shoulders and Cynthe wrapped herself in the deer hide, they needed warmer clothing. Scree got the other blanket. Vassou seemed to fare the best. His fur grew thicker each day, and when they camped, he would go romping with the younger wolves.

It was hard for Diello to find a private moment with Cynthe where they couldn't be overheard, but finally there came an opportunity when they paused to forage. Their meat supplies were not keeping well. Some of the jerky had turned green with mold and, although Scree would eat it, Cynthe threw it away. Weary from trudging up a long, steep trail, they called a halt, and the foraging chores were divided up. Vassou and the wolves went searching for a water source. Scree wandered off to look for edible roots. Diello and Cynthe were supposed to be gathering nuts. She set a few rabbit snares, but—mindful of deeply carved runes on some of the tree trunks, warning them that they were in sprite territory—the twins didn't go far.

When Diello was certain the others had left, he pulled his sister over to a fallen log, sat her down, and told her about Canthroy and what the *nonseen* had said about their mother.

"I *knew* she was important," Cynthe said. "The way she acted, the things she taught us. She never was an ordinary goodwife. Think of it! A great lady with *servants* of her own. And she knew the queen. That meant she was a part of the Fae court."

Jumping up, Cynthe performed a curtsy. "What do you think? I'm out of practice so I may not be graceful enough."

"You can't curtsy properly unless you wear a gown. And you'll never do that."

A faraway look entered Cynthe's eyes. "I suppose I might if it were sewn from enchanted cloth. There must be gowns magical enough to make me beautiful."

Diello blinked. "Uh, let's not worry about that now. We need to revise our plans."

Cynthe curtsied again and began to dance to imaginary music.

"Cynthe! Pay attention."

"I *am*," she said, twirling around to face him. "If Mamee was highborn, then so's Uncle Owain." Cynthe clapped her hands. "That will make finding him so much easier. All we have to do is go to a House of Records and state his name."

"That's exactly what we *can't* do."

"Why not? Every shire in Antrasia has a House of Records. Even if the Fae do things differently, there's bound to be a place where we can inquire. Oh, I'm so relieved! I thought we'd have to wander around Embarthi in search of him."

"Listen to me," Diello said. "Mamee was exiled. Her servants were cursed. If they got into so much trouble, what do you suppose happened to Uncle Owain?"

"Are you saying he's been cursed, too?"

"Maybe. Or driven into hiding. How do we know? But if we go blundering along, asking for him, then . . ."

"We might get in trouble, too," Cynthe said.

"Exactly. We could be arrested, and then the sword might end up in anyone's hands."

"So we can't go to him first," Cynthe said. She sat down next to Diello. "We can't ask his advice or seek his help in getting Amalina back. That means we'll have to go straight to the palace with this stupid sword, just like Clevn wants."

"I guess we never did have much choice." Diello sighed.

"I wish he'd just show up and take it!" she burst out, pounding her fists on her knees. "Then this would be over. Brezog wouldn't be after us anymore, and we'd be free."

Diello's head ached from trying to untangle the knots of this puzzle. Everything was a secret wrapped in another secret surrounded by a lie. Each time he thought he was starting to understand, a new bit of information confused things again. "Why is Clevn playing with us, moving us around like pieces on a gameboard?"

"Not moving us. Blocking us from where we're trying to go," Cynthe said. "I'm afraid that we'll have gone all this way, and then the Fae won't let us into Embarthi at all. It will all have been some cruel joke at our expense."

Diello put his arm around her shoulders. "We'll get there," he said.

"But it could still be for nothing. Clevn will have us arrested, and he'll take the sword. We'll never see Amalina again."

Diello wanted to tell her she was wrong, but he couldn't. "I don't think it's safe for me to try to talk to Canthroy again—safe for him, I mean. Maybe Vassou could do it for us."

She looked up. "Yes. The *nonseen* could know where Uncle Owain is."

"He might tell us where to start looking. I know he's frightened, but he took the risk to contact me."

"We'll have to be very careful. I don't think I noticed the red wolf among the others this morning."

What if he's run away? Or been driven off by Clevn somehow? What if we've already missed our best chance? I should have asked him more questions!

But it was no good beating himself for that now.

"I hardly saw any of them today," Diello admitted. "It worries me when Vassou goes off with the pack."

"You think he'll turn wild? He won't."

"No, I worry about his safety. He's—"

She thumped Diello's shoulder. "Hush! Someone's coming."

It was Scree, carrying the spear Diello had helped him make. Pushing under a cedar tree, Scree sent a shower of ice pellets onto his head and shoulders. He gasped and hopped around, shaking the neck of his tunic.

Cynthe laughed affectionately. "Did you find any stell-plants?"

Scree held out a clump of black soil with a limp piece of vegetation dangling from it. "Is this what you are seeking?"

She examined the wilted leaves. "Um, it's a bit crushed. Where's the tuber?"

Beaming proudly, Scree pulled a fat, oblong root from his pocket. "You see? I listened to everything you said, Cynthe, and I have dug many for our supper. Will these be good to eat? I have sniffed them, and they smell cold like stones. Not tasty. I would rather eat tasty, but even if they are bitter enough to raise blisters on my tongue, I will eat them. I am hungry."

"You're always hungry." She brushed soil off the tuber to examine it. "This looks exactly right. How many have you got?"

"Many. Six and six!"

"Twelve?" she asked.

Scree looked so baffled that Diello came to his rescue. "Not twelve," he said. "Remember that six is the biggest number he knows."

"There are four," Scree announced. "And eight. And six. Many six!"

Cynthe giggled, clamping her hand over her mouth. Diello couldn't help smiling, too. He hoped that Scree hadn't overheard their private conversation. Scree had a habit of creeping about and eavesdropping. Worse, he couldn't control himself from blurting out whatever he learned.

Puffing out his scrawny chest, Scree said, "I have done a good job. I have pleased you both. This is very satisfaction-ary."

"Satisfying," Diello corrected.

"That, too. Come and see!"

"Not yet." Cynthe pulled her sleeve from Scree's fingers. "We haven't gathered enough nuts."

Scree eyed their empty basket. "I do not think you have found *any* nuts. Talking instead of picking is what you have been doing. You are lazy today, if I am permitted to say that." And he allowed himself a sly little grin.

Diello slid off the log. "Why don't you help us?" he suggested.

Scree immediately started trotting back and forth, peering at the ground before gazing up at the naked trees. "Wrong kind. We need to search . . . there!" He pointed.

The twins watched him scurry away.

"Do you think he heard anything?" Cynthe asked.

"I think we'd already know if he did," Diello replied, trying to reassure himself.

"I have found nuts, many nuts!" Scree called, running back to them. He tugged at Diello's tunic.

The twins followed him to what appeared to be a whole grove of trees bearing small, tough-shelled nuts. Most of the nuts on the ground looked recently fallen, and the weathered pods that had contained them were still clinging to the branches overhead, a sign of freshness.

The twins worked quickly, filling their basket and pockets and even the hems of their tunics before they headed back.

The air smelled like snow, and the clouds were a gray wall. Although it was barely past midday, shadows were already lengthening beneath the trees. Thanks to the shorter days, they weren't making very good time, even with the wolves as protectors. Diello looked for the red wolf but didn't see him. Most of the pack was still out of sight, except for a rangy pair following them from a distance. Diello hadn't overheard anything said among the wolves since the first meeting. He kept meaning to ask Vassou about his Gift, but never found the right opportunity.

Along the way, Cynthe checked her snares. All remained empty. She knelt and traced her fingertips along a deer track before shaking her head.

"Too old."

"The wolves look hungry," Scree whispered to Diello. "I wish she would hunt for them. Soon they may decide to eat me."

"No, they won't," Diello said, keeping his tone serious. "You'd be much too tough to chew."

"And tasteless," Cynthe chimed in, puckering her face.

Scree looked at them both, blinking hard before he ventured an uncertain smile.

"It's a joke, silly!" Cynthe reassured him.

"I knew that," Scree said, looking relieved. "I will make a joke on you someday. You will see."

Cynthe gave Diello a light shove, pointing at something moving through the undergrowth ahead. "Look!"

He saw Vassou limping toward them, favoring his front paw. The pup's ear was bleeding, and he was panting heavily.

"Vassou!" Cynthe cried. Dropping her basket and letting nuts scatter as she released her tunic hem, she rushed to him. "Poor boy, you're hurt."

Diello unloaded his share more carefully on the ground and joined her. She was anxiously running her hands over the pup's body, and when she touched Vassou's ribs, he flinched.

"What happened?" Diello asked, gently scratching the pup's throat. "What attacked you?"

Vassou licked Diello's hand and whined. His body was trembling.

"I don't see any bites," Cynthe said. "Just the tear in his ear. But his ribs are awfully sore."

Diello picked up Vassou's front paw, examining the cut pad before he pulled open the waterskin and poured some liquid into his cupped palm. Vassou drank, whimpering a little while Cynthe dabbed healing salve on his ear and foot.

"Did the wolves turn on you?" Diello asked.

"No. Do not blame them."

"Then why didn't they protect you?" Cynthe asked.

"I went alone."

Diello smoothed the thick ruff around Vassou's neck. He noticed that the fur was wet as though something had caught the pup by the throat. *Was it Canthroy? Was I wrong to believe the* nonseen's *story?*

Vassou nosed the waterskin again. Diello poured more water for him, and the pup lapped thirstily.

"Please tell us," Cynthe coaxed, stroking him.

"Sprites jumped me. It was a small group, maybe ten."

"Ten against one is a lot," Cynthe said.

"Usually there are dozens more. I was fortunate."

Diello had never encountered one of these creatures before, but he'd heard plenty about how they roved the wilderness and protected their territories fiercely. A single sprite wasn't supposed to be too dangerous, but a group of them was something he'd rather avoid.

"Are they likely to come this way?" Diello asked. "Those that got away from you, I mean, will they bring more to attack? I've heard that they can live in colonies of a hundred or more."

Vassou gave himself a good shake. "That does not matter. They will not bother us here. My cousins came to my aid and have driven them away for the time being."

Diello frowned. "It's odd that I didn't hear any fighting. Did you, Cynthe?"

"No." Cynthe packed away the salve. "We'd better move on. If sprites are roaming around, this is no place to camp."

"Wait," Vassou said. "Before we go, there is something you must see. Ever since we came to the Westering Hills, I've hoped very much to find it. Leave Scree to guard your possessions. It will not take long."

"What is it?" Diello asked.

"An opportunity that should not be missed."

"Can't Scree come along?"

"No," Vassou said, placing his paw on Diello's foot. "You and Cynthe alone. This is not for goblin-kind."

An awkward silence fell over them. At times like these, Vassou could be coldly oblivious to Scree's feelings.

Averting his face, Scree crouched on the ground and held the gathering basket in his narrow hands.

"Uh, Scree," Diello began, "if you could—"

"I know what is wanted," Scree said, staring at the basket. "I have plenty to do here. I will work. I will pick up the nuts Cynthe threw down."

"I'm sorry," she said. "I shouldn't have dropped them like that."

Scree looked at no one. "I will guard the food and retie the bundles very securely. I will wait, as the wolf has commanded."

"But we can't leave him alone," Diello said to the others. "Not with sprites about."

"The sprites will not harm one of goblin blood," Vassou said. "He is safe enough. And we will not be gone long."

The pair of wolves edged closer, clearly intending to follow. Cynthe gestured at Diello. He looked back as he left. Scree was picking up the spilled nuts. His hands, usually deft, moved slowly.

Diello muttered to his sister, "That was bad. He's upset."

"I know, but he doesn't hold grudges. Maybe he'll be over it by the time we get back."

"It doesn't matter," Vassou said.

"I think it does," Diello replied. "I know he's a nuisance at times, but, Vassou, do you have to hurt his feelings?"

The pup did not answer. Ducking under a branch, Cynthe rolled her eyes at Diello. He shook his head.

The path grew steeper and muddier. Halfway up the hill, the woods stopped. The rest of the way to the summit was open ground. Limping steadily, Vassou never hesitated. A few yips from the wolf pair made Diello look back. They'd stopped at the edge of the trees. The male paced in agitation, while the female dropped to her belly and wouldn't budge. If Vassou noticed their reluctance, he gave no sign.

Diello felt more at ease without them.

Frost-blighted grass covered the ground, dotted with clumps of white heather still in bloom. At the top, they came to a single, gigantic tree. If four people had joined hands, they still could not have encircled its vast girth. It had to be centuries old.

The tree had twisted as it grew, and knobby protrusions jutted along its silvery bark. Diello didn't recognize its variety, but he thought sadly that someday an Antrasin would cut down this old tree for lumber.

The lowermost branches grew horizontally, supporting a canopy that formed an immense, perfectly symmetrical dome. Strangely, despite the cold, the tree had not dropped its leaves. They were burnished a deep oxblood red and veined green on the underside. Although the air was still and hushed, the treetop swayed in constant motion.

Beyond the old tree, Diello could see for leagues. The hill he stood on marked the edge of the Westerings. He hadn't realized they'd come so far. Dense evergreen forest spread before him, and beyond it, the air shimmered with all the hues of the rainbow. It was the hugest *cloigwylie* he'd ever come across. He couldn't see what lay on the other side, but he knew. *Embarthi!*

Diello continued to stare, aware that this *cloigwylie* was far stronger than any Vassou had conjured. It seemed to stretch right and left to infinity. The colors gleamed like jewels in a rich man's strongbox. All that tempting magic in use . . . Even from this distance, he could feel his bones responding to it. He was tired of restraining his developing powers to avoid Brezog's detection. *Once we're inside Embarthi, I can set my Gifts free.*

Cynthe joined him. "What are you looking at?"

"Embarthi's border wall."

Her face filled with yearning as she gazed across the vista. "What wall? I don't see anything. Is there a fortress?"

"Can't you see the *cloigwylie*?"

"No. Just forest. There's a mist over everything else."

He wished he could find the words to describe it to her. "It's beautiful," he breathed. He longed to stretch out his arms and fly over the forest to touch it. If he could just press his skin to its cool surface, some empty place inside him would be filled. . . .

A cold nose nudged Diello's hand. "That isn't what I brought you here to see," Vassou said. "Look at where you stand."

Reluctantly, Diello turned his back to Embarthi. Now he could sense some intangible history here. Perhaps the ground itself was sacred. The faintest of tingles ran through his bones, and he realized that something nearby was waking up. It was slowly growing *aware* of his presence.

"What is this place?" Cynthe whispered.

Diello walked a few steps away from his sister to tug at a

sliver of rusted metal projecting from the ground. It resisted at first, but he dug around it with a jagged stone and finally pried it free of the mud.

He found himself holding the crumbling remains of a war axe, so rusted away its feeble iron didn't even make his hand itch. Diello recalled the stories old Griffudd the peddler had told at his family's fireside. Diello could hear the battle cries and the clatter of Fae chariot wheels over the stony ground. His bones hummed and grew warm. He was tall and valiant, riding through the melee of fighting men with his axe held ready. The wind blew his long warrior braids back from his face. Diello braced himself against the side of his chariot and gathered magic in his free fist, ready to fling it against the enemy.

As his driver whipped the horses to a gallop, something touched his shoulder, and he spun around, raising his weapon.

"Diello!" Cynthe cried.

He barely avoided striking her with the war axe.

"What are you doing? What are you seeing?"

The battle was fading from his mind. The wind and jostling of the chariot vanished. Feeling foolish, he laid the axe carefully on the ground where he'd found it.

"It's an old weapon," he said. "This was a battlefield once."

"You mean from the Great War, long ago, when the Fae drove the goblins back from Embarthi?"

"I think so."

She hooked her hair nervously behind her ears. "The heather. It's supposed to bloom white where it grows over the dead Fae warriors."

"No. Their Death Winds would have borne their dust home. It grows where their blood was shed."

She shrugged. "Something like that. So, Vassou, are we right about a battle being fought here? Who won on this ground, goblins or Fae?"

Vassou's ears flicked back. "What do old battles matter? It is the fighting to come for which you must prepare. And still you do not see."

Diello looked around. There was nothing left except the tree. He elbowed his sister.

"We're supposed to notice the tree," he told her.

"Oh! Isn't it amazing?" she replied loudly. "Wouldn't you love to climb it?"

Before Diello could answer, Vassou snarled at her, "Be respectful. This is the Knower. Many seek it and never find it. But none stand before it unchanged."

"Why is it called the Knower?" Diello asked.

"It knows your future."

"Will it explain why we have so many Gifts in spite of being Faelin?" Cynthe asked. "Will it tell us how to find Uncle Owain?"

"Or who holds Amalina captive?" Diello added.

"You cannot ask the Knower questions," Vassou said sternly. "It tells what it chooses to tell. And it does not speak to all who seek it."

"Diello, you go first," Cynthe said.

He looked to the pup for instructions. "I'm sorry we didn't realize its importance. Please, Vassou, will you tell us how to approach it properly?"

"Cynthe is firstborn between you," Vassou replied. "She must perform the ritual before you do."

Diello flushed and stepped back. *She's not that much older. A few moments only.*

"What do I do?" Cynthe asked eagerly.

"Make an offering of water," Vassou told her.

She slid the waterskin's strap off Diello's shoulder and poured a dribble on the ground.

"Enough," Vassou said. "Kneel at the base of the tree and place your hands on its roots. Remain very quiet, and wait."

Diello watched as his sister knelt gracefully and pressed her palms to the large, gnarled roots.

Nothing happened. Then Diello felt a subtle change in the air. The leaves overhead had stopped moving. He could feel energy building around him. It seemed to be pulling him forward. He took a step.

"Wait your turn," Vassou said.

Diello felt the energy rising up, stronger than ever. His bones itched. No matter what Vassou said, he could not resist the pull. "It wants us both," he whispered. "We belong together."

Vassou made no further protest as Diello brushed past him.

Diello poured his own offering of water before kneeling beside Cynthe. She gave him a quick smile but didn't remove her hands from the roots. Diello pressed his palms to the cold ground.

He felt a ripple in the soil. Startled, he almost jumped back, but managed to remain still.

The ground stopped moving, and he heard a great sigh. A voice spoke—whether aloud or in his thoughts, he couldn't be sure. Although the language was Fae, it sounded different than what Mamee had taught them. Diello struggled to understand the words.

"Who kneels on my ground?"

Diello nudged Cynthe.

She had heard the voice as well. She said, "I'm Cynthe, daughter of Lwyneth and Stephel."

"Lwyneth . . ."

The tree lowered the tips of its bottommost branches to the ground, enclosing the twins in a vast leafy tent. Old and brittle birds' nests fell on top of them, and bits of leaf and twig rained down. The air grew warm and comfortable. Its fragrance reminded Diello of the farmstead orchard.

"I am the Knower. Who *else* kneels on my ground?"

This time Cynthe nudged Diello.

"I'm Diello, son of Lwyneth and Stephel."

"Ah, the daughter and son of Lwyneth."

"And Stephel," Diello added stubbornly. Just because Pa was human, he didn't deserve to be overlooked.

"The prophecy turns," the Knower said. "From daughter to daughter passes the throne. From Sheirae to Lwyneth to—she unnamed until now."

A muffled squeak came from Cynthe. Diello could feel her trembling by his side. *What did it mean?*

"The prophecy turns again," the Knower said. "From daughter to son flows wisdom. So shall the son be mage and counselor to his sister."

Me. Diello's thoughts were tumbling wildly, but he forced himself to pay attention.

"Look to the three Wheels of Silver. Name them."

Cynthe turned to Diello, making a helpless face.

He struggled to remember the small amount of information Mamee had told them. "Uh . . . the Wheel of Life," he began. "The Wheel of Death. And the Wheel of . . . Destiny."

"Yes," the Knower said.

Diello blew his hair out of his eyes while Cynthe gave him a nod of approval.

"The Wheel of Destiny has been changed by the knight called Stephel."

"Pa," Diello murmured.

"Know what lies before you, daughter and son of Lwyneth. Beware the Afon Heyrn and its Watchers."

Diello knew that the Watchers were spirits that used to guard Eirian. "Are they searching for Eirian?" he asked.

"Beware the fight you choose," the Knower went on, ignoring his question. Prepare yourselves for their vengeance, for you are both the chosen and the unchosen."

Mindful of Vassou's warning, Diello held back all his other questions except the most important one.

"Knower," he said, "we carry the pieces of the sword Eirian. Stephel made me swear to return it."

"Eirian must go to its rightful place," the voice replied.

"Who should we give it to? The queen? Clevn? The Watchers you've warned us about? Guide us, please."

The Knower remained silent.

Diello pleaded, "Help us to do what's right."

The leaves around them rustled, and at last the Knower spoke: "Destiny lies broken, changed by Stephel. Nothing shall be given to you. All shall be taken, save that which you seize. Lwyneth's legacy marks your future. The throne passes to Cynthe, yet another shall claim it."

"I—I don't understand," she said.

Suddenly the branches lifted, letting in the cold.

"Is that all?" Cynthe asked.

Isn't it enough? Diello thought.

chapter twelve

hey stood up, backing away from the tree until they were no longer beneath its canopy. It was as though they'd been offered the world, only to have it taken away. All the bits and pieces of information about their parents, gleaned through the years, were fitting together into a story far beyond what he and Cynthe had imagined.

Royalty, Diello thought. *Mamee had been the Crown Princess of Embarthi?* It made sense now—her grace and dignity, her sometimes imperious ways, her love of ceremony and traditions, her magical stories of Fae rituals and luxuries. Yet his mind was crowded with memories of his mother stirring the laundry in a boiling cauldron, plucking chickens to be roasted for dinner, weaving cloth on the loom in the back of the cottage. Pa—so practical and steady—planting and harvesting, caring for his livestock, puttering with his carpentry projects in the barn. Yet Pa had been a Carnethie Knight. Both of them had thrown everything away for a cause they must have believed in. But *why*?

"Well?" Vassou demanded, nudging first Diello and then

Cynthe with his nose. "I heard nothing. Did the Knower acknowledge you? Did it speak of your birthright?"

Cynthe danced a jig around Vassou. "I'm to be queen! Queen of the Fae! Mamee was a princess, and we're—"

"Hold on," Diello said. "That's not exactly the—"

"Queen!" Cynthe rose off the ground. She hovered there and turned a flip in midair. She flipped again, laughing. "I'm a princess."

"And when your head swells, you're going to land on it," Diello said.

She spread her arms wide and floated on her back. "I've always had a feeling we were special. You there, lackey!" she intoned in a haughty voice, snapping her fingers at an imaginary servant. "Bring me roast goose sprinkled with *agligar* spice and double helpings of cake."

"We can do magic now," Diello said. "We don't need any spice to make us giggle and see two of everything."

"I'll never be hungry again," Cynthe declared. "Think of how rich we'll be!"

Diello could imagine never being hungry or cold again, with servants rushing to supply anything he wanted. But dreams, when they had no chance to become real, brought only heartache.

"We're not rich," he said. "Our destiny is broken, and someone else besides you will be inheriting the throne. Or didn't you hear that part?"

Abandoning her silliness, she came back to the ground. "I heard. Vassou, is this really our future, or just what *might happen?*"

"Has the Knower proclaimed you the rightful heirs?"

"Yes!"

"No," Diello said.

Cynthe scowled. "It said we're the chosen."

"And the unchosen."

Her mouth clamped tight. Diello was sorry to dampen her excitement, but he wasn't going to lie.

The wolf pup stretched his front legs on the ground and bowed. "Praise to the Thousand Ancestors of my ancestors! From birth I have been sworn to your service, Lady Cynthe, and now I swear again, of my own will as samal and member of the Kannae pack."

Cynthe grinned.

"You're Faelin, remember?" Diello said. "Faelin can't be royalty. That's what the Knower meant about Pa changing the prophecy. No one's going to let you sit on a throne. It *should* be yours, but another will claim it."

Her grin faded. "Sometimes I don't know why I have a brother like you. Are you *trying* to be a dour old spoilsport?"

"Yes. When I woke up this morning, I decided that should anyone proclaim my sister the future queen, I'd make sure nothing came of it."

Cynthe turned away from him and bent down to Vassou. "Have you always known I'm a princess? Why didn't you tell us sooner?"

"It was for the Knower to say." The pup pressed his nose to her hand before coming over to Diello. "And what was said about you?"

"Cynthe's wrong. The destiny's broken." But Diello couldn't completely ignore the hope he'd felt when the

Knower said he was supposed to be the next mage-chancellor after Clevn. It was the second-highest position among the Fae, almost a king. But again, what good was it to know about a destiny he couldn't have?

"The Knower said that Diello will be my mage and counselor," Cynthe proclaimed.

Vassou bowed to Diello. "On behalf of the pack Kannae, may you grow rapidly in wisdom, my lord. For at present you seem to lack the wits you need."

Cynthe smirked, rolling her eyes at Vassou.

"It's no good joking about it," Diello said. "There are two destinies, the one we were supposed to have and the one we actually do. We aren't the heirs."

"Don't be so quick to throw everything away," Cynthe said. "Isn't there anything you believe in?"

"I believe that if we cross that *cloigwylie* up ahead, we're going to be dealing with a lot of trouble that we didn't cause."

"You've known there were dangers awaiting you since you took Eirian from hiding," Vassou replied. "Fae memories are long. You have seen for yourselves how harsh they can be against transgressors."

"Like Mamee," Cynthe said.

And Canthroy, Diello thought. He told Vassou what he'd learned from the *nonseen*.

"Eirian's return will go a long way toward appeasing the queen and Clevn," Vassou said, "but it may not gain forgiveness for your parents."

"If the queen is our grandmother," Diello said, "then Clevn is our great-uncle. And he's still our enemy."

"Do we have any chance of being accepted by our grandmother?" Cynthe asked Vassou. "Even if she just gives us a home. That's not too much to expect. And we'll never be poor. We'll have somewhere to belong."

Diello stared at his sister. "After what they did to Mamee, you want them to like us?"

"I want a home!"

"You want the throne. Even though you didn't know it until now. Not because you know how to rule or because you've been trained for it—you just want it because it's been dangled in front of you, the way we hold a new toy in front of Amalina. The queen won't give it to you."

"She might," Cynthe countered.

"Tell us, Vassou," Diello said. "Does the queen already have a new heir?"

"Yes."

Cynthe's face turned red, then very pale.

"Vassou," Diello said, "let's make everything clear. Is it really true that Mamee was the royal heir before she was exiled?"

"Yes," Vassou replied.

"Is Uncle Owain her twin?" Diello asked.

"Yes. By tradition, the royal line passes through sets of twins, a sister and a brother. The sister fights and holds the throne. The brother counsels and advises. Had Lwyneth remained in Embarthi, she and Owain would be the successors to Sheirae and Clevn, just as you and Cynthe should be the successors to Lwyneth and Owain."

"Exactly," Cynthe said.

That's why Cynthe's so good at hunting, Diello thought.

That's why I was given Sight and crystal bones.

He felt the rightness of it. A strong sense of longing filled him. He knew that's what Cynthe was feeling now. And yet, he had to let it go, for both their sakes. They would waste their lives wishing for what might have been, and that would be wrong.

"If Pa hadn't been our father," Diello said quietly, meeting Cynthe's green eyes, "we *would* be royalty. But he was, and so we aren't."

"That's not fair!" Cynthe said.

"As the Knower said," Diello reminded her, "Pa changed the destiny."

"All he and Mamee did was steal Eirian."

"No," Vassou said. "That is not all. Stephel stole *your* birthright as well."

Suddenly Diello understood. "It's our human blood. Our being disinherited has nothing to do with Eirian. Clevn doesn't like us because—"

"—the succession to the throne has been broken," Vassou said.

"But all they have to do is accept us," Cynthe said.

"It's not that simple," Diello told her.

"Diello is right," Vassou said. "Fae traditions are like chains."

"I wish I hadn't learned Mamee was a princess!" Cynthe cried. "It's like starving and having to watch your neighbor eat a feast."

"There's nothing I'd change," Diello declared. "I'm Pa's son, and proud of it. The rest doesn't matter."

"Doesn't matter?" she echoed. "You—you *liar!*"

"Cynthe!"

"Don't tell me to face things. Not when you stand there pretending it doesn't hurt."

"But I—"

"It's no good talking to you. Oh, Vassou, why did you bring us here?" She ran blindly down the hill into the woods.

Diello would have gone after her, but Vassou stopped him.

"Let her be," the wolf said. "She must vent her anger, but it should not be against you. More than ever, she needs your support and understanding."

Diello watched until the trees hid her from sight. "She might do anything in this kind of mood. She could set the woods on fire."

"She's become too sensible to do that."

"She's always hated being Faelin. She wants to be purely Fae. And now—this just makes it worse."

"Cynthe will master her feelings," Vassou said. "Meanwhile, we must be practical. Did the Knower give you a warning?"

"Uh, yes. I guess so. Lots of them. They didn't make a lot of sense." Diello paused. "You've talked about the Afon Heyrn before."

"In the old tongue, it translates to River of Iron."

"Iron! I thought the Fae stayed away from iron."

"Yes. It is the name of the religious council, a force to be avoided if possible. Afon Heyrn governs the Watchers, who guard the sacred relics. Their protections are supposed to be as impenetrable as iron."

Not for Pa, Diello thought proudly. "And Eirian was one of those relics?"

"Yes. What did the Knower say to you about the Afon Heyrn?"

"It wants vengeance because Pa took the sword. Just think! He was stronger than their protections, and he didn't even have any magic."

"But don't forget the price he paid."

Diello nodded, needing no reminder of Pa's withered arm.

"Vassou, why did you bring us to the Knower? It didn't tell us anything you don't already know."

Vassou licked his sore paw. "When I return soon to my pack, I must be able to tell them that the Knower spoke to you. It is important that all the samal packs be informed of this. They have decisions to make."

"Return?" Diello said. "What do you mean? Aren't we going to join them when we reach Embarthi?"

"We must part soon," Vassou told him. "I cannot go with you to the palace."

"Why? What have we done wrong?"

"It's nothing you've done. No member of the Kannae pack cán enter the queen's palace."

"Because of Mamee?"

"We have defied the queen in remaining loyal to Lwyneth. We have been banished from the Liedhe Court."

"But—but how will we manage? We need you! And you just pledged your service to Cynthe."

"Yes. But I cannot enter the queen's palace."

"Will you stay close by?"

"As close as I can," Vassou assured him.

Diello began to pace. He hadn't realized how much he

relied on Vassou's calm good sense. "Will we be able to talk to you?"

"Not while you are within the queen's circle," Vassou said. "Soon you will face enemies as dangerous to you as Brezog, yet far more devious. You must be strong in your mind or you will fail. If you are to be mage-chancellor—"

"I'm not," Diello said flatly. "I can't be."

"Why?"

"We just went through that," Diello burst out. "We're Faelin, aren't we? We can't even inherit a little farm, much less a throne. We're nothing."

"Do you truly believe you are nothing? You, who can fly, who can venture into the thoughts and dreams of others, living or dead? You, who can calm your sister's ungoverned powers and face the mage-chancellor's wrath without flinching? You have channeled spell fire and swept goblins to the winds. Do you not expect to one day command storm and lightning?"

"I don't know," Diello said, drinking in Vassou's compliments. "We've been told Faelin can't do such things."

"Ordinary Faelin, no. But never before has royal Fae blood been mingled with a human's. You are not ordinary, Diello. Nor is your twin. Your powers grow daily. Were you not fearful of attracting the goblins to you, you would be practiced and strong by now."

Diello stared across the hilltop past the Knower. "You've already said the Fae don't forgive and we'll never have a chance to be accepted as part of the royal family."

"I am saying do not make judgments yet. They can forgive, but not easily. Fae law is the queen's will.

Nothing more. Soften her heart, and there could be a chance."

"But what about this heir, this other girl who's supposed to take the throne away from Cynthe? You know who she is, don't you?"

"Yes. She lives in the palace and is known by all the Liedhe Court, but she is not the official heir. In the Liedhe Court, the weak perish quickly. Possession of Eirian makes you strong."

"What are you trying to tell me?" Diello asked. "I've had enough riddles for one day."

"I'm trying to prepare you for what is to come. You will be walking into old troubles, but the anger behind them is still sharp. If you use what you've been given, you can shield yourself against grudges and—"

"I can't worry anymore about Fae politics," Diello broke in. "Maybe we're royal and maybe we aren't, but what matters most is gaining Amalina's freedom."

"That is a small task."

"Not to me!"

"You think as a child. You believe that once the sword is returned, all will be forgiven. It is not that simple."

"Then why don't you speak plainly?" Diello cried. "Why can't the Knower? Why does it all have to be hidden?"

Vassou's blue eyes clouded with disappointment. "You hold the key to the world, and yet you will not use it. What else can be said to you?"

Diello touched the pouch containing Eirian's hilt. *Make me whole*, the sword whispered in his mind.

He jerked his hand away. Once again, he felt like a

playing piece on a gameboard. But this time, instead of Clevn moving him, it was Vassou. The games of kings—or queens—were not for him. All Diello wanted was to be allowed to grow up with some kind of home for himself and his sisters.

"I will go after Cynthe," Vassou said at last, and trotted away.

chapter thirteen

iello turned to gaze toward Embarthi. He didn't want to quarrel with Cynthe or Vassou.

I'm just trying to be sensible, like Pa, he thought, kicking at some pebbles.

A flock of rooks broke from the trees below, flying past in a flutter of dark wings. Feeling dizzy, Diello put his hand to his face. The rooks circled overhead, then vanished. Diello's head cleared.

The Death Flock!

Their appearance foretold someone's death. But he was alone up here. Were they foretelling *his* death?

He heard warning yips from the wolf pair standing guard. Diello saw the red wolf crouched as though about to attack the grays. All three animals had their hackles raised and their teeth bared. There was a brief, vicious fight before Canthroy came streaking uphill toward Diello. The others gave chase, snapping at his heels.

"Canthroy," Diello whispered.

Something pushed against his mind, and then the *non-seen*'s thoughts were inside his own.

Run! Run!

Canthroy's panic infected Diello. Yet he refused to flee. He couldn't outrun wolves. He backed against the Knower's trunk with his quarterstaff ready, wondering if the Knower was watching this. Would the ancient tree help him?

Who do I trust?

Canthroy had reached the summit and was less than twenty paces from Diello. But the gray wolves were gaining. One leaped, biting at the *nonseen's* spine, and nearly pulled him down.

Dirt flew in all directions as the creatures rolled then sprang apart. The *nonseen* attacked the gray pair with a savagery too terrible for Diello to watch.

Run! came the frantic command inside Diello's mind.

Run where? he wondered. *Run from what?*

The common wolves had been approved by Vassou, and they certainly seemed determined to keep Canthroy away from him. Uncertain, Diello edged away from the fight. He heard a shrill cry and saw Canthroy stagger. But the *nonseen* wasn't finished yet. Canthroy hit the female and knocked her down. Her mate leaped at the *nonseen's* back, but Canthroy had already opened her throat. As the other two fought next to the dying female, her form grew shadowy and indistinct.

Diello rubbed his eyes, but she was still changing, her fur melting into grayish-brown scaly skin, her muzzle becoming a long, needle-thin nose, her paws transforming into curled, knobby hands tipped with black talons.

The wind shifted, and the rotten stink of goblins reached Diello's nostrils.

At Diello's back was a sheer drop off the hill's summit. He had no choice but to run past the wolves.

As he gained speed, Canthroy barreled into him and knocked him over the edge.

Diello went tumbling down the steep hillside, bouncing and skidding, unable to stop. He finally crashed into the undergrowth at the forest line, landing hard against a tree.

He hurt all over. The knee of his leggings was torn, and he'd lost a sleeve and part of the skin off his elbow with it. His forearm was aching badly. As Diello staggered to his feet, he heard a wolf howl in triumph. Diello scurried deeper into cover before he peered uphill.

There, on the jutting rock above, stood the victorious gray wolf. The red wolf's body lay motionless, near where Diello had fallen.

Diello understood now that Canthroy had died to save him. *Are all the wolves shape-shifters? How can I warn Cynthe? Does Vassou know?*

As Diello watched, the gray wolf transformed into a gor-goblin, like Brezog, the cruelest of all the breeds. The goblin stared in Diello's direction.

If I run now, he'll see me pushing through the evergreens. Be still. Be still, Diello told himself.

All he had with him was a waterskin, his quarterstaff, his bronze knife, and the hilt of Eirian. Canthroy's sacrifice had gained him a few moments' lead, but he must use it wisely.

A faint cry rose on the air. Another came, and another, until a chorus echoed through the hills. A handful of green bloidy-goblins came trotting into sight, soon joined by more. The gor-goblin shouted to them and pointed toward Diello.

Diello careened deeper into the evergreen forest. He found himself cut off by more goblins. They seemed to be combing the woods. Diello bolted back the way he'd come.

They'd talked often about what to do in case of a goblin attack. The plan was for the twins to stay apart until they each reached safety, then wait for Vassou and Scree to find them. Easy to talk about around a campfire, but not so easy to do. Diello didn't want to abandon Cynthe, not even for Eirian's sake.

Has she had any warning? Was it just the pair shadowing me?

And how could he have been so close to goblins without sensing a disguising spell? He'd been so confident about that ability. Now, he felt like a fool. If not for Canthroy, Diello would be the one lying dead on the hillside right now.

Thank you, Canthroy. May no one hinder your Death Wind from taking you home.

The pitch of the slope changed unexpectedly, and Diello stumbled. He paused a moment to rest and listen. He was afraid of never seeing Cynthe again. He hated that they'd parted with a quarrel.

"Cynthe's probably doing better than you," he muttered to himself.

Pushing himself onward, he went at a slower pace. He could no longer run in a blind panic. He had to stay calm and use his wits. The goblins would be following his tracks and scent, although they could guess where he was headed. Worried about being ambushed before he reached the border, Diello knew it was time to try some tricks.

He needed running water. He sniffed at the light breeze. Detecting nothing, he turned west, resisting the urge to look constantly over his shoulder.

The afternoon was waning into long evening shadows when he stumbled onto a stream. Shallow and very clear, it was running fast despite the white crusts of ice along its banks. Diello heard a guttural voice call out and another goblin's reply.

They were far too close.

Diello waded into the water and walked upstream away from the voices. Knee-deep in the freezing water, he went as far as he could endure, then paused. It was hard to concentrate, but he did his best before lifting both arms above his head and grabbing air.

Up!

For once, his ascension worked exactly as it should. He soared high into the treetops before grabbing a stout branch and swinging himself onto it. Settling into a fork, he wrapped one arm around the trunk and pressed his cheek against the rough bark. His wet feet felt like chunks of ice. Diello couldn't think of any way to warm them, and shivers kept running through his body. He jammed a wad of pine needles in his mouth and bit down hard to keep his teeth from chattering.

Running water was the best way to throw goblins off his scent. He hoped that it had also concealed his brief use of magic. Still, he was hiding too close to where his trail vanished. He should have taken a bigger risk and tried to fly farther away.

But if he'd fallen, the goblins would have him by now.

Oh, Guardian, have mercy upon me and my friends, he prayed.

Then he heard the goblins coming. They were running along the creek bank, their footsteps loud over the brittle snapping of twigs. Diello pressed against the tree trunk. The gathering twilight helped hide him among the dark pine boughs, but if the breeze shifted and they caught his scent . . .

A voice called out. They came into the open near his hiding place and trampled up and down the edge of the stream, pointing in various directions and arguing.

Diello bit down harder on the foul-tasting pine needles. He would've given anything for the ability to cast a spell of invisibility around himself.

Ten or so goblins splashed into the water, yelped, and leaped out, shaking their feet and pushing one another. Diello didn't see the gor-goblin and feared that creature must be leading the search for Cynthe. One of them crossed to the other side of the stream and trotted into the woods, only to return a moment later, his head bent as he tried to find tracks.

At last their arguments ended. Grumbling, they wandered off, trailing their spears dejectedly.

Diello waited a long time, but they didn't return.

He spat out the pine needles. His perch offered safety,

but it was too cold up here. He needed a fire so he wouldn't freeze to death, and he couldn't very well light a blaze—however small—in the top of a pine tree.

Eventually he found enough courage to climb down. His half-frozen feet ached, but he stamped them hard and trudged on, knowing the movement would help restore his circulation. *Soon*, he kept promising himself. *Soon I'll build that fire.* He forged onward, afraid of running into sprites, and even more terrified of building a fire that might draw the goblins straight to him. Diello was no longer sure of anything except that he must reach Embarthi.

He tried to fill his stomach with frequent sips of water, but soon his hunger was fierce. The night grew dark and frosty. Exhausted, he was hardly aware of what he was doing.

Just as his eyelids grew so heavy he couldn't hold them open, he bumped into something. It bounced him backward. He scrambled on all fours, pausing to reach out. His fingers grazed the smooth, slightly cool surface of the *cloigwylie* around Embarthi.

He pressed his face and chest to it, feeling the hum of its magic inside him. He'd made it! Now all he had to do was pass through the wall and make camp until Cynthe caught up with him.

And if she doesn't? What about Vassou? What about Scree?

He ignored his doubts. He would make a fire to thaw himself. He'd be safe, and it wouldn't matter how tired and hungry he was.

But Diello found he couldn't walk through this *cloigwylie*. It was so thick he couldn't even thrust his hand through it.

"I'm Fae enough to go through," he said aloud. "Why is it keeping me out?"

He couldn't believe it. The difficult journey, the hunger and the cold, the endless leagues of walking on sore feet, now to end like this . . . He threw himself at the barrier, and bounced off. He hammered at it with his fists and kicked it. He even flicked fire and tried to burn a hole in it, but nothing worked.

Embarthi—that fabled place of plenty, beauty, and every imaginable comfort—might as well be as far away as the two moons. It would not let him in.

He raised his arms.

Up! Up! Up!

But it seemed he'd used up his store of magic eluding the goblins. His feet rose slightly off the ground, but his body felt heavy and sluggish.

Up!

Diello pushed as hard as he could and ascended a little more. He struggled to stay aloft. He dipped lower and placed his palms on the *cloigwylie*, hoping to find some way to climb it.

But his fingers could find no purchase. The barrier flexed beneath his touch, making it even harder to hold on. He slid down to the ground with a thump.

I'll try again in the morning. I'm too worried about Cynthe and the others to concentrate.

Diello took shelter in a nearby grove of pine saplings. He scooped needles into a pile and burrowed into what paltry cover they afforded. They prickled under the collar of his tunic and jabbed his ears and made him sneeze. Diello huddled in a tight ball and told himself that soon he would be warm. If he just kept his back pressed against the *cloigwylie*, he couldn't freeze.

Build a fire.

He sat up, shivering, and cleared a space around a heap of pine needles and twigs. But he couldn't even flick fire.

He fumbled in his pocket for his tinderbox, but before he could pull it out, he heard a noise.

Whatever it was moved away. Other sounds came from within the forest. They seemed normal night sounds, but his hands were clenched in fists. He didn't try to eavesdrop on the animals, fearing that Brezog might somehow seize control of his mind. Fire was too risky, Diello decided.

He lay down again in the dry brown needles, listening. Exhaustion finally won out, and he slept.

Diello awakened under sunshine and raised his head to peer blearily around him. He was curled in a small depression under the trees, and when he tried to sit up he nearly cried out from the aches in his body. His head felt as heavy as a millstone, and he was still shivering. The skin on his hands was pale. He could barely feel his fingers or toes. Picking up his quarterstaff proved impossible.

He didn't feel all that hungry anymore, but thirst drove him to gulp almost all of his water supply. His thoughts were woolly, and it was an effort to remember what he was supposed to be doing.

Find Cynthe.

He dragged himself to his feet. Frost sparkled on the pine boughs, and the sunlight reflected off the *cloigwylie* in molten sheets of gold and silver. He pressed his face to it, trying to peer through. But it was like trying to see underwater. He glimpsed distorted shapes, but couldn't tell what they were.

And still he could not push through it.

Must find Cynthe, he thought and hobbled on, running his hand along the *cloigwylie* for support. As he kept going, his body loosened and moved more easily. The farther he walked, the more confident he grew that nothing would bother him while he was touching the *cloigwylie*.

Then Diello came to a ravine. The magical wall spanned it, shimmering all the way to the bottom. Diello sighed. He wasn't going to climb down and then back up just to keep following the wall. The last time had landed him in a trog den.

"Fool me twice, shame on me," he muttered, repeating one of Pa's sayings.

The sun was climbing above the treetops now. He shrugged his blanket off his shoulders and let it hang from his belt while he pondered whether he should try to fly over the *cloigwylie* again.

He squinted upward, shading his eyes. He couldn't see the top of the wall. He wasn't sure he could ascend that far, and yet why not try?

A gigantic bird circled over him. Eagle or vulture, he couldn't tell, but he heard its thoughts.

This one carries the magic, but it is not whole. You are clever, groundwalker. I must seek other pieces of the magic before I strike. The bird flew away.

Diello drank more water, and found the skin nearly empty. He must do *something*.

He piled his blanket and the waterskin on the ground. Fresh chills almost made him reach for the blanket again.

He lifted his arms. They were heavy. His whole body was heavy.

No, he thought in frustration. *I must be light.* He thought about paleweed fuzz and soap bubbles and lovely darterflies skimming the creek's surface in summer. Gradually, he felt magic swirl around his ankles and rise through his legs. He lifted his arms, spreading his fingers wide.

Up!

He rose slowly but steadily, feeling the thrum of the *cloigwylie* next to him. He went higher, and still the barrier shimmered.

Up!

Diello rose farther than he'd ever gone before, not daring to look down, and still he could not find the top.

"Please," he whispered hoarsely, touching the barrier. But it remained as impenetrable as ever.

He knew then that he'd failed, and even if he soared as high as the clouds, he would not get past it.

Tears pricked his eyes, and he felt his strength ebbing. He began to drop, rapidly at first, then more slowly as he struggled for control. By the time Diello reached the ground, he was wheezing and his head throbbed. Sitting at the base of the magical wall, he rested awhile, trying in vain to catch his breath. Gray dots kept swimming across his vision. The ground felt cold beneath him, but it seemed too much effort to pull the thin blanket around his body.

So much for prophecy and destiny and plans, he thought.

If only he had the entire sword, he would've plunged it

through the *cloigwylie*. He would've shown the arrogant Fae just what they could do with their barriers.

But maybe, just maybe, the hilt might be enough.

Diello sat up, wincing as his headache intensified. Pulling out the hilt, he curled his fingers around it.

Make me whole, the sword said in his mind.

He jabbed at the *cloigwylie*. When the pommel struck the barrier, the *cloigwylie* trembled.

Diello flinched. Then he struck again and a third time. The barrier shook, but held.

Diello stared at the hilt a long while before tucking it away. His throat was burning. He reached for his waterskin, but it was gone.

Something thumped him between the shoulders, nearly knocking him flat. He turned around but saw nothing.

A taunting whistle came from his left. He turned, glimpsing only a blurred shape. It whistled again.

He pretended to turn in that direction, but instead spun the other way—and found himself face to face with a tiny, brown-skinned creature no taller than his knees. It had a puckered face, like an apple left too long in the root cellar. Tufts of white hair grew from its scalp. Its eyes were bright and beady black. In one hand it held a pointed stick. In the other, Diello's waterskin.

A sprite, he thought in dismay.

"Give my water back," Diello said. Clearly it understood his meaning, for the sprite held up the waterskin and shook it.

Diello reached for the waterskin, but the sprite sprang to one side. As it moved, it jabbed his arm with the stick.

"Ow!" Diello cried. He ran at the sprite and missed.

The sprite swung the waterskin just out of reach.

Diello crouched in the dirt, feinting one way and then the other, so that the sprite skipped around. While the creature was on the move, Diello picked up a stone. As soon as the sprite paused a moment, Diello threw the rock.

His aim was true. With a squeak, the sprite toppled over backward. Diello grabbed his water and the pointed stick. He finished the water and threw the stick in the ravine.

The sprite bounced to its feet and jumped up and down in rage.

Suddenly a stone hit Diello's leg, hard. Another struck his foot. Now, instead of one angry little sprite, he faced two. Both were picking up rocks.

Diello dodged, but not quickly enough. One rock bounced off his hip. The other got him in the ribs. He rushed at the sprites, but they eluded him easily. He heard a sound behind him and turned to find himself confronted by a half-dozen more.

Using his fists, he knocked several away, but more swarmed him from behind. Some climbed his legs and others jumped on his back, clawing their way onto his shoulders. They bit at his ears and neck, their teeth painfully sharp, and for every one he brushed off, at least three more took its place.

He staggered back and forth. He slammed against the *cloigwylie* and managed to dislodge several sprites, but they came at him again, pulling him to his knees. Flicking fire, he forced several to retreat. The rest crawled over him like ants.

Diello held his arm across his face, protecting his eyes. A chomp on his ear made him cry out.

Then he felt little hands pulling at his belt and the rabbitskin pouch.

"No!" he cried.

He fended them off until he grew short of breath. His throat was so dry he started coughing. He sank down.

A sprite jumped on Diello's stomach and banged his forehead with a rock. He fought to hang onto consciousness. To be so close to Embarthi and yet unable to drag himself to safety was maddening.

"*Let me in!*" he yelled.

The rock struck again, smashing into his temple. The last thing he heard was the sprites whistling in triumph.

chapter fourteen

iello heard voices talking above him. Now and then he felt gentle hands lifting him, but that hurt so much he cried out, and then there was darkness again.

He was very hot. There was a thick warm moisture that clung to his skin in droplets. It was urgent that he find Cynthe, but no matter how far he waded through the dense mist, he couldn't see her.

"Cynthe!" he called. "Cynthe!"

He feared the goblins had killed her. He searched until his legs trembled and could carry him no farther. Ahead, he saw a slim figure waiting in the misty shadows.

"Cynthe!"

The figure turned and threw back its hood. It was Brezog—red eyes gleaming in that scaly face. The gorlord reached out for him with long talons. Diello tried to run, but once again, he found himself caught in the creature's spell.

Brezog's hands reached closer and closer until they fastened around Diello's throat. He screamed.

A light surrounded him, driving back the mist and

gloom. A pale hand touched Brezog's shoulder, and the gorlord vanished.

Sinking to his knees, Diello looked up to thank his rescuer.

Mamee.

She wore a gown of simple white cloth, falling in folds from her throat to her feet. Her hair—silver streaked with copper strands—swept back from her brow and fell unbound to her waist. Her skin sparkled. She had never looked more beautiful.

He flung his arms around her, but grasped nothing. She drifted away from him, still smiling serenely, and he knew that she was only an image, a memory. He began to cry.

"Hush, my dear halfling," she said. "Do not fear what lies behind you."

"I've failed," he said. "Cynthe is missing. I can't get into Embarthi. I don't know where Amie is."

Mamee placed her hand on his cheek. "None of your terrors are real. You have done well."

"Not well enough. I can't find Cynthe."

"She is not lost. You will be with her soon."

"Where is she?"

"Close by. Be strong for her, Diello. Cynthe needs you more than ever."

"Everything's so hard. What do I do about Amie?"

"Do not lose your courage. You should not have gone to the Knower. Sometimes you can learn too much."

"We don't know *enough*," Diello protested. "Vassou says there's a chance Cynthe might take the throne, but I don't understand how."

"Do not be guided by the samal in this matter," Mamee said. "The throne is unworthy of your sister. Do not let her waste my sacrifice. There are other, more important tasks for you both to accomplish."

"Like saving Amalina?"

Little sparks danced in Mamee's hair. "Keep your promise to your father. Honor him."

"Eirian must be returned. But I've lost it."

"Why do you say that?"

"I don't know. I—I can't remember. Is it here? Is it safe?"

"Let your bones guide you."

"But how do we find Uncle Owain? How do we find Amie?"

Mamee was fading from his view.

He lunged for her. "Don't leave!"

But she'd gone, and the mist was returning.

Mamee's voice came to him, faint and far away. She was singing her old lullaby from when he and Cynthe were little.

Bide quietly, my sweetest.
Close your eyes and sleep.
Trust your heart to keep
All your dreams at rest.
Till the morning dawns
And doves coo their song,
Bide quietly, my sweetest.
Close your eyes and sleep.

He grew calmer. The fog lifted before him, and then he was ascending slowly and with perfect control. He saw the shimmering *cloigwylie* above him. Diello put out his hand and passed through it.

Opening his eyes, he found himself lying in a soft bed. His warm blankets were gossamer-fine and spun in the pattern of cobwebs. Cynthe sat beside him, holding his hand. She was staring out a window and humming the old lullaby. She looked different somehow.

He stared at her for a long moment before he realized the change: she was clean. Gone was the ragged, gaunt, almost feral girl she'd become on the journey. The leaves and twigs had been combed from her hair, which was longer than he remembered and hung loose to her shoulders. *How long have I been asleep?* A green ribbon held her hair out of her eyes, and she wore a matching green jerkin over a tunic.

Nothing around him looked familiar. But he was just relieved that Cynthe was with him. Diello lay there and listened to her song.

She turned her head his way, and a smile lit up her face. "You're awake! Praise the Guardian. You're awake! I must tell the healer!"

"No . . . Stay." His voice sounded so thin and weak.

"I promised I would tell them if you woke up."

"Stay."

"All right." She leaned down and kissed his cheek.

"Are you crying?" he asked.

She blinked away her tears and shook her head. "Why would I cry over you? Just because you've been sick for weeks and we thought you might die? I—I knew you wouldn't give up, no matter what *they* said. I've sat with you every day, and I've talked to you, trying to make you wake up."

"I couldn't find you."

She rubbed her fingers across the back of his hand. "But I was here, even when they tried to keep me away. I paid them all the gold in your purse, and some of Scree's goblin gold, too, to make them take care of you."

"They?"

"The healers in this place. Imagine, a whole compound devoted to healing."

A rush of memories came back. "The goblins!" Diello cried. "They tricked us. They killed Canthroy. I had to run, had to leave you. I didn't want to. I've tried to find you ever since."

"Shush," she said. "You must stay quiet."

"I thought they got you."

"I'm here, aren't I?" She grinned, but there was something she wasn't telling him.

"What about Vassou and Scree?"

"They're not . . . allowed in the compound."

He was about to ask more questions, but Cynthe was swept aside by a woman with a white headdress covering her hair and throat. Her wide-set eyes were dark gray.

"So you are with us at last," she said. She was speaking Fae. She frowned at Cynthe. "You were to call us at once."

"I got through?" Diello asked. "Is this . . ."

"Yes." Cynthe leaned close to him. "We're in Embarthi. This is the healer assigned to your care. Her name is Marshana."

"Stop upsetting him," the Fae woman said. She filled a cup with blue liquid and lifted Diello's shoulders slightly off his pillows. She was gentle, but being moved made his head ache.

He kept his gaze on Cynthe and smiled a little. "Safe."

"Drink," the woman said impatiently.

Diello swallowed the liquid. It was cool and thick, and tasted of sweet fruit. Before he could finish it, he grew tired.

Falling asleep, he was dimly aware of more voices murmuring around him until they were shushed and quiet fell. He managed to open his eyes enough to glimpse shadowy figures along his bedside.

When he next awoke, the figures were gone. His room was dark, and a panel of cloth covered his window. At the foot of his bed, a glass lamp was shining by some means he didn't understand. It burned no flame that he could see, yet the light it cast was clear and lucid.

A slender man stared down at him. He had violet eyes and ears with long pointed tips.

"Uncle?" Diello called hesitantly.

"No. I'm one of the attendants." The man turned back Diello's blankets and washed him with a sponge dipped in warm water. Just as Diello began to shiver, the man finished and tucked the blankets securely around him again.

"What's your name?" Diello asked.

"That's not important," the attendant replied. He spoke Fae slowly as though he thought Diello might not understand him. "Are you in pain?"

"A little," Diello admitted. When he tried to move his head, agony stabbed him sharply behind the eyes.

"More than a little, I think. Lie still."

The attendant left, but returned shortly with Marshana. She bent over Diello and prodded his scalp in various places.

When he flinched, she stopped her examination and snapped her fingers at the attendant.

"The spheres."

The man held out a bowl, and Marshana chose a small orb from among several. It looked like a clear glass ball, but when she held it over Diello, it turned murky inside. Making a tsking sound, she picked up another orb and held it over Diello's chest. It turned a putrid green with streaks of yellow. A third orb held over his head turned crimson, almost purple.

"Hmm, yes, the pain is still severe." She tossed the crimson orb back in the bowl. Diello heard it smash.

"What happened to me?" Diello asked. "Did I fall?" He coughed a little, and pain flared through his whole body.

"Be quiet." Marshana held up another orb over his stomach. This one changed to brown, like swamp water. "Interesting. We shall change your diet."

I might as well be a beetle for all she cares. Diello shut his eyes. He wished Mamee were here, taking care of him.

The male attendant smiled and slyly held out the bowl to catch the used orbs that Marshana tossed away, one by one. As each orb smashed, noxious odors mingled together.

Diello wrinkled his nose.

"No, you're far from a beetle," Marshana said, wiping

THE CALL OF EIRIAN

her hands and draping the cloth over the bowl. She gestured for it to be taken away. "Don't look so astonished. Of course I can read your strongest thoughts. I wouldn't be a healer if I couldn't. Be proud of yourself. It's not every Faelin boy who can recover from a fractured skull and lung fever. The Fae in you has made you strong. If you were human, you'd be dead by now."

"Oh," Diello said, not sure what else to say.

"You are mending well, unless you decide to do something foolish. Your sister may visit you once a day. I will consider extending her visits to twice a day."

"Did I fall?" Diello asked again.

"No. We will discuss it later. Now, enough questions! I will give you something to ease your chest so you can sleep. Here." She thrust a cup of the sweet blue liquid at Diello, supporting him skillfully so he could swallow. "Drink all of it."

He had no choice but to obey.

In the next few days, Marshana fulfilled her promises. Once the orb held over his lungs stayed clear, Cynthe was allowed to come twice a day. As Diello grew better, he asked her how she, Vassou, and Scree had eluded the goblins.

"Were the wolves all shape-shifters?" Diello asked.

"No. Just the pair following us around that day. The wolves fought the goblins, and then Vassou and I ran. I've never gone so fast."

"And later?"

She was watching the closed door. "What?"

"Tell me what happened later."

"Oh. First, we, uh, we doubled back and found Scree. Then we tracked you. Why do you want to hear all this again? I told you yesterday and the day before. Can't you remember?"As she said it, her eyes widened. "I'm sorry! I didn't mean that."

"The man that tends me . . . there's something odd about him."

"Who? Dhrui?" She glanced at the door and bent closer to Diello. "He spies on us."

"Why?"

Cynthe shrugged. "They aren't very nice. We seem to make them nervous."

"Have you been mistreated?"

"No. It's just—I can't explain it. It's a feeling I have. They stop talking when I'm around. They stare at me. No one answers my questions."

"They can read minds," Diello told her.

"I know. But just strong thoughts, the way Mamee could."

"We could trick her a lot of the time," Diello remembered.

Cynthe nodded.

When he and Cynthe were children, they'd devised simple codes to thwart Mamee from knowing about their plans to sneak off from chores or play in areas of the forest where they weren't supposed to go. All Cynthe had to do was drop a duck feather next to Diello when he was pulling weeds in the field, and he knew that she wanted to spend their afternoon swimming. If she tapped her foot against the pail while they were milking, Diello knew they'd soon be venturing into the woods. One tap meant *let's go to the hills*, and two taps meant *let's explore all the way to the road*. Whenever Mamee grew suspicious, they changed their code.

I wonder if we ever really fooled Mamee.

"Let's talk about something else," Cynthe said quickly. "When we found you, it was awful. You were lying there all bloody and unconscious, with eagles circling overhead."

"Vultures," Diello said. "I saw one."

"No. Eagles. Huge ones. Vassou said they must have protected you by keeping the vultures away."

Diello didn't understand, but at the moment he wasn't interested in birds. More memories were returning. "Do you have the—"

"Wait!" She looked at the door, and in the quiet Diello heard footsteps walking away. Cynthe swung back to him. "Now we can talk freely, but not for long. Keep listening for him."

"The hilt," Diello said, suddenly thinking of it and amazed that it took him this long. "Is it safe? Who has it? Is it with my clothes and things? Where's my quarterstaff?"

"I couldn't find your quarterstaff. The hilt's gone, too. . . . I'm sorry."

He groaned. "The sprites took them?"

"We hunted for the hilt but never located the sprite lair. All I found were a few pieces of the pouch." She sighed. "At the time, your quarterstaff didn't seem to matter."

"And now the goblins have Eirian's hilt," he said grimly.

"You don't know that. I don't think the sprites are in league with the goblins, if that helps," she said. "Scree says sprites are nasty thieves and will take anything they see. Maybe they threw it away. What use would they have for it?"

The idea of the hilt lying in the brush gave him a chill. "We have to get out of here and go back for it."

"Not till you're well enough. I marked where we found you, but goblins had trampled out the sprite tracks."

"Maybe they *do* have it."

"I don't think so. I've overheard the soldiers in the garrison—"

"What garrison? I thought we were in Embarthi!"

"Stay calm! We are. But there's a Fae garrison across town from the healing compound. I guess they guard the border. The town's big, maybe double the size of Wodesley, but it's nothing like I expected."

Diello shifted on his pillow. "What about the goblins?"

"Oh, they've been seen roaming up and down along the *cloigwylie*. On the Antrasin side, I mean. They're still looking, so they must not have it."

Diello didn't feel very reassured. "What about the blade?"

She twisted around so that he could see her quiver. Nestled in among her arrows was the slim, leather-wrapped blade. Hidden in plain sight. If only he hadn't failed his part.

"The Fae here think we're stupid," Cynthe said. "That gives us an advantage."

"If I could have gone through the *cloigwylie*, it would be safe now," he said. "I tried everything! I flew higher than

I've ever dared before and still I couldn't make it."

She placed her hand over his. "You mustn't blame yourself."

"How did you and the others get through?"

Cynthe hesitated. "Vassou spoke in Fae, and the *cloigwylie* parted."

"A magic word? Why didn't he tell me before we split up?"

"No one expected the shape-shifters, and how was Vassou to know you'd be attacked by sprites? He's been very worried about you. So has Scree."

"I want to see them. Where are they?"

"At the garrison."

"Why there? Aren't they allowed to visit? Tell me everything. Stop holding back."

"Vassou and Scree are prisoners," she admitted at last. "I've seen them twice since we came into Embarthi. Otherwise, I haven't been allowed out of the compound at all."

"Where exactly are we?"

"I told you. It's a border town. The garrison guards a road and checkpoint across the border. They open the *cloigwylie* only at certain times, and all the travelers are questioned before they can pass. When Vassou brought us through, they were furious. They arrested him and Scree on the spot. You were hurt, so they sent you and me to this compound." She twisted her hands together in her lap. "I thought Embarthi would be warm and beautiful, with everyone singing and playing games. I thought they'd be kind, but it's not like that at all."

"Are you held as a prisoner, too?"

"Not at first, but now . . . I leave my room only to visit you."

"Why?" he demanded.

Biting her lip, she shrugged. "It's because I had a tempest."

"What?" He thought of Cynthe's last tempest, when she'd nearly burned them alive in the castle storeroom at Wodesley before discovering she could fly. His Gifts just *came*, while Cynthe suffered more violent changes because she was a girl. Diello didn't know why it worked that way, but he was glad he hadn't gone through what Cynthe had.

"Are you saying you manifested another Gift?" he asked.

She nodded. "Now they know I can do magic."

"Were you alone when it happened? Did they help you? Were you scared?"

"No, I wasn't scared. I'm not a baby."

"But no one helped you?"

"It wasn't like before," she said softly.

"Were you angry? Had you lost your temper?"

"Yes. I was yelling because they wouldn't release Vassou. They keep him caged." She tossed back her hair. "And the way they treat Scree is worse. I think if we weren't here, they'd let him starve."

Diello grimaced. "How do they treat *you*?"

"I do all right. My room looks a lot like this, only smaller. The food's served hot. Mostly I'm bored."

He stared at her, waiting.

Finally she said, "They won't talk to me, either. They

look at me like I'm a trog. I really don't care. These healer folk are so strange. There's a bell that rings from a tower in the compound, and they stop whatever they're doing immediately and start a new task. They all eat together at long tables, but no one says a word. If they didn't look Fae, I'd swear they weren't." She paused. "They have no joy. Not like Mamee."

He thought of their mother's songs and how she had made the most mundane task into a special activity. Even when she'd been sad, it was never for very long. "Tell me more about your tempest."

"There wasn't much to this one. I was yelling about Vassou, and then I felt hot, *scorching* hot. I thought I might start flying or set something on fire—like that stupid commander who ordered Vassou caged—so I went off by myself. While I was throwing a few stones at the compound wall, I started calling the garrison commander some bad names. Each time I did, my voice got lower and stronger. I'm not sure what I said, but part of the wall cracked."

"Luck," he said, scoffing. "Stray magic."

"Stray—I've never heard of that. You're making it up."

"That wasn't a real tempest."

"It was. And I handled it myself," she insisted. "Now I have a new Gift. If I hit a certain tone of voice—not loud but just really, really stern—I can break things." She pitched her voice low. "Like that *bowl.*"

The glass bowl of water shattered, sending shards flying everywhere. Ducking, Diello whistled in awe.

"Sorry," Cynthe said. But she was grinning. "They'll have an awful fit over this mess."

"Let them," Diello said. "We can get out of here."

The door burst open, and a harried female attendant looked in. "What happened?"

Cynthe said, "Clumsy me. I broke a bowl. I'll clean everything up."

"You'd better." The attendant slammed the door.

The twins looked at each other and laughed.

"I've got everything planned," Cynthe said. "As soon as you're on your feet, we'll break out."

Diello sank a bit lower on his pillows. He was tired of being cooped up and envious of Cynthe's new Gift.

"Did they punish you for cracking the wall?"

"Not that first time. They didn't understand. Then I got the idea of breaking the wall where Vassou is caged, but they caught me. That's why I'm now locked up here inside the compound. I haven't seen Vassou or Scree since. There's no point in breaking out until we can all escape."

"I'll be better soon."

"They hate us, you know. Really hate us. They're so polite, but I can see it in their eyes."

"You didn't tell them who we really are, did you?" he asked.

"I'm not *that* witless," she replied. "But they already know."

"Perhaps they read your mind. Or it could be Clevn."

"I overheard yesterday that there are plans to move us when you're well enough to travel."

"You seem to overhear a lot," Diello said. "I hope you're a better spy than that attendant."

"Of course, even if I can't read minds." Cynthe shrugged.

"If I don't eavesdrop, how else am I going to learn anything? We're to be taken to central Embarthi. I think that's where the palace is."

"We can't do that," Diello said. "We can't be delivered into Clevn's hands without—without everything we're supposed to have."

"Agreed. We'll go there on our own and not as prisoners."

"Help me sit up," Diello said. "I can make it if you help me."

"Stay put. You can't get up. Stop!"

She pushed him onto his pillows. Diello closed his eyes against the spinning room and cursed.

"That's a nasty word," she said in admiration. "Where'd you learn that one?"

He grinned feebly, cracking open one eye.

"We can't do anything yet," she said. "Promise me you won't try something stupid."

He didn't respond.

"Promise!"

"I promise."

She released him reluctantly, straightening his blanket. "They didn't think you'd live. And Marshana said that if you did, your wits might be affected. You really scared me."

"I'm fine, Cynthe. I remember more every day about the attack. I almost wish I didn't."

"You kept calling for me, but you didn't know me for the longest time. It was awful. Sometimes . . . you talked to people who weren't there."

"I saw Mamee."

Her eyes filled with tears. "Oh, Diello!"

"It's all right," he said, touching her shoulder. "She told me—"

He felt something brush across his mind.

People were talking outside the door now, their hushed voices rising.

Cynthe leaned in. "I'll bet it's all the healers, coming to stare at you again. They've done it before."

The latch clicked on the door, but it didn't quite swing open. The argument grew louder. Cynthe straightened, but Diello caught her sleeve.

"Be careful," he whispered. "Have they seen you fly or flick fire?"

She shook her head.

"Then keep it secret. No more tempests. No losing your temper," he warned her. "At least, not until we're ready to get out of here."

tall Fae man wearing highly polished armor stepped into the room with Marshana. From breastplate to shin guards, the stranger gleamed. He carried a helmet under his left arm, its plumes curling behind him. In his right hand he held a scroll glittering with tiny gold chains that revolved around it in continuous motion.

Clevn! Diello thought, before he realized this couldn't be the mage-chancellor. He'd seen Clevn before, and this man—although equally stern—looked nothing like him.

The visitor stared at both Diello and Cynthe. "Great Hand of Mobidryn," he muttered. "It's true, then. A pair of them."

"Yes, General," Marshana said. "It's quite true."

Diello managed to push himself up on one elbow. Immediately, Marshana brushed Cynthe aside and assisted Diello in sitting up. She made quite a business of plumping pillows to prop him on and then pulled his blankets higher.

"You see how we care for the queen's grandson," she said. "We make sure he is kept warm." She touched the walls nearest to Diello's bed. Sparkles danced across their surface, and the air grew warmer.

Marshana shooed Cynthe into a corner out of the way before positioning herself at the foot of Diello's bed. Several other soldiers crowded in the doorway but did not enter.

Diello wondered if Cynthe and the others had been imprisoned on this man's orders.

Diello had always imagined Fae warriors to be elegant— capable of felling an enemy with bolts of magic and silver arrows. He hadn't expected them to look this weathered. This general might wear fancy armor, but he was grizzled and gnarled. His nose jutted hawklike from his face. A jagged scar twisted down his left cheek, and his pointed ears each had a gold ring pierced through the tip, from which dangled a tassel made from coarse black animal hair. A long, curved dagger sheathed in leather studded with jewels hung at his belt. His spurs featured barbed fighting rowels.

The man approached Diello. "There's nothing of her in you," he said. "I see only the Carnethie peasant that sired you." He turned his glare on Cynthe. "And are we to call this gawky creature a maiden? Who lets her go about garbed like a boy and slung with bow and quiver in a house of healing?"

Cynthe took a step forward before she stopped herself. Diello lay stiff with fury.

"As you can see, General," Marshana said, ignoring his criticisms, "the queen's grandson has improved, but he is far from fully recovered."

The general thrust the scroll at Diello. "A message from the palace," he barked in Fae. "For you. Or the girl. It concerns you both."

Diello made no move to take the scroll.

"Healer!" the man said. "Make him understand."

"He speaks Fae," Marshana replied.

"I doubt very well. Are his wits as damaged by his injury as you expected?"

Before she could answer, the general snapped his fingers at Cynthe. "Come here, girl. Come, come, come! Take the message, if you can read at all."

Cynthe's face was stony. Marshana shoved her forward.

"Take it. Take it!" the man ordered.

When she refused, the general gripped her arm.

"Stop it!" Diello said. "Let her go."

Cynthe wrenched free.

The officer swung back to Diello. "So you do have a tongue in your head."

Diello asked Marshana in flawless Fae, "Who is this empty wind that dares disturb my sister and me?"

Marshana averted her face, allowing herself the faintest of smiles. The soldiers in the doorway withdrew, and the room grew ominously quiet.

Diello felt Sight coming upon him, making the room waver and then fade into the scene of a battlefield. He saw the general standing on a vantage point overlooking a sea of warriors. The man was holding a sword aloft, and lightning danced off its point.

The jingle of spurs brought Diello back to the present. The general had retreated slightly from his bedside.

"Healer Marshana," the general said, "would you introduce us properly?"

She folded her hands. "Lord Diello, may I make known

to you Lord Rhodri of the Black Lion regiment? He is general of Her Majesty's army."

"Thank you," the general said.

Cynthe edged over to Diello. "She called you 'lord,'" Cynthe whispered in Antrasin.

Marshana cleared her throat. "Lady Cynthe, this is Lord Rhodri."

Cynthe said nothing. Diello kept silent also.

"Let us begin again," Lord Rhodri said. "I bring you a message from Her Majesty. With your permission, may I offer it to you?"

Diello didn't know how to refuse this formal request. Warily, he nodded.

Rhodri proffered the scroll once more.

The parchment was rolled tightly between two disks of polished ebony. The tiny chains still sparkled and glittered around it, and Diello's bones tingled. He didn't know how to open the chained scroll and felt too embarrassed to admit it.

Cynthe took it from Rhodri's hand. "From our grandmother . . . For both of us?"

Rhodri nodded. "I suppose neither of you can read Fae?"

"Of course we can!" Cynthe turned it over and over in her hands. "How does it open?"

Taking the scroll from Cynthe, Diello gave it a twist. The chains vanished with a pop, and his fingers felt as though he'd touched fire. Diello curled his aching hand and ignored Rhodri's raised eyebrows. Apparently that wasn't the proper way to open the thing, but Diello didn't care.

When he unrolled the parchment, gold-colored words—written in elaborate cursive—flowed off the page and hung suspended in the air before him.

With their heads together, he and Cynthe looked at it.

The message began with what seemed to be all of Queen Sheirae's titles, including Her Most Esteemed Majesty of Highest Estate, Ruler of the Golden Lands, Inheritor of the Silver Wheels, Keeper of the . . .

Diello skipped to where he spotted his and Cynthe's names. It was hard to read for all the extra flourishes. Still, it was a summons to the palace, all right. They were to come without delay. Diello read on, looking for some welcoming word, some indication that their grandmother truly wanted to meet them. But there was none. The final lengthy paragraph held nothing but praise and compliments to the queen.

"Done?" Diello asked his twin.

She nodded, and Diello dropped the scroll on the blanket. The floating words shimmered and flowed back onto the page. Then the thing rolled itself up with a snap, and the golden chains reappeared around it.

"So?" Diello said.

Rhodri glared. "Is this all you have to say at the honor extended to you? A personal message from the queen herself, and this is your response?"

Diello shrugged.

"Great Guardian! Can you truly be so ignorant of its value?"

"Any scribe could have written it for her," Diello said.

"I tell you it was written by the queen's own hand. I saw

her do it. Have you no understanding of what it took for her to extend this opportunity to you?"

"When do we go?" Diello asked.

"Today, preferably. Tomorrow at the latest."

"Impossible!" the healer said. "In a few weeks perhaps, but not this soon."

While the healer and the general resumed an argument that they'd apparently started earlier, Cynthe gripped Diello's hand. "What are we to do?" she whispered in Antrasin. "How can we ransom Amie without the whole sword?"

"There's nothing we *can* do right now," Diello said. "We'll need Uncle Owain's help more than ever."

"Do you think I can persuade Lord Rhodri to release Vassou and Scree?"

"Try," Diello said.

"My patient's well-being must be my chief concern," the healer was saying coldly.

"And you think the palace is oblivious to that?" Rhodri replied. "He'll travel in comfort. We'll take him by sleigh."

Marshana looked astonished. "The royal sleigh?"

"What else? Her Majesty shows great benevolence here. We'll wrap him in plenty of furs, and he'll never feel the cold. The journey won't take half a day. He'll be coddled like a shipment of the finest Imjarian nectar."

"If anything goes wrong, I will not be blamed," the healer said. "I wish that clearly established."

"Lord Rhodri, will you order the release of our friends?" Cynthe asked. "They're being held prisoner in the garrison."

The general shook his head.

"Cynthe," Marshana said. "Please leave now."

"Talk to him," Cynthe said to Diello. "Make him understand, or we'll never see Vassou and Scree again."

Marshana shooed Cynthe out into the corridor. The general followed them, but Diello called out, "Lord Rhodri, may I speak with you?"

"If he is to travel," Marshana said, "he must rest now."

The general walked back to Diello. "Yes?"

"Privately," Diello insisted. "Please."

"I protest!" the healer said.

"Then do it in the corridor." Rhodri gestured. "Out."

Marshana went out, slamming the door behind her.

Rhodri stared down at Diello. "Yes?"

"My sister was asking you about our friends. Please have them released."

"Friends? You call a samal wolf and a half-breed goblin your *friends*?"

"I do. Will you order their release?"

"Why should I?"

He wants me to grovel. And I may have to do it. "Scree and Vassou don't deserve any punishment. They're not really a part of—of this situation."

"They joined your cause, didn't they?"

"We don't have a cause, except to find our uncle Owain and have a home again."

"You expect Owain to welcome you?"

"We're hoping he will. We need his help." Diello paused. "We have a little sister, only three—"

"Bah." Rhodri turned away and began to pace the room,

his spurs spinning. "Stick to the point. Why should I have any interest in your sister?"

"Will you please let Vassou and Scree go?"

"Set them loose to spy and cause trouble?"

"They aren't spies!"

"And what do you think a half-goblin is made for, eh? They're always spies or assassins. Their allegiance is always to the goblins, and don't you believe differently."

"You're wrong. I saw what Brezog did to Scree, and I know he—"

Rhodri spun around. "Brezog, you say? You've seen the gorlord? Where?"

"He killed my parents and burned our farm," Diello said. "He tortured me. He threatened the life of my little sister. His horde has tracked and chased us halfway across Antrasia, trying to stop us from getting here."

Rhodri stared at him a moment. "Impossible! You're mere children, spinning a tale for the attention it brings you."

"Don't call me a liar," Diello said furiously. "You weren't there! You didn't see my mother murdered or my father dying with a spear in his chest."

"Then the mage-chancellor must be informed that the gorlord is on the move."

"He knows!" Diello looked up, swiping his eyes with the back of his hand. "He's been watching it all. He even stopped Mamee's Death Wind from taking her to Embarthi."

Rhodri's gray eyes bored into Diello. "You can't know such things. Clevn would never—"

"I saw it happen. I saw his face in the lightning storm."

"*You?*"

"I have the Sight."

"A Faelin child with Sight? Nonsense. You couldn't possibly have such a Gift."

Diello wished he could retract the boast. What did it matter if this man believed anything he said?

"Prove it to me," Rhodri said. "Make me believe you!"

I can't, Diello thought. His Gift was hard to control. He couldn't risk failing.

But the room wavered again, and this time he saw a much younger Rhodri kneeling at the feet of a girl. Her hair was bound with pearls and roses. When she turned her gaze, Diello saw that it was Mamee. She looked no older than Cynthe. Jewels were sewn to her gown like flower petals, and her pale skin glistened. She shook her head and touched Rhodri's bowed shoulders.

"No," she said. "I love another now. I cannot pledge my heart to you."

"Well?" Rhodri's voice demanded, shattering the image.

Diello raised his hand to his aching brow.

"Come, come, enough of your tricks."

"I'm sorry," Diello said, lowering his hand to his side. He understood now why Rhodri hated him and Cynthe. "You loved my mother, didn't you? And she rejected you for my father. Is that why you're acting so cruel to us?"

Rhodri stiffened. "You little *cur*! How dare you!"

"You shouldn't be angry with Cynthe and me for what happened all those years ago."

"A—a guess, nothing more! That doesn't prove you have Sight."

"She wore roses and pearls in her hair. Her dress had jewels on it. Your cloak was crimson and black, but you didn't have tassels in your ears then. You—"

"Be silent!" Rhodri said. His voice was shaking. He slid something from beneath his wrist-guard and threw it at Diello.

The object looked like a tangled ball of yarn, but it unfurled into a web that struck Diello in the face.

Knocked back against his pillows, Diello felt invisible threads binding his thoughts. He was filled with an intense need to babble everything he knew. But before he could utter a word, the threads broke inside his mind. Diello screamed, aware of nothing except the pain that seemed to go on and on. He could hear himself whimpering, and then the web was ripped away. Rhodri was lifting him, roaring for help.

"I'm sorry, boy," he murmured. "It was the truth. I'm sorry."

Attendants rushed in, all talking at once. Diello was laid on the bed, but the pain was driving him mad. He kept screaming and crying. Over it all, Rhodri was shouting orders. Someone forced Diello's mouth open, and a thick potion was poured down his throat.

He swallowed, gulping and choking. Gradually the agony faded away. He felt his body slowly relaxing.

"No wonder he hasn't improved faster, if this is your level of care," Rhodri declared. "Potions, pah! Use *aegeth* on him. The magic will force his skull to heal."

"We don't practice *aegeth* here," Marshana replied. "We don't believe in mending injuries unnaturally fast. Sedation and a serene environment promote a more natural—"

"Rubbish! He should be well enough for questioning."

"And we don't use Webs of Truth on children. If you distrust him so much, you should have asked a mage—or even me—to sift his thoughts for possible lies. Not this barbaric test. You could have killed him in his present condition."

"Tend him well," Rhodri said. "Make him ready to travel in the morning."

"You've set him back days, perhaps longer."

"Whatever you have to do, make him ready tomorrow."

Rhodri strode out. Marshana stared at the door, then down at Diello. Her narrow face held no compassion. Without a word to Diello, she rose and left.

I made everything worse, Diello thought.

Footsteps approached. It was the attendant called Dhrui—the spy—who tucked Diello's blankets smooth and tight, then stood over him.

"They should not be so mean to you," the attendant said quietly. "Children should not be punished for their parents' crimes."

"Help us escape," Diello pleaded. "Tonight. *Please.*"

"I can't," the attendant said without apology. "You're of the Liedhe Court. I . . . can't."

chapter sixteen

Just after daybreak, swathed in a thick fur robe, Diello was carried across the gardens of the compound to an open area where the Fae soldiers waited in formation. Standing stiffly at attention, they stared straight ahead.

Fat snowflakes were falling, stinging Diello's face.

He was grateful to be outdoors again and eager to get his first glimpse of Embarthi. The compound disappointed him. With white walls surrounding the gardens and plain white buildings, the place seemed drab, not at all what he'd expected the Fae to build. The arrow-straight paths were made of raked gravel. He didn't see a single weed. The shrubs—precisely clipped cubes beneath their dusting of snow—stood like sentinels.

Even so, Diello couldn't help inhaling the cold air gladly. When he thought no one was looking, he stuck out his tongue to catch some of the flakes.

"Good morning," Lord Rhodri said gruffly, walking up. Wearing a long crimson-and-black cloak, his cuirass polished to mirror brightness, he nodded to the soldier who was holding Diello. It wasn't clear if his greeting was to the soldier or Diello, so Diello kept silent.

"Everything's ready," Rhodri said. "Carry on."

"Sir!" The soldier carried Diello out the compound gates.

It was like entering a different world. Past the regimented drabness of the healing compound, the street wound off between houses made of colored glass—too opaque to see through—and roofs of hammered metal. Many of the buildings stood on stilts, and instead of four exterior walls like the typical abode in Antrasia, these dwellings had five or even seven walls, making them look crooked and whimsical.

But Diello was more interested in the enormous craft just outside the compound gates. Painted silver and lavender, it looked like a river ship, except it lacked sails or mast. It was so wide it couldn't have fit through the drawbridge gate at Wodesley Castle, and it towered nearly as high as the compound walls. The front end curved into a point that jutted out. At the back, three tiered sections rose to a canopy stretching across a row of four large chairs. Their plump cushions bore the ornate, interlocking initials SS beneath embroidered crowns. Around the chairs, pots of flowers unaffected by the cold and snow were blooming cream, palest apricot, and blush pink. Their fragrance filled the air.

Diello also caught the unmistakable scents of fried ham, heated jams, and hot bread. His stomach rumbled.

What amazed him most was that the royal sleigh didn't touch the ground. The whole craft hovered in midair, its hull about shoulder height above the paving stones.

Cynthe came crawling out from beneath the bottom of the sleigh. Her cheeks were flushed. She'd pulled back her hair and tied it at the nape of her neck. She wore a traveling robe like Diello's. Hers was much too large and swallowed her, but she'd rolled up the sleeves and belted it around her waist. She was clutching her bow and quiver tightly to her chest. He noticed that she'd wrapped all her arrows in the piece of leather that had been covering Eirian's blade. Nothing called attention to it.

Good work, he thought, but he worried about the lost hilt they were leaving behind.

"Diello!" she cried, running to greet him as the soldier gently set him on his feet. "Have you ever seen anything like it?"

Diello's gaze wandered back to the sleigh, marveling over it again. The railing and hanging steps were carved of ivory.

"They said you took worse last night." Her voice was soft. "You look poorly."

"I'm just tired," he said. With the soldier listening to every word, he was afraid to tell her what Rhodri had done. "And Marshana gave me a different potion than usual. It turned my stomach."

"There's more to it than that."

"Later," he said. "What about Vassou and Scree?"

"Already aboard. Not as I would wish—still caged—but not left behind. Whatever you said, well done!"

"I want to see them."

She pointed at the sleigh's undercarriage. "They're inside. Underneath there're all sorts of storage places and little cubicles. It's called the hold. Isn't that odd?"

"Why? Because it *holds* things?"

She grinned. "Don't be so clever. That end with the point is called the prow. And the back, where the chairs are, is the stern. They say 'deck' instead of floor. The initials are the queen's: Sheirae Suprema."

"I figured that out by myself," Diello said.

She ignored his sarcasm. "I wish you could come explore it with me."

"I wish I could, too."

"Are you warm enough?" She chattered in a falsely cheerful voice. "Aren't these clothes unusual? So much warmer and lighter than wool. They're made of *viculla*. Very costly, I hear. Gifts from our grandmother, I suppose. *Viculla* is spun from the belly hair of some kind of goat that lives in the mountains."

A loud roar silenced her. Diello twisted around.

Cynthe stepped closer to him as six huge, black-furred beasts came padding through the snow in single file. They looked like gigantic cats.

"What are they?" she asked.

A young officer came up to them and saluted. "They're black lions." He wore rings with tassels in the tips of his ears, like Lord Rhodri, and he touched one, making it swing. "We're the Black Lion Regiment. When we fly our first lion, we cut hair from its tail as a trophy. It's an honored tradition for every officer."

"Black lions," Diello echoed, fascinated. He'd never heard of such beasts. They were nearly as large as ponies and had shaggy manes and coarse tufts of hair at the ends of their long tails. Their paws were the size of Diello's face.

"What do you mean by 'fly our first lion?'" Cynthe asked.

The officer seemed pleased that she was asking questions. "We catch young lions from the wild. The trick is to capture them just as they're old enough to fly but not yet strong and experienced in the air. Bring one in—a good one, mind you, suitable for training—and you get your tassel . . . and first promotion."

Cynthe's eyes were shining. "I'd love to try that."

Diello nodded, trying to imagine such a hunt.

The great cats wore harnesses of red leather and although they milled about for a moment, displaying enormous teeth and slapping casually at their handlers, they were soon organized in pairs and hitched with long, braided-leather traces that reached up to the hovering sleigh. A driver's seat perched above the prow, and Diello saw a man in a cloak flying up to sit there. When he snapped his fingers, long reins rose magically within his reach.

"Are the lions going to pull it?" Cynthe asked. "Does it float behind them as they go?"

"Why don't they have wings?" Diello wanted to know.

The officer shrugged. "What have wings to do with anything?"

Lord Rhodri came up, his breath puffing white. "Getting the tour, I suppose?" Avoiding Diello's gaze, he seemed contrite this morning—his tone far more courteous than before.

He's ashamed of what he did, Diello thought, *but he's not really sorry.*

Rhodri gestured at the young officer. "This is Ffoyd, my aide."

Ffoyd saluted Diello and Cynthe again.

"Take them aboard," Rhodri ordered.

A soldier rushed ahead and skipped nimbly up the dangling steps before turning around and reaching out his arms. Tingling bands of magic swirled around Diello. He found himself floating up to the man before he was caught and efficiently settled into one of the cushioned chairs on the top deck. Ffoyd saluted and strode away. The soldier spread another fur robe across Diello's lap.

"All right there, m'lord?" the man asked.

Diello gave him a tiny nod. He felt like he was in a dream.

Cynthe floated up and sat down next to him. Rhodri climbed aboard and took a seat one over from her, leaving the largest, central chair empty.

A man approached, saluting smartly. "All's ready, sir, and the men have come aboard. Will you give the word?"

"Given."

Shouts rang out, and the lions roared in unison. The animals bounded forward, and Diello braced himself for a jolt. But the lions flew into the air, drawing the sleigh smoothly behind them in an arc that sent them soaring high over the compound. Both Diello and Cynthe cried out in amazement. Cynthe raced to the railing, leaning over, while Diello craned his neck to see. They circled over the town with its curved, meandering streets adjacent to the healing compound. At the other end of the community stood the garrison Cynthe had told him about. Its fortress walls featured turrets as high as the *cloigwylie*.

So it does have a top, Diello thought, gazing down at the barrier. *It doesn't reach to the sky like I believed.*

And there was the gate Cynthe had described, with the road from Antrasia stopping at the massive portal. From this height, the guards at the gate looked as small as beetles.

Then the sleigh took a long, banked turn and sailed high toward the dark bellies of the snow clouds filling the sky.

Cynthe came back to her chair, grinning. "Look, Diello! We're going so high!"

"Don't be frightened," Rhodri said.

"I'm not afraid," Diello told him.

"Nor I!" Cynthe declared.

When Rhodri looked away, Cynthe mimed grabbing air and rolled her eyes. Diello smiled at her.

When the sleigh leveled off, the cold wind vanished as though some force were blocking it. Snowflakes swirled around the sleigh without falling on it. The air became as warm as springtime. Cynthe shed her warm robe. Soon Diello did the same. A steward rolled a cart to them and raised covers off silver trays. The food was steaming hot and smelled delicious. Diello was ready to eat it all.

Cynthe popped a morsel of hot bread into her mouth and closed her eyes. "Mmm."

Everything tasted even better than he expected. Diello couldn't remember when he'd last had a meal as wonderful as this. *Trying to bribe us*, he thought, but that didn't stop him from chewing as rapidly as he could. He ate all of his ham and bread, munched on juicy, heart-shaped berries, and sampled a warm jam tasting of spices he'd never encountered before.

And then, entirely full, he felt so tired he couldn't hold his spoon.

Cynthe was still gobbling. She'd eaten three times the amount he'd managed. "Almost as good as Mamee used to make," she mumbled around a mouthful.

"Almost." He sighed.

Some time later, he awoke with a start, certain he'd heard someone say his name. He rubbed his eyes and sat up. Cynthe and Rhodri were no longer beside him.

It had stopped snowing. The sun glimmered now and then through the dark-streaked clouds, and they were still flying smoothly, heading toward a range of jagged mountains topped with snow and cloaked with forest.

He spotted Cynthe down on the main deck, leaning over the railing. One of the younger soldiers was talking to her, pointing out the scenery.

Diello wasn't sure that making friends was a good idea.

"Awake again, are you?" Rhodri sat down beside him.

Diello would have moved away, but he didn't want to appear afraid of this man.

Rhodri held a bottle of blue liquid and began turning it around and around in his fingers. "It's time for your dose," he said. "According to that healer's instructions."

"I don't want it," Diello said.

Rhodri tossed the bottle over the railing. Diello leaned forward to watch it tumbling end over end, its contents spilling in a trail behind it. He almost grinned.

"I agree," Rhodri said. "Silly potions are good enough

for commoners, but not for the likes of us, eh? Once we reach the palace, you'll be seen by a proper *aegeth* healer."

Diello wasn't sure exactly what *aegeth* involved, and Marshana's strong opposition to it worried him, but he kept quiet. So far the general hadn't actually offered an apology for last night. Until he did, Diello had no intention of thawing.

"Your sister's full of questions," Rhodri went on. "About how we fly the royal sleigh and what other types of craft we use and how we train the lions. What about you? Haven't you anything to ask?"

"No."

Rhodri said something else, but Diello didn't hear it. He felt a sudden chill and pulled the fur robes tighter to his stomach.

Looking up, he saw an enormous pair of eyes peering down at them from the sky. The face was obscured by cloud, but he felt the magic tingling in his bones and knew it was Clevn. Thunder rolled in the distance.

"Boy, did you hear what I just said?"

Diello jumped to his feet. "It's an attack!" he shouted.

A bolt of lightning speared down from the sky, striking one of the black lions. The others roared in rage and terror, twisting frantically in their harnesses while the dead beast hung limply. The sleigh listed dangerously, and the men were running and shouting. Cynthe was shoved across the deck and strapped to a pole for safety.

Swearing, Rhodri tackled Diello, knocking him to the deck. Another lightning bolt sizzled right over them.

The sleigh was falling. Rhodri's weight was crushing

Diello. He tried to crawl out from under the general, but the man clutched his tunic and held him.

"Stay put," Rhodri muttered.

"No," Diello said, wriggling again. "Clevn will kill us."

He pulled free and scrambled weakly to his feet, staggering as the sleigh wobbled beneath him. *Whose power is flying it? The lions?*

"Get . . . *down!*" Rhodri roared, hitting the back of Diello's knees.

Diello collapsed as another lightning bolt cracked above his head, smashing into one of the royal chairs, which burst into flames. Diello slid across the tilting deck. One of the flowerpots sailed off into the air, and he was about to follow it.

"Diello!" Cynthe screamed.

At the last moment, his flailing hand gripped a canopy pole. Fighting to hang on, he felt the deck buck beneath him.

A soldier scrambled to Diello, sliding a leather strap around his waist and fastening it to the base of one of the chairs. Another soldier was pointing at the fire, shouting a phrase that doused it.

Ffoyd had arrived and was lifting Lord Rhodri. A splinter of wood projected from Rhodri's upper arm.

"Secure the boy!" Rhodri gasped.

"He's fine, my lord," Ffoyd said.

The sleigh was still falling. Diello saw Clevn's eyes appear once more, right over him. A bolt of lightning hardly bigger than a sword struck the leather strap, and suddenly Diello was sucked right off the deck and into the air.

chapter seventeen

As Diello fell, he felt a sense of calm acceptance flow through his body. He was too weak to fly. He didn't know whether the soldiers' magic couldn't stop his fall or whether they hadn't tried to catch him. On his own, he had no chance of stopping his long plunge to the ground. *I'm done. I can stop fighting. Cynthe will have to save Amalina now.*

The air whistling past his ears grew gentler. He realized that he was slowing. He started to float and swirl around like a leaf on the breeze.

He remembered what Cynthe had said. Don't try to force the magic. The ability to fly was part of him. All he had to do was *be*.

He grinned, drifting a bit, letting the wind currents toss him around, and knew he would never fear falling again.

"Diello!"

Cynthe's voice sounded far away. He lifted his head and rolled over onto his stomach.

Soon he could see her, flying toward him. *Up!* he thought, and rode a breeze in her direction.

"Diello!" She stretched out her arms to catch him. "I've got you."

"I'm not falling." He smiled at her, and her eyes widened. "You're different. You know how to fly!"

"You don't have to know how," he said. "You just let it happen."

Flinging her arms wide, she arched her back and let the air lift her before she glided down again. "Exactly."

"This is our chance," he said. "Do you think you can guide us back to where I lost the hilt? I can't find my bearings."

"I've been watching for landmarks all the way," she said briskly. "And I know I can do it. But are you strong enough?"

"I'm tired out," he admitted. "But we've got to try."

"Listen," Cynthe said.

Diello heard a shout coming from the sleigh above them, which was still falling, although much more slowly than before.

"They're in trouble," he said. "And Scree and Vassou are with them."

Cynthe put her arm around him, and they lifted together until they were nearly even with the sleigh.

Some of the soldiers were floating around the lions. Uncooperative, the animals snarled each time they were approached. They would not let anyone near the dead lion. Other soldiers had positioned themselves beneath the sleigh, trying to make it level. The driver was standing on the seat, shouting instructions and throwing off surges of magic with every frantic wave of his arm.

"The lions are scared," Cynthe said. "Don't they know what to do?"

"I think the problem is the dead lion," Diello said.

"Poor thing. Why kill it?"

"Clevn was trying to kill us. I guess he missed."

"But doesn't he want us to come to him?" Cynthe asked.

"That's what I thought," Diello replied. "I'm going to help."

"No! You aren't well enough."

Ignoring her, Diello flew closer to the lions. Some of the men shouted at him, but he concentrated on the frightened animals. His bones were tingling as the magic swirled around him.

"Restrain your spells!" he called up to the astonished driver. "You're confusing them!"

Then, before anyone could stop him, Diello floated next to the lion paired with the dead animal. When he touched the struggling beast's shoulder, he could feel waves of grief and he heard its—and the other lions'—silent speech:

"*You must pull with us again.*"

"*Tiambe is dead. Tiambe is dead!*"

"*Let us break free and attack those who strike us from the sky!*"

"*I would rather die with Tiambe.*"

Diello didn't know whether the grieving lion could speak aloud like Vassou did, or even if it would listen to him.

"I'm sorry," he murmured to it, concentrating on being

as calm and comforting as possible. "The attack was against me. I'm sorry you lost Tiambe, your friend."

Baring its teeth, the lion roared right in Diello's face, but it didn't bite him. The baffled fury in its eyes faded. Lowering its head, it stopped trying to guard its comrade.

"*You know my harness-mate's name?*" it asked him.

"*Only because I overheard you and the others,*" Diello responded. "*Can you stop our fall?*"

"*With help,*" one of the other lions answered. "*Pull together, my brothers!*"

Their descent stopped, leaving the team and sleigh suspended in the sky.

Swiftly, the Fae soldiers cut the dead animal free, and it spiraled away while its companions roared. But now all the lions were calmer and submitted to having their harnesses checked and tightened. The single lion was shifted into the lead position, and the traces reconfigured.

Diello moved from lion to lion, rubbing their broad skulls or patting their shoulders, giving each animal soothing encouragement. "*You're doing well,*" he said over and over. "*Be calm. Let your handlers help you.*"

"That's good!" called the driver. "You've been handling lions all your life, young lord, by the looks of you. Well done, and thanks!"

Diello flushed at the praise.

More soldiers pushed from beneath the sleigh, righting the tilting frame. The fires on the deck had been put out. The canopy, ripped in half, flapped in the wind. The men climbed back aboard the sleigh, many of them calling to Diello and Cynthe.

"Diello!" Lord Rhodri shouted from the railing. "Cynthe! Can you manage to stay where you are? I'll send a man to you."

Cynthe rejoined Diello as he moved away from the lions. "Since they know what we can do now, we might as well show them more," she said.

He nodded, and together they glided to where eager hands could catch hold of Diello's arms and legs. He was pulled onto the deck and steadied upright. Cynthe came aboard on her own with a flourish, landing gracefully on one foot. The men applauded.

The sleigh's magic slid around them, providing warmth. Diello blew on his numbed fingers, grateful when someone wrapped a robe around his shoulders.

A sudden lurch made everyone stagger, then the sleigh surged forward as the lions began to pull again. The driver called out encouragement to the animals, and more cheers went up from the men. The twins were brought hot foamy drinks. Diello sipped his, warming his fingers on the cup.

Lord Rhodri's injured arm had been bound in a sling. He was busy reprimanding Ffoyd when Diello and Cynthe joined them. "I want everyone who was serving on watch today put on report. I don't know which is worse, the treason committed by whoever attacked Her Majesty's sleigh or the dereliction of duty exhibited here."

"Sir, the men did their best," Ffoyd said.

"Then tell me why no one detected the magic rising against us except this boy." Lord Rhodri turned to Diello. "It goes without saying that we're very grateful to you. How did you do it all? Where did you learn to handle lions? More important, what told you there was going to be an attack?"

"I saw the face in the clouds, looking at us," Diello replied, choosing to answer only the last question. "And— and I just *knew*."

"My brother has the Sight," Cynthe said.

Rhodri dismissed Ffoyd, who seemed glad to hurry away. "Great Guardian above," the general said hoarsely. "Sight . . . Flying . . . Controlling a lion with the ease of someone trained to it. Had I not been a witness, I would have sworn none of this could be true. You *are* Lwyneth's children."

"Well, of course we are," Cynthe said. "What did you expect?"

"Faelin don't fly." The man sounded shaken. "They can't. They never have."

Diello squared his shoulders. "We do."

"It's the royal blood in you," Rhodri said. "There have never been royal Faelin before. The queen will have to be told. And it will be up to Clevn to investigate this attack."

"Not him!" Diello said.

"Why not?"

"Uh . . ." Diello struggled to find an answer. He didn't trust Rhodri enough to tell him the truth. And Rhodri hadn't believed him before.

"Come! Spit it out."

"He's the one who attacked us," Diello finally declared.

"No, of course not!"

Diello caught Cynthe's eye and didn't explain further. If

Rhodri wasn't going to believe him, there was no point in discussing it.

"That's a dangerous accusation," Rhodri said. "I wouldn't go repeating it, if I were you."

"It's true if Diello says so," Cynthe insisted.

Rhodri looked at them sternly. "Don't be so quick to blame Clevn. He could prove to be your best ally."

"We know he isn't," Diello said. "He's used his lightning against us before."

"He's not the only one who controls lightning. As for today's attack, when you gave warning before the lion was killed, what *exactly* did you see?"

Diello thought back, trying to recall precise details. "A pair of eyes," he admitted. "Dark, angry eyes."

"Doesn't sound a bit like Lord Clevn," Rhodri said. "His eyes are pale."

"But he—"

"This Sight of yours," Rhodri went on. "It's unusual. Foreknowledge is far different from peering into the past. Extraordinary. You're both . . . I think that there is more to come with these Gifts of yours."

"No," Diello said quickly. "You've seen everything we can do."

"That's right," Cynthe agreed.

"You need to become better liars if you expect to fool me. I'd like to know if there are any other important Gifts manifesting." He turned to Cynthe. "What about breaking walls, eh?"

"Oh." She shrugged. "Well, it happened. I'm not sure if it's a real Gift or not."

"You know very well that Voice is a powerful ability indeed. Don't try shattering bowls in the palace. And what about you, my boy?"

Think of something, Diello told himself. *Anything to throw him off track. Don't trust him. Don't believe all he says.*

"Isn't it true that you'd never seen a lion until today?" Rhodri asked. "You didn't even know what the creatures were called, did you? Yet you weren't afraid of them just now. Can you—"

"It's nothing," Diello said. "I felt sorry for them and wanted to help. That's all."

In the awkward silence that followed, Rhodri rubbed his palm across his gray hair and cleared his throat. "Well, I understand if you don't want to confide in me. I owe you both an apology. But you, Lord Diello, most of all."

Diello put down his empty cup. "We're just Diello and Cynthe. Don't give us titles that aren't real."

"As you wish. But please accept my apology."

"For what?" Cynthe said. "Diello, what's he talking about?"

"You hurt me," Diello said flatly. "You did it deliberately."

"Yes," Rhodri replied. "I was wrong. You caught me by surprise. I . . . was striking at someone else."

"My father."

"From the moment I met the pair of you, I could see nothing but Stephel. Even your voices . . . those Antrasin accents so similar to his. I felt the old jealousy, the hurt, as though Lwyneth had rejected me yesterday instead of years past. And when you saw into my memories . . . I wanted to hurt you as I'd been hurt."

"What does he mean?" Cynthe asked.

"If Mamee hadn't married Pa," Diello said, "Lord Rhodri might have been her husband."

Cynthe gasped. "Did you love her?"

"With all my heart," Rhodri said. "I always will. When I heard she was dead, I—well, we won't speak of that. I do not expect forgiveness for my actions, Diello, but still I offer my apology." He swallowed. "And my allegiance. We're in your debt today."

"Allegiance to us," Diello said scornfully, "children of a Carnethie peasant?"

"So that still rankles, eh? Well, let it." Rhodri's face grew bleak. "Do not ask me to forgive that man. He took her away from me and her people. He got her . . . killed." Rhodri paused. "I cannot think of you as his, only hers."

"Then I don't accept your apology," Diello said. "I carry my father's lineage with pride."

"So do I," Cynthe said.

"And you're wrong, blaming Pa. The goblins killed them, not—"

Rhodri turned his face away. "Enough. You ask too much."

"We've asked for nothing but fairness," Diello replied.

"Fairness be damned." Rhodri strode away.

"Not much of a thank-you, was it?" Cynthe muttered.

Diello shook his head glumly. Then, keeping his voice

low in case some of the Fae understood Antrasin, he told Cynthe what Mamee's spirit had said about the Knower's prophecy.

Cynthe didn't argue as he'd expected. Instead, she sighed. "Maybe Mamee was right to leave Embarthi forever. I saw the lightning cut your strap and make you fall, Diello. You could have died today."

"Except I didn't."

"Faelin aren't supposed to fly. We all know that. So whoever attacked us tried to murder you. Do you really think it's Clevn?" Cynthe whispered. "And if it wasn't him, then who?"

Diello could only shrug.

"I wish we'd never come here," she said. "It's pretty. There are amazing things to see, and we can use our magic, but—"

"The food's good, too."

Cynthe almost smiled. "But just because we left Brezog behind doesn't mean we're safe."

"We're here to get Amalina back," Diello said. "That's all. No matter what they say or do, we have to focus on that."

"You're right." Cynthe nodded. "We have to watch out for each other more than ever."

In the afternoon, the sun broke through the clouds, and the sleigh soared between immense mountains before beginning a slow descent into a valley blanketed in snow. A frozen lake spread across part of it. Halfway up one of the mountain slopes stood a palace. It looked as though it were made of glass and mirrors, reflecting the sunlight.

Diello thought of his and Cynthe's tenth birthday, when Mamee had boiled sugar and water and topped their cake with spires and loops until it looked like a castle. Diello saw now that she'd been recreating what had once been her home.

Poor Mamee, he thought, *how you must have missed all this.*

Cynthe squeezed his hand, and he knew his sister was remembering the same thing.

On the tier below them, Rhodri abruptly sat forward and spread his gnarled fingers wide. A tiny whirlwind sprang into existence on his palm, and he spoke to it for a long time before it vanished.

"Come here," the general called to the twins. "At once please."

Reluctantly, they joined him.

"We shall arrive very soon," Rhodri said. "There are a few things you should know."

"What's going to happen to Vassou and Scree?" Cynthe asked. "How long are they going to be treated like prisoners?"

"As long as necessary. There are more important things to discuss at the moment."

"Our friends *are* important," Cynthe said. "Vassou told us it's forbidden for him to go to the palace, yet you're taking him there."

"I have orders to do so."

"Are they going to punish him for disobeying the rules?" she asked. "That would be wrong."

Rhodri scowled. "What's wrong is a girl who doesn't know when to mind her manners and keep quiet."

Flushing, Cynthe sat back.

"Now," the general said, "I don't know how much you two have been taught about the Liedhe Court, but you shouldn't enter it completely ignorant of its ways."

"We'll manage," Cynthe muttered.

"I want to know," Diello said.

"Very sensible. There are protocols to follow, and you need to have some idea of what's expected. First and foremost, there's Queen Sheirae. Her word is law, but she's bound by traditions and the expectations of her nobles. Then there's the mage-chancellor."

"Clevn," Diello said. "How do we avoid him? We'd rather meet our uncle first. Is that possible?"

"Owain? But—"

"It's important," Cynthe said. "We really want to go to Owain first."

"Do you even know him?" Diello asked Rhodri.

"Of course I know him! But he's hardly going to be friendly."

"Why not?"

"Are you truly that ignorant of the situation?"

"We need him," Diello said.

"My dear boy—"

"I'm not your boy. Will you help us find Owain or not?"

"No."

"No?"

"Absolutely not."

"Then we'll find him on our own," Cynthe said.

"Wait! You must understand that Owain is not your ally."

"Tell us why," Diello demanded.

"Do you understand the pattern of succession in Embarthi?"

"Yes, we know it," Cynthe answered.

"When Lwyneth renounced her right to the throne, she destroyed Owain's chance to rule."

"Won't he be mage-chancellor anyway?" Diello asked. "After Clevn, I mean?"

"No. He can never rule under the present laws of succession."

"But aren't mage-chancellors just advisers?"

"They are far more than that. The queen is a warrior. She defends the realm, both from within and without. The mage-chancellor is a governor. He supports her magic, guides and counsels, and keeps the realm in order."

"So Clevn runs things," Diello said. "That gives him a lot of power and importance."

"Yes, the position of mage-chancellor is vital. Owain has every reason in the world to hate your mother."

"We know there's a new heir," Cynthe said. "A girl. Who is she?"

"Owain's daughter."

"So he should be pleased about that," Diello said. "There's no need for him to be angry."

Rhodri gave him a pitying look. "My dear boy—"

"You'll have to excuse him," Cynthe broke in. "Sometimes my brother thinks everyone is as good and honest as he is. Diello, pay attention!"

"I am! Can't Owain be a mage-chancellor to his daughter, the way he would've been to our mother?"

"The problem is," Rhodri said, "that the succession isn't settled yet. Owain has no son. There are no twins to rule jointly. Your arrival is going to complicate the situation. Now do you understand why Owain's unlikely to welcome you?"

"We didn't come here to cause complications," Cynthe said. "We still need our uncle's help to find our little sister, Amalina."

"You have enough ahead of you with the queen," Rhodri said. "She may well refuse even to see you. She may wish to protect you by ignoring you."

"That doesn't make sense," Diello said.

"Your claim to the throne could start a civil war."

"We have no claim."

"Maybe we do," Cynthe said. "We keep meeting folk who think we do. But we just want our sister back."

"You'll be wise not to mention these supporters at court," Rhodri said. "Even a discussion such as we're having now could be misunderstood by eavesdroppers and troublemakers."

"How will we know who we *can* talk to?" Cynthe asked. "Who do we trust?"

"Each other," Rhodri said.

Had the general overheard their previous conversation?

Diello wondered. Did he read minds, too? *We've got to be a lot more careful. I wish I still had my quarterstaff.*

"Well," the general said, "you've been warned now. The Liedhe Court looks pretty and carefree, with its games and merriment, but you must expect to meet enemies. People bearing grudges, like me. People who still hate your mother. People prepared to flatter and manipulate you for personal gain. I misjudged you both when I first met you. So will others. Today I've seen enough to change some of my views. Don't expect everyone else to do the same. And if there's been one attempt on your life already, there will be more."

"Lord Rhodri," Ffoyd interrupted, coming up and saluting. "We're preparing to land."

chapter eighteen

the *aegeth* healer lifted his hands from Diello's head. Eyes closed, the man brought his palms together, then parted them. A tiny swirl of gray mist floated up, fading as it went.

"And that," the healer said, opening his eyes, "is the last of your injury."

Diello believed him. This was his third session with the healer, and he'd never felt better in his life. There was no more pain. Instead of colored orbs and doses of medicine, there had been this healer's cool fingertips drawing away the headaches and lethargy. Today, Diello was bursting with energy, and eager to get outdoors and find his sister.

"Thank you," he said. "I'm grateful for all you've done."

The healer—so slender he hardly seemed to exist—drew his hands into his wide sleeves and bowed. "It has been my privilege to serve one with crystal bones."

Diello left the man's rooms deep within the palace. Exiting through the door of polished alabaster meant a sheer drop of two stories to the floor far below. Diello descended with practiced ease and headed through the maze of corridors with the two Fae guards who were his constant escorts. In the past three weeks, Diello had explored as much of the vast palace complex as he was permitted, which wasn't very much. The walls were made of thick, semi-opaque glass tinted with the palest green. The sun shone through, casting a watery light. Some of the ceilings were low and ordinary. Others soared so high that the walls beneath featured multiple doors stacked vertically.

Most of the doors were like the healer's, made of alabaster panels cut so thin that any light shining behind them made them glow. The gleaming marble floors had patterns of inlaid jewels or bands of silver. No one seemed to use rushes or carpets here, yet Diello had never felt an icy draft across his ankles. Although there was plenty of room for flying, curved staircases stretched across some of the spaces.

His favorite room was long, rectangular, and empty of furniture as though made for dancing. The ceiling was glass, with each pane stained a different color—amethyst, peacock, and amber. He liked it best because a wall of windows overlooked the grounds.

Although it was winter, no snow fell on the grass, and flowers still bloomed along the paths. A takia tree— recognizable from Mamee's descriptions—grew near the windows, its graceful white racemes swaying in the breeze. Small creatures with round amber eyes and puffs of tan fur on their ears scampered along the branches, nibbling clusters of nuts. Diello had tried to hear what the animals were thinking, so far without success.

Twice, he'd glimpsed courtiers—men and women

wearing elegant silk clothing and jewels—walking through the grounds or skipping through games. Some of them had miniature stars and moons orbiting their heads. Others dragged slender whirlwinds on sparkling magic leashes. Dancers performed intricate steps in midair. Diello especially wanted to watch the game where lions soared and pounced so their riders could whack silver balls with long mallets. But Diello's guards would not allow him to watch the Liedhe Court at play. They always made him leave.

In all his imaginings while listening to Mamee's stories, he had never dreamed he could be so lonely inside the palace. Other than Cynthe, his guards, and the healer, Diello had yet to meet the people living here.

Exiting the gallery, he emerged onto an open landing, with broad stairs winding to other floors. Above, he could hear the sounds of doors closing, footsteps pattering, and chatter, yet he saw no one.

A door popped open just as he passed. One of his guards spoke sharply. A woman with her hair wrapped in ropes of pearls whisked herself back the way she'd come, slamming the door. She didn't even glance at Diello.

Sighing, Diello walked on. He'd describe the woman to Cynthe later. Without trips to the healer, his twin was even more confined.

At night, the two of them would open their window overlooking a private walled garden. Unlike the spacious grounds where the courtiers strolled, this one lay buried in snow. Diello and Cynthe would listen to strains of beautiful music coming from one of the spires while snowflakes drifted down or the cold distant stars glittered above them. Sometimes there was singing. One voice in particular sounded so tender and exquisite that Diello would get goosebumps. Cynthe always pretended that listening to it didn't make her cry.

He couldn't complain about their quarters—a far cry from the ratty old storeroom they'd stayed in at Wodesley Castle and certainly leagues beyond their rustic lean-tos and campsites on the journey here. Now they had a spacious suite of three rooms: a sitting room furnished with a desk and comfortable chairs, and a bedchamber for each of them. Cynthe's bed looked like a swan. Its wooden wings formed the sides while the graceful neck and head curved at the foot. Every feather was intricately carved. She said she often dreamed of flying on the swan's wings.

Diello's bed was shaped like a boat, low-slung and flat, with a tall prow carved like a dragon's head. He tended to have nightmares about drowning.

He and Cynthe had tried switching beds, only to find themselves back in their assigned places in the morning. A few times they slept on the floor of their sitting room, yet always woke up in their beds with no memory of how they got there.

Servants were never seen, even if the twins stayed in their suite all day. Two trays laden with delicious food appeared at the appropriate times. Their baths were filled with warm, fragrant water each evening. Fires burned on the hearths without anyone coming to replenish the logs.

Despite the luxury and comfort, Diello felt like a prisoner—like he and Cynthe were something to be ashamed of. After Rhodri's warning and urgency, it was a letdown to be kept isolated like this. Worst of all, Diello had the sense of time trickling away.

Today, eager to tell Cynthe that he was completely cured, he stopped by the suite, but she wasn't there.

Lord Rhodri was sitting at the desk, waiting for him. "Good morning, Lord Diello."

Diello was almost glad to see the familiar face. "Good morning," he replied cautiously.

"You're looking well."

"So are you." Rhodri was no longer sporting a sling.

"I've come to ask your advice."

"Mine? Regarding what?" Diello asked.

"A scout report reached me this morning about a sighting of goblin forces in the Westering Hills. Much larger than the usual raiding party."

"Brezog?"

"We'll soon run him off. I want to know if you have any information as to what he's after."

"*Me.*"

"Why you?"

"I told you Brezog killed my parents. He's been after us ever since."

"He can't touch you here. Anything else you want to tell me?"

"Nothing of any importance," Diello said, digging his toe into the rug. "I wish I could help you more."

Rhodri snorted. "Then tell me, what have you done with Eirian?"

Diello tried to slow his rapid breathing. "Who?"

Rhodri shifted in his seat, and Diello sprang back from him.

"Easy, boy. I'm not going to attack you. Neither of us are fools. Let us, in these circumstances, be allies. There's only one thing Brezog could want from you, and that's the sword."

"I don't know what you're talking about."

"Lwyneth put it somewhere. Even if it lies at the bottom of a river, it's *somewhere*."

Diello gnawed at the inside of his lip. *Is Clevn using him to test me?*

"My mother didn't tell me anything about a sword."

"I see." Rhodri strode out past Diello's guards without another word.

Diello went racing outdoors to the private garden. Even draped in snow, it was lovely. A sundial stood in the center, where all the paths intersected, and each path led to a different exit. Guards stood at all four gates.

Cynthe was wandering around the garden, wearing her bow and quiver. Fortunately, she was allowed to take them everywhere, and no one had questioned her being armed. Still, Diello worried about how long they could successfully hide the blade among a quiver full of arrows. He wondered if maybe the Fae knew it was in their possession and hadn't decided to take it away just yet.

A distant shout rang out. Glancing up, he saw several lions pulling chariots through the sky. They were too far away for him to see much. How he wished he could climb the garden wall and see everything that was happening out there.

Then the chariots soared higher, vanishing beyond the palace spires.

"Well?" Cynthe called to him.

"Cured," he said.

She ran up and gave him a big hug. "Finally! Now we can—" she lowered her voice, and spoke in Antrasin, "—start doing something."

"They'll be expecting that."

"So we'll surprise them."

"How?"

She shrugged and kicked at the snow banked along the path. "We've got to do something, anything. I hate all this waiting."

He started to explain about Rhodri's visit when Cynthe gripped his arm. "Someone's coming."

He turned around, watching the west gate open.

Scree came trotting into sight with his hand on Vassou's back. Only twice before had the guards brought the pair here to visit Diello and Cynthe. They knew that Scree and Vassou were being kept caged in the stables. The injustice of it infuriated Diello.

Set free, Vassou tore around the garden, zipping past the twins. Finally, he leaped at each of them in greeting.

Scree stood near Diello, grinning widely when Diello patted his shoulder.

"Oh, Vassou and Scree," Cynthe said loudly. "We've missed you."

"We need to get out of here," Diello whispered in Antrasin.

"Yes," Scree agreed cheerfully. "I have been eating half

my food and thinking of how to become smaller. Yesterday I thought that I could slide between the bars of my cage. It worked. The guards do not know this."

"Good," Diello said. "Can you figure out a way to release Vassou?"

"He and I have talked much about the problem, but I do not know how it can be done," Scree said. "He is growing all the time, and his cage is different from mine with a magic lock I cannot pick."

"Vassou," Diello said, "can't you use your magic to break free?"

"No. They're expecting that and have too many safeguards," Vassou replied. "Scree's method is the best, but even if I starved I could still not crawl out."

"Perhaps I can sneak in and out of the palace," Scree volunteered. "There are many old passages. I will learn them quickly so I can lead all of us to freedom once you find a way to release Vassou."

"It's not as easy as you think," Diello told him. Before he could say more, Vassou nudged Diello.

"Has the queen sent for you yet?"

"No."

"You look well. Perhaps she has been waiting for that."

"Perhaps."

Across the garden, one of the guards cleared his throat, warning them that they'd been huddled together too long.

"Snowfight!" Cynthe said. Scooping up snow, she threw it in the air.

Diello packed a snowball and tossed it at Cynthe. She ducked, and the snowball hit Scree in the face.

"Oh!" Scree cried out, sitting down hard. "That is cold!"

Yipping, Vassou dashed toward Scree and began digging, throwing snow over him.

Diello ran to Scree's rescue, pulling him back onto his feet and brushing him off before throwing snowballs at Vassou. The four of them ran and romped and chased each other until they had to rest. Diello hadn't played like that since last winter when he and Amalina built a wall of snow and then tore it down.

The sound of a gate opening caught their attention.

"Not yet," Cynthe said. "It's too soon for them to take you away."

"Wait," Diello said. "Look!"

A figure in an emerald-green cloak and gown spoke briefly with the guards, and despite their apparent protests, pushed past them to walk along a path toward the garden's center.

She stopped next to the sundial and stared at their group.

She was about the twins' age. Her hair was chestnut brown streaked with silver, held back from her brow by a narrow gold diadem. Sparkles glinted in her hair where the pointed tips of her ears peeped out. Her eyes were a deep rich green, even more vivid than her clothing. At her waist swung an ornamental bow on a chain. It struck Diello as an odd choice of jewelry.

He walked forward.

"Hello," he said. "I'm called Diello. This is my sister, Cynthe, and our friends, Vassou and Scree."

The girl went on studying them without speaking.

"Don't you have anything to say?" Cynthe asked.

"You've no right to wear that bow here," the Fae girl said. "Take it off at once."

"I won't!"

The girl seemed shocked by Cynthe's refusal.

"What's your name?" Diello asked, trying to distract them.

"Don't you know?"

"Then I wouldn't be asking. And if you didn't want to talk to us, you wouldn't have come here."

"I came to see if the court rumors about you are true. It seems they are. Considering you face execution, you are very cheerful."

Diello and Cynthe exchanged an uncertain look, but then he glimpsed the girl's fleeting smile.

"You have a strange idea of a joke," he said.

"Who says I'm joking?"

"We do," Cynthe told her. "Are you a courtier?"

"I'm Penrith. You really don't know anything, do you?" she said. "How amusing. It's exactly as my maid said. But what is this game you play?"

"What, the snowfight?" Diello asked.

"Is that what you're doing? Fighting? Is it a contest of skill?"

"No, we're just being silly. We're glad to be outdoors, and Vassou especially loves the snow."

Penrith swished her long skirts a little before extending her slender hand. A mound of snow appeared on her palm. "Like this?"

"You pack it together. I'll show you." Bending, Diello picked up some snow and formed it into a ball.

Penrith imitated his movements.

"That's right," he said. "And then you—"

Her snowball smashed into his cheek. He gasped, then grinned and hurled his own snowball. It went splat across her gown.

She looked outraged. "You dared strike me! Guards!"

Two of the men hastened forward.

"That's not fair!" Cynthe shouted. "That's the way the game works."

Penrith gestured, and the guards retreated.

"It's supposed to be fun," Diello said. "That's all. I wasn't attacking you."

"Your game is foolish," Penrith said. She spun around.

"Don't go," Diello called after her. "Do you know the queen's son, Owain?"

"Of course."

"Does he live in the palace?"

"When he is not visiting his private estates, he has apartments here."

"Could you do us a favor?"

"Why should I?" she asked suspiciously.

Scree ventured closer to her, reaching out as though to touch her bow ornament. She frowned, stepping away from him.

"Scree." Cynthe beckoned, and he came back to stand between her and Vassou.

"Please," Diello continued, "would you tell him that we need to speak to him urgently?"

Penrith began to play with a lock of her hair, twisting it around her finger. "He's very busy. I hardly ever see him."

"But could you try?"

"What would you give me for doing you so great a favor?"

"Be careful," Cynthe muttered to Diello.

"What would you expect?" he asked.

Penrith laughed, turning away.

"No, wait!" he called. "We really do need your help."

"So you can pester Lord Owain with idle requests?"

"No. Nothing like that. He's our uncle. We're hoping he'll—"

"He won't claim kinship with you!"

"Our little sister has been kidnapped," Diello said. "We need his help to get her back. All you have to do is give him my message."

"Messages are sent by Talking Winds, not by me," Penrith said. "Even if he is my father."

"The heir," Vassou murmured.

"And our cousin!" Diello declared.

"Do not call me cousin. I do not acknowledge such a connection."

Cynthe's smile faded. She glared at Penrith. "Did you come here just to be mean?"

"Don't, Cynthe," Diello said softly.

"Why not say what I think?"

Diello turned back to Penrith. "I'm sorry you don't want to be cousins. But will you still ask your father to speak with us?"

"I don't quite know what to make of you," she said. "You aren't exactly what I expected."

Then she spun with a flare of her cloak and ran out the gate.

"She was just toying with us," Cynthe said. "She doesn't care what happens to us, or if we ever find Amie."

"Maybe she has to get used to us," Diello said. "We didn't expect to be liked here, after what our parents did."

"I didn't expect it, but I hoped," Cynthe choked out.

"I'm sorry." He rubbed her arm, but Cynthe pulled away.

"I guess you think I'm jealous and petty. It isn't just that," she said.

"Are you sure? She *is* our grandmother's heir."

"I wouldn't mind so much if she were nicer about it."

"She didn't rub it in your face, Cynthe."

"She didn't have to. She's no friend to us. She never will be."

"I hope you're wrong," Diello said. "We need her help."

"We'll never get it."

chapter nineteen

Later that day, someone tapped on their door. Diello jumped up to open it. A gust of wind blew past him, swirling around the room and ruffling his hair.

"You will attend Lord Owain this evening," a voice said. "You will be sent for."

The wind blew out again.

"She spoke to him," Diello said.

Cynthe nodded. "Perhaps I misjudged her . . . a little."

The rest of the afternoon they paced and fidgeted. As soon as they finished their supper, there was another knock at the door. Palace guards stood outside, a larger escort than usual.

"Come with us," one of the men said.

The twins were conducted through the passageways until they reached a *cloigwylie*. Passing through alone, they found themselves in a spacious room filled with people. Everyone was frozen. Some had paused in the act of drinking, others were reaching for food, and a few sat with their mouths open in conversation.

Diello felt tension in the air like before a thunderstorm. There was a peculiar smell, like singed paper about to catch on fire. *Magic?* he wondered. *This is a trap!*

Grabbing Cynthe's hand, he started to retreat, but the *cloigwylie* would not let them through.

"What is this?" Cynthe asked.

"Trouble."

"No, it isn't," said a voice that Diello recognized.

"Clevn," he whispered.

A lithe figure came threading its way through the frozen courtiers. Framed by snowy hair flowing to his shoulders, Clevn's face was like fine marble, his eyes so light they looked nearly white. A golden nimbus shimmered around him. He carried a long ivory staff, carved with symbols. The magical power pulsing within him was so strong that Diello's bones began to burn.

"Where is Eirian?" Clevn demanded.

"Where's our sister?" Diello replied.

"There's more at stake here than a child."

"Return her or you get nothing."

Clevn raised his hand, and Diello was knocked across the floor. He bumped into a woman in a rose-pink gown. It was as if he'd hit a wall. Stunned, it took him a moment to stand up.

Cynthe ran to him. "Are you all right?"

Diello shook her off and looked at Clevn. "We want Amalina."

"Where is Eirian?"

"Tell him what happened," Cynthe said. "Don't argue with him."

"What is it you have to tell me? What are you hiding? You're frightened. Why?"

"Why shouldn't we be scared of you?" Diello said.

"I did not attack the royal sleigh. Lord Rhodri should have made that clear."

"Like you didn't block my Sight when I was talking to Canthroy."

"I have better things to do than trouble myself with boys and treasonous servants," said Clevn.

"We made a deal. The sword for our sister. You asked us to bring it to you, and we're here. So where is she?"

"I do not have Amalina. I never did."

"Then there's no point in talking. Let's go, Cynthe."

"No deal was struck between us! You are the children of the Betrayer. You took Eirian from its hiding place. Now *you* are responsible for returning it to me."

"We've—"

Clevn gestured for Diello to stop talking. The mage-chancellor closed his eyes, turning his head from side to side. "It is here," he murmured. "I sense the ancient tracings of its magic." He opened his eyes and pointed at Cynthe. "You carry it with you. Hand it over."

"Leave her alone," Diello said.

"If I use Voice to command her obedience, she'll suffer needlessly."

Cynthe braced herself, but Clevn did not attack her.

"Why don't you just take it?" Diello asked. "We can't stop you."

"You know that Eirian resists being taken against the will of its possessor. Your father was crippled by it when he stole it from its rightful place." Clevn's gaze swung back to Cynthe. "Hand it over, girl. And be quick about it."

"You're afraid of it," she said.

"I respect how dangerous it can be when mishandled. You've been lucky not to get hurt."

"We aren't as stupid as you think," she said.

"No, but it's foolish to be so stubborn. You've accused me of crimes I did not commit. You approached Owain without my permission."

"How long did you expect us to wait?" Diello asked.

"I warn you," Clevn went on without answering, "if you give Eirian to Owain, then you will be guilty of treason, with full penalty of death. And no tie of blood will save you."

"Where is our little sister?" Diello pleaded. "If you don't have her, then who does? Why won't you tell me?"

"The sword is not for paying ransom. You seek to use it for a trifle."

"Amalina isn't a trifle!"

"Would you give your life for hers?"

"Yes!"

Cynthe clutched at him. "Diello, no! He's tricking you."

"I don't care. If you won't help us, Clevn, there's only one thing left to do. I'll give Eirian to the queen."

Clevn paused. "You will give Eirian to Queen Sheirae?"

"Yes."

"Before the Liedhe Court?"

"I—I prefer to do it in private."

"Then hand it over now. I will arrange a meeting."

"No! I'll give it to her myself."

"This is how you bargain for a private audience with Her Majesty? What do you think you'll gain by it?"

"I'll know the sword is in *her* hands."

The mage-chancellor glared at Diello, and the burning sensation grew in Diello's bones. But he didn't back down.

"Surrendering Eirian is your duty," Clevn said. "The Betrayer will not be forgiven. You will not speak of her in the queen's presence."

Diello had no choice. He needed the queen's help to get Amie back. He might never reach Owain.

"Agreed."

Clevn lowered his staff. "Then in the queen's name, I accept these terms. Go back through the barrier. The guards will escort you to Her Majesty's reception chamber. Wait there."

Across the room of frozen people, the shimmering *cloigwylie* opened. Diello and Cynthe hurried out.

"Diello?" Cynthe began.

"It's the only thing we can do."

"But it's not enough."

"I *know*."

They were back in the passageway. Glowing orbs of light floated in the air overhead, lighting their way. Through the closed door, they could hear people talking and laughing again.

The guards marched the twins along.

After all they'd gone through, Amalina remained as lost to them as ever. Diello had no idea where to search. *Let your bones guide you*, Mamee had said, but what did that mean? Even if by some miracle he located Amie, he would soon have nothing with which to bargain for her.

I will not cry, he told himself. *And I will never give up.*

A double set of carved doors opened before them. They passed through an empty chamber into a square room furnished with gilded chairs, a gleaming floor, a screened-off corner, and an entire wall of mirrors. More orbs of light floated near the ceiling. Smaller sparks of illumination gleamed here and there. Diello realized these were tiny creatures the size of winged insects. They gathered in a swarm and abruptly flew out of the room just as the doors closed behind the twins.

The guards remained outside again. The room was windowless.

"Look at our reflections," Cynthe said.

The wall of mirrors showed multiple images of them. When Cynthe reached out to touch a mirror, her reflection did not move. "How strange," she said.

"Please give me the quiver," Diello said nervously.

"You can't trick them. Whatever you're about to try, it won't work."

He heard footsteps approaching. Someone was addressing the guards.

Diello took Cynthe by the arm and led her to the corner behind the screen. The space contained a table and a glass box about the length of Diello's forearm. It looked half full of water, and although Diello didn't touch it, the water was shifting in constant motion. A tiny ship with a sail tossed on the surface, and Diello thought he could see an even smaller person on board, struggling to control the vessel.

There was no chance to marvel at it.

The doors swung open, and a man stepped inside. He had auburn hair and a short-cropped beard covered his jaw, the first beard Diello had seen on any Fae. His garments were made of red velvet. Thumb-sized rubies studded his sleeves. Another ruby dangled from one of his pointed ears.

A gust of wind blew into the chamber. "Lord Owain, come away," called the Talking Wind. "You're expected in the Council Room."

Owain! Diello hurried from behind the screen, but guards had already surrounded his uncle and escorted him out.

"Uncle Owain!" Diello called out as the doors slammed shut.

"Let's go after him!" Cynthe said.

Diello tugged on the door knob, but it wouldn't turn.

Glancing over his shoulder, he saw a portion of the mirrored wall sliding open.

The queen had arrived.

chapter twenty

Clevn walked beside the queen. It was clear that they were twins. Queen Sheirae had the same haughty features as her brother, the same narrow face, pale skin, and high brow. Her long hair flowed down her back and was streaked with glittering strands of silver, white, lavender, and gray. A silver diadem covered with diamonds adorned her brow. Her flawless skin glistened and glowed. Her eyes weren't near-white, like Clevn's, but an icy amethyst-blue.

Her gown was fashioned from silver cloth so encrusted with diamonds and pearls that the skirts stood out stiffly. Long strings of diamonds hung from the tips of Sheirae's ears, dusting her shoulders. She wore huge cuffs of diamonds on both wrists and an enormous diamond pendant the size of a duck egg at her throat.

Ice queen, Diello thought. He stared at her, yearning for some sign of recognition, some acknowledgment that he and Cynthe belonged to her. Had she ever loved Mamee? Couldn't she find any affection in her heart for them?

At her waist hung a small bow—as tiny as a toy and crusted with diamonds. There was also a dagger with a jeweled hilt.

Diello thought the diamond bow even more absurd than Penrith's, but the dagger was real. She looked as though she knew exactly how to use it.

Beside her walked the largest wolf that Diello had ever seen. His pelt was glossy black, and his eyes were blue and intelligent. A chain of gold links encircled his neck.

It's not fair that the queen has her samal wolf in the palace but Vassou has to stay caged.

Halting in the center of the room, Sheirae stared at Diello and Cynthe for a long time without speaking. The sight of them seemed to sadden her. Eventually she gave the mage-chancellor a nod.

Clevn beckoned to the twins. "Come forward."

They obeyed, kneeling before the queen. One of Sheirae's brows lifted ever so slightly.

"Which of you is the eldest?" she asked. Her voice was like crystal.

"I am the firstborn," Cynthe replied.

"Clevn, look on her with Sight. Tell me what lies within her."

The mage-chancellor stepped forward, but Diello thrust out his hand to shield Cynthe from Clevn. He didn't know if it would work, but he was determined to keep her safe.

The mage-chancellor's eyes were glowing white. Diello met his gaze, returning Sight with Sight. And suddenly he was looking at a vision of Clevn stumbling alone through a vast cave. Diello felt the rawness of grief and shock, like a sword thrust through the ribs. He saw Clevn pick his way through shards of glass and drop to his knees before the smashed remnants of a display case. A jeweled scabbard—

identical to the one Diello had seen Brezog wearing—lay empty on the floor. Smoke and ashes hung in the air. A dead man in a hooded robe lay crumpled nearby. One hand was outstretched, clutching a tunic sewn with the Carnethie star.

Diello turned his gaze and the vision faded. It was hard to shake off Clevn's emotions while dealing with his own. *Was that Pa's tunic? Did Pa kill that man? Or did he just defend himself? Will we ever know the truth?*

When Diello swayed, Cynthe held his arm. He gave her a little smile of reassurance.

The mage-chancellor glanced at Sheirae with a frown and shook his head.

"Rhodri told me you have Sight, boy," the queen said. "But you'll have to grow wiser and a great deal stronger before you can best my brother."

"Anyone can place a tunic at the scene," Diello said. "Is that all the proof you hold against my father?"

The queen looked surprised. "You saw *inside* Clevn's mind? Tell me your vision."

"It's not important," Clevn said.

The queen pointed at Diello. "Tell me!"

"I saw a cave filled with smoke and a dead man by a smashed case. I saw Eirian's empty scabbard and a tunic with the Carnethie star on it." He paused. "I saw Clevn kneeling there."

"You chose a dark memory indeed to gaze on." Sheirae looked at Cynthe. "As for you, girl, what do you suppose Clevn saw inside you?"

Cynthe's lips parted, but she didn't answer.

"Well?" Sheirae turned to Clevn.

"Nothing," he said.

I am stronger! Diello thought. *She'll have to accept us now.*

"I saw nothing in the girl worth mentioning," Clevn added.

Is he just trying to cover his weakness? Diello wondered.

"Tell me," the queen said. "Let me decide."

"I saw the Betrayer's shroud and her Death Wind failing to bring her back to Embarthi," Clevn said. "I saw anger and grief in this girl in the aftermath of a goblin attack that killed her parents."

Sheirae closed her eyes.

Diello held his sister's hand, fighting back his own memories. *What a liar he is!*

"You stopped her Death Wind," Diello shouted at Clevn. "You haven't Seen anything! You were there, and you ordered the Death Wind away. You condemned our mother even after her death."

"By the queen's order," Clevn snapped. "So this is how you force us to discuss the Betrayer. We had an agreement!"

"Silence!" the queen commanded her brother. "Why do you tell them I gave such a cruel order? What have you done?"

"It can be discussed later."

"We'll discuss it now! Does this boy speak the truth? Did you interfere with my—with the Betrayer's Death Wind? Has her dust not gone to Dweigana?"

"It has not," Clevn said.

The queen's mouth drew very tight. "Then there is no

hope. When I, too, am dead, there will be no reuniting with her, no chance—ever—of reconciliation."

"I know Your Majesty has found this situation difficult."

"Difficult!" Sheirae spat the word. "You kept me in ignorance. You deliberately misled me in your report."

"I gave you the essential facts. The law is clear. Any Fae who is banished is exiled even beyond death."

"Unless special pardon is granted." Sheirae pressed her fists against her jeweled skirts. "Which I gave the moment I received the report of her death."

"By then it was too late."

"How? There should have been time in the day or two following her . . . demise."

When Clevn didn't answer, Diello spoke up. "Mamee's Death Wind came almost immediately. We hadn't finished preparing her. Even so, it would have taken her dust. But *he* stopped it."

"You rushed this, Clevn?" the queen asked. "Knowing I would give a pardon, you made it impossible for me to do so?"

"The Betrayer did the unforgivable. Need I remind Your Majesty how important it is to maintain political stability? Any sign of weakness is an opportunity for your enemies to erode your power."

"Weakness! No one in my realm can accuse me of it!"

"No," Clevn agreed. "And let us be diligent in keeping it that way."

The black wolf moved closer to Sheirae, and the anger in her face faded as she regained control of her emotions.

"Yes, I see," she murmured. "Well, it is done now, and there can be no undoing it."

Diello rose to his feet. He'd been dreading what was to come, but now he wasn't sure he cared anymore—except for Amie's sake. *How can someone like this be Mamee's mother? She's letting Clevn get away with his lies.*

"Let's be finished," Clevn said. "Boy, will you—"

"Keep your place, Clevn," Sheirae broke in. "It is for me to deal with this." Her gaze went to Diello. "I am told that you have brought Eirian back to us and are willing to restore the sword and scabbard to my hand, with nothing in exchange. This is well done of you."

Diello swallowed.

"Eirian has kept the Fae safe for countless generations. Without it, Embarthi has suffered. In returning Eirian, you are closing a circle that was broken, and the Wheels of Silver can turn once more." Sheirae held out her hands. "I will receive the sword now."

Diello pulled the wrapped bundle from Cynthe's quiver and unrolled the leather, letting the arrows fall with a clatter.

The engraved glasslike blade glimmered, casting its radiance across his arms and face. Diello left it lying on the leather instead of touching it directly. He knelt again before the queen and held it up to her.

"I'm sorry," he said. "This is all we have to give you right now."

"The blade alone?" she cried, stepping back. "Where is the hilt? Where is the scabbard?"

"The goblin gorlord has the scabbard," Diello told her.

"I don't know how he got it."

"Treachery begets treachery," Clevn said, scowling. "Presumably Stephel took it. He could have sold it to the gorlord."

"Never!" Diello declared. "Pa left it behind. You're forgetting that I just saw your memories. The scabbard was still there."

"Who is correct, Clevn?" the queen demanded. "You or this boy?"

"The boy." Clevn's eyes narrowed. "There was much confusion that day. I must investigate further, for it seems we have another traitor in the Liedhe Court."

"What of the hilt?" Sheirae asked Diello. "Tell me that!"

"I had it until I reached the Embarthi border. We carried Eirian in pieces, Cynthe and I, for safety."

"Sensible," the queen said.

Clevn leaned forward. "And then you fools lost it!"

"*I* lost it," Diello said. "Cynthe isn't responsible."

"You mustn't blame him," Cynthe said. "He was attacked and nearly killed. It was stolen."

Sheirae turned on her mage-chancellor. "You told me the boy was very ill. You did not say why. How long have you been censoring the reports sent to me?"

"You must stay strong," Clevn argued. "Dwelling on the past can only distress you. Even meeting these children tonight was a mistake. I can see how they tear at your resolve. You know where your duty lies."

"All too well! But don't forget that it was *you* who brought them here."

"They tricked me."

"You admit it?" Sheirae stared at him. "Then you must acknowledge their royal blood, *her* blood, for otherwise they couldn't deceive you."

The queen's not as cold as she tries to be, Diello thought.

"Don't lose sight of what's most important here," Clevn said. "Without the sword, Embarthi falls into greater jeopardy."

"And still we don't have it," Sheirae said. "Take the blade, Clevn. The audience is over."

Make me whole, Eirian whispered in Diello's mind.

Clevn spun around as though he heard it, too.

"Wait!" Diello cried to Sheirae. "I know where the hilt is. And if you'll promise to get Amalina back, then I'll—"

"I do not bargain!" the queen declared. "You have broken faith with me. You lied in order to obtain this audience. I will tolerate no more deceit this day."

"So your mage-chancellor's allowed to get away with lies and tricks, but we aren't," Diello said. "Who really rules here, you or him?"

"Silence!" the queen said. "Clevn, take the blade."

The mage-chancellor approached Diello. "Are you surrendering the blade?"

"Take it!" the queen ordered. "There is no need for this caution and formality when it's not complete."

"Enough power remains for there to be danger, Your Majesty." Clevn's pale eyes met Diello's. "Are you surrendering the blade?"

"No!" Cynthe shouted. "We aren't!"

Eirian must be returned. Diello recalled Pa's dying words.

Bowing his head, Diello held out the blade to Clevn. "I surrender it."

The mage-chancellor folded a portion of his sleeve over his hand and reached gingerly for the blade. It flashed briefly before its radiance dimmed.

"You have Her Majesty's leave to withdraw," Clevn said solemnly.

"Can't you even thank us?" Cynthe asked.

"You will withdraw," he repeated.

"After all we've gone through to bring it back?" she said. "Don't you care anything for us?"

"Don't," Diello said. "It's no use."

"Yes, it is." Cynthe stood before them. "I would have chucked this horrid old sword away and left you without it forever, but Diello wouldn't give up. We may not have the hilt, but Brezog doesn't have it, either. Can't you be glad of that?"

"Enough, girl," Clevn said.

Sheirae turned and walked away.

"It's not enough!" Cynthe shouted after her grandmother. "Our little sister has been stolen, and you haven't even offered to find her when you're probably the only person who can. Now that I've met you I'm sorry we ever came here. If we could've saved our little sister by giving away the sword, we'd have done it."

The queen was stepping through the opening in the wall panel.

"I understand now why our mother ran away from here. She was worth a thousand of you! She was beautiful and kind and good, and even if you cut out my tongue I am proud to say her name."

"No!" Clevn commanded.

"Lwyneth!" Cynthe screamed. "Lwyneth! Lwyneth!"

She ran to Diello's arms and wept against him.

Diello thought the queen might look back, but she continued out of sight, her diamond gown rustling around her. The black wolf hesitated, however, gazing at them before it followed her.

Clevn stayed behind. "You do not understand."

"I think we do," Diello said. "She might have liked us, if not for you."

"A queen has responsibilities that separate her from others. She cannot be simply a woman . . . or a mother. She must always consider the good of the realm."

"Would the realm have suffered if the Death Wind brought home my mother's dust?"

"It would have been enough to ignite civil war. You think only with your hearts and ignore our traditions and laws just as your mother did."

"My mother advised us not to seek the throne. She said it was unworthy of her sacrifice. We came here to get our sister back, not to cause trouble."

Clevn didn't seem to be listening. His gaze was on Cynthe. "Owain's daughter, Penrith, will soon be named officially as Her Majesty's heir, although the girl has no twin brother to rule with her. That is unfortunate, but the queen must have an heir. No matter what you may think, we are grateful for the return of this blade.

Soon you'll be taken back to Antrasia, where you will be provided for."

"We don't need anything from you," Diello said.

He put his arm around Cynthe and led her out of the chamber.

chapter twenty-one

they were headed back to their suite when a Talking Wind blew in their faces. "Go back to Lord Clevn," it said. "You are wanted immediately."

"We won't go," Cynthe said, but the guards shooed the twins back to the chamber of mirrors.

Clevn was examining the blade on its piece of leather. At the twins' arrival, he frowned. "Diello, come and look at this. What have you done to it?"

"Nothing."

"No," Clevn said. "The tracings have been altered. And now . . . Step closer."

Diello obeyed, gazing at the blade with curiosity. "I don't see anything."

"Feel the magic within it. See with your senses, not your eyes!"

Squinting, Diello looked again. He still had no idea what Clevn was so upset about. The blade was just lying there, looking ordinary—except for its beautiful engraving.

"Hold your hand over it."

Diello reached out. The blade began to glow brightly.

Now Diello could see tiny patterns swirling through the light, as though the weapon were coming to life.

Make me whole.

"Don't touch it!"

Drawing back, Diello blinked at his great-uncle. Clevn's eyes were shining with a light similar to Eirian's. He stepped away from Diello, and the sword's radiance dimmed. Clevn's eyes returned to normal, but he looked furious.

"Did you put the sword together? Answer me quickly! When you had both pieces, did you assemble the sword?"

"Why would we?" Cynthe asked warily.

"Don't lie to me. It's obvious by these indications that you have. How much have you handled it? Played with it?"

Neither twin spoke.

Muttering to himself, Clevn laid the blade carefully on a chair. Diello didn't see the mage-chancellor move, but suddenly he had Diello in his grip. He pressed his fingertips to Diello's face.

"No!" Diello cried, wrenching away. He backed against the mirrored wall, holding up his hands. "Don't!"

Cynthe stepped between them. "Don't you dare hurt him! I don't care who you are, you've no right to force yourself into his mind."

"You—a Faelin—know of Mind Walking?" Clevn said. "I suppose it was your mother who—"

"Mamee wasn't cruel," Cynthe said. "If you must know, it was Brezog, trying to force Diello to tell where the sword was hidden."

A soft sound escaped Clevn's lips. "Then it was a harsh

experience indeed. I assure you that my sifting through your thoughts would not be so unpleasant."

"And no Web of Truth, either," Cynthe said. "He's gone through enough."

Clevn nodded although he didn't apologize. "Will you please answer my questions?" he asked, keeping his voice mild. "This matter is very important. I need honesty from you and cooperation. Not evasions and lies."

"I don't see that we owe you anything," Cynthe said.

But Diello asked, "What's wrong with the sword?"

"One problem is that it still carries residue of an *amddif* spell—"

"The protection our mother wove to conceal Eirian when it was hidden on our farmstead."

"Yes, the one you so rashly unlocked. The other problem is that it's awake. Have you fought with it?"

Awake? Diello shook his head. "Not really."

"Explain!"

Diello told his great-uncle about the night in the forest when Brezog had caught up with them. "I swung it at him, but he wasn't really there. Just a projection of his spirit."

"What happened the very first time you held the sword?"

"It was like grasping something enormous and scary, something too big to understand, and yet I—I liked it," Diello admitted.

"The usual reaction, I believe."

Diello felt a rush of embarrassment.

"He couldn't let it go," Cynthe said. "I had to pull it from his hands."

"So you've both handled it?"

They nodded.

Clevn swept his palm the length of the weapon without actually touching it. Delicate patterns swirled in the air before tendrils of light wound themselves around Diello's wrists.

Diello gasped. Clevn spoke a sharp command, and the tracery of light vanished.

"What is it?" Diello asked.

"The sword is trying to bond with you."

"You mean control me? Take possession of me?"

"Not precisely. It involves a joining of your soul to the intelligent force residing in the weapon. A commingling of spirits. Most of the truly ancient weapons were made this way—not for mortals. That's why they're so dangerous." Clevn looked at Diello. "Especially for individuals with weak magic."

"We've been careful," Cynthe said. "Diello hasn't been practicing swordplay with it, if that's what you're asking."

"Does it speak to you, Diello?"

How does he know? "Sometimes."

"I didn't know that," Cynthe said.

Diello looked down. "It's like a voice in my head, always saying the same thing."

"And what does it want?" Clevn demanded.

"It says 'Make me whole.' From the moment Pa handed me the—" Diello broke off.

"Go on."

But Diello didn't want to describe Pa's final moments to this man that hated him so much. "It's private."

"I need to know."

"That's all. There's nothing else."

"Then I must consult with the Afon Heyrn," Clevn said. "As it is now, the weapon cannot go back to its place within the first Wheel."

"The Wheel of Life?" Diello asked.

"The Wheel of Destiny. And who has been telling you about the Mysteries?"

"I'd rather not say."

"You *will* say, but we'll leave that for later," Clevn said. "Cynthe, bring the blade. Both of you, come!"

Cynthe barely had time to rewrap the blade and slide it into her quiver before Clevn was stepping through an opened wall panel. As soon as the twins were in the passage with him, the opening closed. For an instant they stood in total darkness, then an orb of light appeared, casting soft illumination. It floated ahead of them as though it knew where Clevn wanted to go.

The mage-chancellor led them through a maze of passages and then started down a tight spiral of stairs. They descended to a level where the air smelled dank and cold. Rough stone surrounded them.

Overhead, a stone arch was engraved with Fae symbols. Diello couldn't read what they meant, but he felt uneasy.

"Could he be taking us to the Cave of Mysteries?" Cynthe whispered.

"Mamee said it wasn't for Faelin."

"Quiet, both of you," Clevn said. "Hurry."

They followed him under the arch. The air smelled

different. A breeze blew in their faces, carrying the scent of water tangy with salt.

And then they were outside, standing on a cliff edge at the mouth of the cave. It overlooked the largest expanse of water Diello had ever seen. The air was warm and moist. The mountains that should have been looming over them were gone.

"That's not the lake by the palace," Cynthe said. "Where *is* the palace?"

"Is this the sea?" Diello asked. "Where are we?"

Clevn pointed across the water. Staring hard, Diello could make out a shape on the horizon.

"Is that land?"

"Yes, the Isle of Woe."

Diello looked at him. "That's where the Fae go when they die."

"No. Their mourners gather there, but Fae dust is carried by the Death Wind to Dweigana. It's a—"

"—cloud. We know," Cynthe said. "Our mother will never be there, thanks to you."

"Come." Clevn started down a precipitous set of steps carved into the cliff.

When Diello tried to follow, Cynthe gripped his tunic.

"Where's he taking us? What's he up to?"

"The Wheels of Silver are on the Isle of Woe," Diello replied. "I don't think we'll get any answers unless we go with him."

Cynthe sighed and followed Clevn.

At the foot of the cliff, they found Clevn waiting on a thin strip of beach. Waves splashed over the rocks, throwing sprays of foam. A framework of weatherbeaten timbers supported a large bronze gong. Clevn took a mallet off a hook and struck the disk.

The sound vibrated through Diello's bones, making him cry out. Clevn struck a second time, and Diello had to grit his teeth to keep from screaming. His bones trembled.

"Can't you see how it affects him?" Cynthe shouted at Clevn. "Stop hitting it!"

"The gong must be struck three times," Clevn said. "There are occasions when having crystal bones is a disadvantage."

The gong rang a third time. Cynthe held her hands over Diello's ears, but it didn't help. The sound was inside him, a part of him. He closed his eyes until it finally faded.

Lightning streaked across the cloudless night sky. Thunder rumbled, and then the waves began to churn and toss. They grew into bigger waves, rising higher into the air.

Cynthe retreated. "The water's going to wash over us."

"No," Diello said. "Look!"

The waves had parted, leaving a calm channel of water between them. It seemed to stretch all the way to the island.

A raft was approaching on the channel, poled along by a Fae robed in silver. As the raft drew up to shore, the silver robes began to move. What had appeared to be cloth now separated into individual fish that wriggled free and leaped into the water. The boatman stood there as dark and insubstantial as a shadow.

"Who desires to cross the Sinking Lands?" he asked.

"Clevn, and three who shall not be named."

Diello glanced behind them.

"Who's the third?" Cynthe asked.

Catching Clevn's look of warning, Diello pointed at Cynthe's quiver without saying the name Eirian aloud. She nodded in understanding.

The boatman extended his hand and caught the light orb from where it floated in the air. As he cupped it in his hands, its illumination faded to such a low glimmer that Diello could hardly see anything.

Cynthe edged closer to Diello. "Why was he *wearing* fish?" she whispered, but Diello could only shrug.

Clevn stepped aboard the raft. "Come."

The raft was narrow, forcing them to crowd together. While the boatman poled them across, Diello gazed up at the ocean waves frozen on either side. If the magic failed, they would drown. But only he and Cynthe seemed worried. Diello listened to the steady splashing as the pole lifted and sank.

Clevn pointed at the wall of water on their right.

Dim light, distorted and wavering, shone from within the water, and Diello saw what looked like a forest. Huge trees, each as large as the Knower, stood beneath the sea. Their trunks and leafless branches were gray and worn.

"Ghost trees," Diello murmured.

"And there," Clevn said, pointing to the left.

Diello saw a stone building with tall columns along its front. Some of the stone blocks had fallen. Green weeds grew on them, and a school of fish darted between the blocks.

"What happened?" Diello asked.

"In the long ago," Clevn replied, "this land and forest were home to the Fae. Then the ground began to sink slowly, year by year, until the sea claimed all of it except the Isle of Woe. The island was too small to live on, and the Fae moved to Embarthi."

Maybe they did drive the goblins out of Embarthi, like Brezog once said, Diello thought.

"The island still contains what is oldest and most truly Fae," Clevn said. "I warn you to behave with the utmost respect while we are there. No Faelin has ever seen the Mysteries before. And the Watchers have never forgotten that your father slew one of them. They will not be welcoming."

"Nothing new about that," Diello muttered to Cynthe.

"Hush," Clevn said. "Your attitude will not be tolerated. Perhaps you would prefer to swim back to shore."

Swallowing, Diello shook his head. Cynthe nervously pushed her hair behind her ears.

There was a splash, and a glistening fish leaped from the water and clung to the boatman. Another fish did the same, and another—until he was robed in silver once more. He stopped poling, and the raft glided to a stop against a flight of stone steps leading up to a railing.

The twins climbed quickly, needing no encouragement to keep close to Clevn now. A roar of water behind them made Diello look back. The raft was gone, as though it had never been, and the ocean surged together violently.

"Where did the boatman go?" Cynthe asked.

"To where he belongs," Clevn answered. "He is of the

water. I conjured him from the waves to serve us."

"Why do the fish cover him like that?"

"He is of the water," Clevn repeated. "The fish left him while he served us. They returned to him when his task was done."

Cynthe frowned. "I still don't understand."

"How did Pa do this?" Diello blurted out. "Did he come here by boat? Not the raft, I suppose, but did he use—"

"Your father did not take this route," Clevn interrupted. "There are many possible paths."

"All magical ones?"

"Not all. Enough talking. Come."

Ahead of them, another light orb appeared, bobbing in the air. At the top of the steps, they passed beneath another stone arch and found themselves inside a wide chamber lined with white marble. Stone columns carved into the shape of trees rose in each corner, their branches appearing to support the roof. Round stone vessels held fires burning with flames of blue and green. Chiseled words in ancient Fae script covered the walls. They blurred when Diello tried to read them.

At the far end of the chamber, Clevn gestured for the twins to stay back before he stepped inside a circle inlaid on the floor. Kneeling, he dipped his fingers into a bowl resting there and murmured something too low to hear as he touched his forehead with his fingertips. Then he rose and turned to Diello and Cynthe. His eyes were glowing white.

"Leave your bow and quiver here, outside the circle. Your knives as well," he ordered. "Bring only the blade."

In silence, they did as he said. Cynthe handed the

leather-wrapped blade to Diello, and he took it with shaking hands.

When they stood inside the circle with Clevn, he pointed at the ceiling, showing them a circular hole directly overhead.

"We shall ascend to the altar of the Guardian. Do not fear. I am powerful enough to shield you from the magic emanating there, but take care. If you stare directly at the altar, you could go blind."

Diello found it hard to breathe. He nodded to show he understood.

"Beyond the altar, we'll enter the Chamber of Memory. You will not be permitted to go farther or enter the Cave. You won't see the Wheels or the sacred relics. The Watchers will come to us."

Cynthe opened her mouth to ask a question, but then stopped.

"Good," Clevn said. "Perhaps you've begun to learn a little prudence."

Lifting his hands, he rose into the air.

Cynthe pushed out a breath and closed her eyes. She ascended smoothly.

It was Diello's turn. He was so nervous he froze for a moment before he remembered that all he had to do was be one with the air. And then he was floating up through the opening in the ceiling. He landed on a platform next to Cynthe and Clevn. Close to them, a black oblong stone was hanging suspended without support. Strange symbols were carved along its sides.

Diello averted his eyes. Even so, they stung and watered. He could feel a throbbing presence inside the stone rectangle. He had no desire to go closer to it.

Clevn stepped off the platform into midair and flew through a doorway into a room with plain white walls and ceiling. There was no floor.

No, Pa definitely couldn't have come this way, Diello thought.

At Clevn's gesture, a floor appeared. Diello's feet had barely touched it before a shimmering column of light appeared at the opposite end of the room. It was joined by another and another . . . until there were twelve.

Diello found that he couldn't stare very long at the columns without his eyes hurting. So he focused his gaze on the floor instead.

"The Watchers have come," Clevn said. "Both of you, stay where you are. Neither of you should speak unless directly addressed."

As Clevn walked toward the Watchers, each column of light faded before changing shape into a man. All the Watchers wore long tan robes with hoods that concealed their faces. Several of them turned to stare at Diello and Cynthe, and Diello could feel waves of hostility coming their way.

He and Cynthe stayed close together. She didn't even try to whisper.

"Diello," Clevn said, "bring the blade."

He obeyed, gripping it tightly in both hands. Although he'd expected Cynthe to follow him, she remained behind, as though she didn't dare move without a direct order.

Clevn spread his hands wide as he addressed the Watchers: "Eirian is not complete, but this portion of it has returned. Behold!"

Diello unwrapped the leather partway to reveal the shining blade.

One of the Watchers stepped forward. "Why have you brought this to us?" His voice reverberated, the words echoing and overlapping, making it hard for Diello to understand him.

"The blade belongs here," Clevn said.

"The *sword* in its scabbard belongs here!" the Watcher said. "This is not the sword. It is a fragment—awake and aware. The *amddif* that clings to it no longer keeps it dormant."

"I know. That is why we have brought it to you."

The Watcher started to turn away.

"You won't accept the blade?" Clevn asked. "Can't you reconsider?"

"There is no balance. There can be no harmony. Without all three pieces, the sword is dangerous to any who would use it—" the Watcher looked at Diello "—or be used by it."

Clevn edged slightly apart from Diello. "When the other pieces are recovered," Clevn said, clearing his throat, "they'll be returned here to complete Eirian."

The Watcher said nothing.

"Meanwhile the blade is not safe anywhere except within the Wheel—"

"Eirian cannot pass the portals of Afon Heyrn unless it

is complete. And even then . . . rituals of separation would be required."

"That's why we have come."

"No element of magic brought here can be so strong that it destroys the delicate balance of the Wheels. They must be able to turn without interference."

"Eirian was here before. It belongs here again."

"Not awake. Not like this. The fragment is too potent. It may awaken other relics that have long lain dormant. Eirian must sleep if it is to remain here. Only asleep does Eirian's power create good."

"I know all this," Clevn said. "We have brought the blade here so that it can be made dormant once more."

"Impossible unless it is complete."

"Something can be done," Clevn insisted.

"No. Unless it's complete, it cannot be parted properly from this boy or any other who seizes possession. Only then can its power be controlled and bound by the scabbard."

"Can the rituals be started now?" Clevn asked. "This boy should be separated from Eirian—even a piece of Eirian—before more harm is done."

"Their bond is weak as yet."

Diello felt something lightly tickle his wrist. He saw a thin thread of magic reaching out from the blade. It was trying to entwine itself around his arm. *Make me whole,* Eirian whispered. *Do not put me in this prison.*

Jerking, Diello nearly dropped the blade.

"Put it down, Diello," Clevn ordered. "Carefully."

Diello obeyed quickly, leaving the blade on the floor. He stepped back several paces, wiping his sweaty palms on his tunic.

"You will take it now," Clevn said to the Watcher. "Guard the blade while we regain the rest of it."

But the Watcher turned and left. The others followed. Eirian's blade was left lying on the floor.

Cynthe came up behind Diello and touched his arm.

The mage-chancellor rewrapped the blade and, carrying it with him, strode from the Chamber of Memory. Diello and Cynthe had to hurry to keep up with him. This time they walked down a curve of stairs instead of flying. Outside, a strong wind buffeted them and drove the waves until they were white and rough.

"May we speak now?" Cynthe asked.

Clevn's head was lowered in thought.

Diello ventured closer to him. "If we—"

"Don't bother me now with questions!"

Thunder boomed overhead, and Clevn vanished.

The twins gaped at where he'd been standing.

"The old wart," Cynthe said in disgust. "He's left us here. How are we supposed to get back?"

Diello ventured halfway down the steps to the churning water. A wave slopped across his feet, nearly pulling him into the sea. Another surged behind it, throwing spray in his face. He retreated to the top of the steps.

"If that raft comes back for us," he said, "I'm not taking it."

"It's going to start raining soon," Cynthe shouted over the wind. "Should we seek shelter inside?"

They headed for the arch that led to the room of white marble, but now thick gates barred their way.

Diello thumped his fist on one. "Locked out!" he yelled. He kicked it before shouting at the dark sky, "Damn you, Clevn!"

"So now what? Do we fly?"

"Not in this wind. It could blow us into the sea."

Cynthe rubbed her arms. "I'm getting cold. Clevn said there are several ways back. Maybe we can figure out how Pa did it."

"Mamee must have told him what to do," Diello said. He ran his fingers along the side of the arch. "The place is full of illusions and magic."

Cynthe was staring behind him. "Diello, look!"

He saw a whirlwind spinning across the water, coming right at them. He had just enough time to grab Cynthe's hand before they were engulfed by it and sucked into a maelstrom. Swirled and tumbled about, Diello tried to hang onto Cynthe, but the wind was too strong. It tossed him higher and higher until he was dizzy and half-conscious.

Then—as abruptly as it had come—the wind was gone. And Diello and Cynthe were sitting on the floor of the queen's reception chamber with its mirrored wall and gilt chairs.

It was as if they'd never gone anywhere with Clevn—except their clothes were stiff and damp with salt spray, and the blade was gone.

chapter twenty-two

In the soft evening light, their suite looked like a fancy prison cell. As the guards who'd escorted them back closed the door, Cynthe shrugged off her bow and quiver. She rushed over to the fire burning on the hearth and warmed her hands there.

"And you thought my tempests were bad," she said. "What do you think of Great-Uncle Clevn's tantrums? It's not our fault the Watchers wouldn't take the blade."

"At least he didn't leave us there," Diello said.

"Being pulled backward through a thorn bush would've been more fun. I'd prefer not to travel in any more whirlwinds."

"He made sure we can't find the Isle of Woe again, didn't he?" Diello said.

"Clever Clevn. Except I don't mind if I never return."

There was something odd about their quarters tonight. Diello felt a faint trace of power humming in the air. Puzzled, he looked around and touched Cynthe's arm in warning.

A sound came from inside his bedchamber.

Cynthe picked up her bow and quiver and tiptoed over

to his closed door. When she was ready, Diello flung the door open.

Amalina was sitting in the middle of his bed, playing with a pair of dolls.

"Amie?" Cynthe breathed. She tossed her weapon aside.

The child looked up with a big grin and flung down her toys. She came running over to Diello, hugging him around the legs.

"Del!" she cried. "Oh, Del!"

He picked her up, hugging her small body tightly before handing her over to Cynthe.

"Cynnie!" Amalina cried, kissing her cheek. "Where have you been? I have lots of new toys. And here, Del, I saved this 'specially for you."

She handed over the deed seal—a silver disk engraved with the legal title to the family farmstead. It had been Pa's, and his father's before him. When Pa died, he entrusted the deed seal to Diello. Only then had Diello discovered that there was a magical spell on the disk. It had proven to be the key to where Eirian had lain hidden for years. The old piece of metal felt warm and heavy on his palm. He traced the engraved words with his fingertip.

Amalina giggled, her blue eyes dancing. "Ninka can't see it. Isn't that funny? Uncle can't, either."

"Who's Ninka?" Cynthe asked.

"My nursemaid. She's old and likes to sing."

Diello slipped the chain back around Amalina's neck, tucking the seal beneath her dress. He'd first given it to her because Mamee had told him its magic would protect her, and perhaps it had. She seemed well cared for. Her hair had grown into longer ringlets, tied with a ribbon of blue velvet that matched her dress. Her shoes were made of kid leather, with decorative beading on the toes. *I forgot that we missed her birthday*, Diello thought. *She's four now.*

Amalina squirmed, and Cynthe put her down.

"Are you all right, Amie?" he asked, stroking her curls.

"I missed you lots and lots. No one tells me my story before I go to sleep. I don't like 'adishes, and I have to eat them every day." Amalina grimaced. "And Ninka washes my ears too hard."

"Is that all?" Cynthe asked.

"Uh-huh. Do you like my dress?" Amalina swished back and forth. "It's my favorite color, you know."

"It's beautiful," Cynthe said. "Just like you."

Amalina whirled and ran back to the bed, scooping up her dolls and introducing them to the twins by name.

While she chattered, Cynthe whispered to Diello, "She's fine."

"And Clevn lied again. Telling us she wasn't here."

Amalina tugged at the hem of his tunic. "You're not listening!"

He lifted her up. "And you need tickling."

She squealed and squirmed while he spun her around and around. "More! More!" she shouted.

"What is going on here?" a man's voice said from behind them.

"Uncle Owain!" Diello cried.

"Uncle!" Amalina shouted. "Uncle! Look who's come!"

Owain smiled at her, and something in the tilt of his head reminded Diello of Mamee. "And who are your visitors?" Owain asked her.

Amalina laughed. "Del and Cynnie. And I'm visiting *them*."

He made an exaggerated face of astonishment. "Really? Are you sure?"

"Uh-huh. I wished and wished and wished, just like you told me. And here they are!"

He tapped her nose lightly. "Then you must be an excellent wisher. Now it's getting late. Tell them good-bye."

"But I want to stay here."

"It's time for bed." He spread his hands wide, and a blue band of light glowed between his palms. "Go back to Ninka."

Rubbing her eyes, Amalina waved. "'Bye, Cynnie. 'Bye, Del."

"No, wait," Diello started, but the blue light encompassed Amalina, and she was gone.

"Where is she?" Diello demanded. "What have you done with her?"

"She's safe." Owain gave Diello and Cynthe a broad smile. "Well, now. At long last, I meet my nephew and niece. Clevn's a wily one, but he didn't hide you quite as securely as he thought. When I got your message from Penrith, I realized that the 'guests' in this wing had to be you."

"Uncle Owain," Cynthe said, "we're so glad to see you."

Owain turned to Diello, reaching out his hand.

Diello backed away, but Owain's hand came down on his shoulder.

A spark of magic made Diello's bones burn. He wrenched free.

"Crystal bones, as I suspected," Owain murmured. "Young and untrained, of course, but as powerful as Clevn's. Excellent."

"You took Amalina from us," Diello said.

"Well, of course," Owain replied. "It's been amusing, watching you struggle to get here and blaming the old mage for everything that went wrong."

"Watching!" Cynthe exclaimed.

"Not every moment. But now and then."

"Did you watch when the sprites attacked Diello?" she asked.

Owain shrugged. "No, I missed that."

"Why didn't you help us when the royal sleigh was attacked?"

"Penrith was right. You really are innocents."

"It was *you*!" Cynthe cried.

"Don't you have any questions for me, Diello?"

"Stop the games," Diello said. "Tell us what you want."

"Who is playing the game here?" Owain asked. "Hand over Eirian."

There was no use now regretting that he'd given up Eirian. A part of Diello was glad he'd done the right thing, even if the Watchers hadn't appreciated it. *But what about Amalina?*

"We don't have the sword," Diello confessed. "I gave it to Queen Sheirae."

Owain's phony smile faded. "A silly thing to do,

considering I have what you value most. Poor little girl."

"You tricked us!" Cynthe declared.

"No, Clevn tricked you. He's the mage-chancellor. He rules the storms and the lightning." Owain lifted his hands. "I am but a minor player at the Liedhe Court, to be pitied and gossiped about, never to fulfill my own destiny, thanks to my dear sister. I rejoiced when I heard that she was dead. Do you know why?"

Diello sent his uncle a stony look.

"Lwyneth cost me everything. And for what? An empty prophecy too old to matter."

"What prophecy?"

"Lwyneth tricked *me*, and now you've done the same. She's paid dearly—I was forced to betray her hiding place to the goblins—and now so will you."

"That's how the goblins attacked—"

"Who do you think you're dealing with, boy? What do you think is at stake here?"

Amalina's life. Diello's eyes were stinging, but he wouldn't cry. *Lord Rhodri warned us about Owain. Why didn't I believe him?*

"We're going to get Amalina back," Cynthe said. "The queen will see to that. If you really wanted the sword, you could have helped us. Why didn't you?"

"And be caught committing treason? Certainly not. I don't believe in taking unnecessary risks."

"No, you'd rather sneak and betray people who've trusted you," she said. "And now our grandmother's very grateful to us."

Owain looked startled, but swiftly recovered. "A good try, but I doubt Sheirae welcomed you with loving arms."

"Are you sure of that?" Diello asked, continuing Cynthe's bluff. "Penrith hasn't been named heir yet. And Cynthe's here now."

Owain gripped Diello's arm, his fingers digging in. "Don't attempt that game with me. Penrith is the queen's favorite. Her place is secure. But Clevn opposes my bid to rule jointly with my daughter. With the help of your crystal bones, I will be stronger than he is."

Owain closed his eyes. Diello felt his uncle's touch crawling in his thoughts. A burning sensation spread through Diello's limbs.

"Stop it," Diello gasped.

Instead, Owain sent magic coursing through Diello. The burning increased until Owain finally pulled away.

Diello staggered, pressing the heels of his hands to his eyes.

Owain shook him. "Never lie to me again! I am a mage, with no need of Webs of Truth to sift your thoughts. You didn't give Eirian to the queen. Not all of it. I just learned that you've lost the hilt. You *fool*!"

As Owain raised his hand again, Diello stepped back.

"Leave me alone!" he shouted.

Their uncle didn't move, but Diello was suddenly pushed across the room. He caught himself on a chair.

"You will be quite useful," Owain said, "once you learn a few lessons in obedience."

"I am not helping you."

"Not even for Amalina's sake? I've been kind to the child, so far. My kindness can continue."

"You wouldn't hurt her!" Cynthe said.

Owain turned to Cynthe. "I need this boy and the child, but not you. Perhaps it's time you were given to the goblins, as well."

"Guards!" Cynthe cried.

"They can't hear you. I've seen to that."

"Let her go free," Diello said quickly. "I'll do whatever you want."

Owain laughed. "Of course you will."

chapter twenty-three

"Come along," Owain said to Diello. "If we hurry, we can reach the borderlands by dawn."

Diello's eyes widened. "To look for the hilt?"

"Smart boy. You can find it, can't you?"

"I—I think so."

Diello didn't need to glance at his sister. He heard the slight change in her breathing. Diello ran for the door. When Owain blocked his path, Cynthe swung a chair at him.

The chair bounced harmlessly off Owain's *cloigwylie*. Diello dashed to the window, but the lock wouldn't release.

Picking up a stool, Diello slammed it at the glass. Owain twisted the stool from Diello's grasp.

Cynthe ran into the sitting room. To give her a chance to fetch her bow, Diello grabbed the stool again and tried to smash it through the window. Owain shouted, and Diello felt his limbs go weak.

Owain's magic wasn't as powerful as Clevn's, but it was capable of slowing down Diello. By now, Cynthe was in position behind Owain. She drew her bow. Would an arrow pierce his protection?

If she kills him, Diello thought, *we'll never find Amalina.*

Owain turned to face Cynthe. He pressed his hands together, and blue light glowed around them before he revealed a small orb on his palm. An image of Amalina could be seen inside it. "Be very careful," Owain said.

Instead of releasing an arrow, Cynthe pitched her voice flat and harsh. "*Break!*"

The chair lying on the floor next to Owain shattered into kindling. Swearing, he jumped to one side.

"You cannot do that!" he yelled. "Faelin cannot do that!"

Cynthe grinned. "Who says?"

Rushing at Cynthe, Owain hit her with his fist and knocked her sprawling.

"Cynthe!" Diello cried. When he tried to go to her, Owain grabbed his arm and swung him around, slamming him against the wall.

Twisted ropes of blue light bound Diello's wrists. Another band of light covered his mouth. Owain wrapped a cloak around him and spoke a word that unlocked the window. Then he pushed Diello out.

They were one story above the ground. Diello sailed through the air, too startled to fly. His fall was broken by a snow-laden bush. Tumbling down through its branches, Diello landed with a jolt. Snow cascaded on top of him.

Before Diello could stand, Owain landed on the ground beside him and pulled him upright. He shoved Diello through the garden and opened the west gate.

A servant muffled in a cloak was waiting with a white lion and chariot. He had a cloth thrown over the lion's head, but the animal was growling and lashing its tail.

Diello refused to walk another step, but Owain picked him up and tossed him into the chariot. Owain jumped up behind him. He picked up the reins, and the lion roared.

"I'd hold on if I were you," Owain murmured in Diello's ear. "Let him go!" he called to the servant.

The cloth dropped from the lion's head. Shaking its mane, the animal leaped into the air, drawing the chariot behind it. The servant leaped, too, catching the back of the chariot as it left the ground and swinging himself aboard. They soared high over the palace. Then Owain pulled on the reins, and the lion leveled off, flying above the lake before turning eastward.

Diello craned his neck to see as much as possible in the darkness. His hair whipped back from his face, and the wind was bitterly cold. The ground beneath them was a blur.

If Owain had Clevn's power, we'd be at the border in a few moments. Diello still didn't understand how Clevn's magic had taken them so far from the palace in such a short length of time.

Maybe Owain could keep them from being followed. *Or maybe he's not a very good mage.*

Diello expected Owain to read his thoughts and comment.

"Easy, Meseiros," Owain called to the lion instead. "We're not racing tonight. Easy now."

The chariot slowed down a bit, but Diello could still feel the creature's urge to go faster.

"Magnificent, isn't he?" Owain said. "I bred him myself, and his sire before him. White lions are the fleetest, and my racing stables contain the best stock in the realm. Meseiros has never been defeated. Find the hilt for me quickly, and I'll teach you how to handle the reins on our return flight."

Still gagged by the band of blue light, Diello could say nothing. *Does Owain think I can be bribed that easily?*

"No need to arrive before daybreak," Owain said. "The border *cloigwylie* is strongest at night. I wonder if Clevn has rushed the blade to the Watchers or decided to wait. He's bound to come seeking the hilt as well, for without it, Eirian is useless."

Exhausted, Diello dozed off and awoke when Owain brought the chariot to a bumpy landing. They were on the Antrasin side of the *cloigwylie.* The scent of pine forest filled Diello's nostrils. Through the trees, he glimpsed the sun just cresting the horizon.

"*Release,*" Owain said.

The bands vanished from Diello's mouth and wrists. He flexed his sore wrists and winced.

"Get out and start searching," Owain said. This order held no magic command, but Diello didn't argue.

He jumped off the chariot and looked around, unsure of where to start.

The ground was trampled here. He could see broken branches through the undergrowth. *If the sprites left any tracks, they're gone now.*

There was a whiff of goblin stink. It was several days old, probably, but the odor made Diello uneasy.

"Get on with it," Owain growled.

"Aren't you coming?"

His uncle gestured, and the servant walked over to

Diello. "Iones will help you. I prefer to watch from the air."

"I need something to protect me from the sprites," Diello said.

"Like that?" Owain pointed.

Half concealed beneath a bush lay Diello's quarterstaff.

Diello ran to pick it up, glad to have it in his hands again. "How did you know where to find it?" he asked, but the chariot was gone.

"If you can find this, why can't you find the hilt?" Diello shouted at the sky.

I'm watching, Owain's voice whispered in Diello's mind. *Hurry!*

Diello ran into the forest. Iones followed at first, but then veered away. When the servant was out of sight, Diello halted to lean against a tree.

He was very hungry and thirsty, and Owain had supplied him with nothing. The last thing Diello wanted was to face the sprites again. How he wished Cynthe were with him now.

Keep moving, Owain said.

Diello walked on. He wasn't finding any territory markings, and he was no tracker. Now and then he heard Iones crashing about, but Diello knew they weren't going to find the hilt by trailing through the woods. He wished he'd kept the deed seal when Amalina gave it to him. It might have guided him to the hilt, the way it had led him to Eirian before. That time, helped by a riddle spell-engraved on the seal, he'd located the hilt and blade hidden in the farmstead's cistern where water was stored.

Closing his eyes, Diello tried to shut out all thoughts of sprites, goblins, and Owain.

He remembered Mamee's words: *Let your bones guide you.*

Diello concentrated. The magic of the border *cloig-wylie* overwhelmed his senses, but gradually, he figured out how to ignore it, to listen deeper. He didn't move; he just listened.

He heard the natural rhythm of the forest around him. The sap in the trees, moving sluggishly through their trunks; the sigh of air through leaves and the sleeping-breaths of the animals hibernating in hollow trunks or dens dug beneath sheltering roots; the decomposition of the leaves, turning slowly into the cold winter soil; a trickle of water slipping over rocks and down a shallow slope, still moving beneath its crust of ice.

And beneath all that, he felt the hilt's power. Its force was something different. It was foreign to the woods. Magic instead of nature. It was barely thrumming, but he found it.

Well? Have you found it?

No, Diello replied in his mind, angry at the interruption. It was obvious now that Owain wasn't monitoring his thoughts or the man wouldn't have needed to ask that question.

Hurry! You're taking too long.

Diello tipped his head back to stare at the sky. He still couldn't see where Owain was hiding. "Stop it!" he shouted. "You're distracting me! Go away!"

I thought you were afraid? You wanted my help.

"I can't focus with you in my head. Leave me alone!"

There was no reply. But Diello no longer felt watched. He didn't hear Iones moving around, either. Diello pushed his fingers into the soil.

Listen, he told himself. *Listen. Eirian . . .*

He found it—the most delicate thread of magic—and this time he stayed calm, controlling his emotions. Carefully, Diello rose to his feet and, using Sight, looked through the forest around him.

He saw through the trees right down to the heartwood at the core of their trunks. He saw beetles living in their bark. Then his vision grew momentarily blurry. When it cleared he understood that Sight was now showing him the past. As though from a distance, he saw several shadowy sprites forming a circle. They were tossing the hilt back and forth.

Again his perspective shifted. He found himself watching a group of goblins rushing into the clearing where the sprites played. The sprites scattered, tossing the hilt aside as they fled for safety. Then the goblins vanished, too.

Holding onto his vision of the clearing, Diello walked and walked until he came to the place where the sprites had played. His Sight faded. He blinked, rubbing his aching eyes. The sun was well up now, filtering through the evergreens. His fingers tightened on his quarterstaff. If the sprites attacked him, he didn't think Owain or Iones would help.

What if the goblins took the hilt when the sprites ran away? This is all for nothing!

The clearing was bigger than it had looked in his vision. Diello searched first along the edges of the trees, hoping to find the hilt and get out of there fast. Finally, he moved into the open and stood where Sight had shown him the hilt had been dropped.

It wasn't there. He tried to use Sight again, but he was too drained and nervous to control his Gift. He kicked at the ground.

His toe connected with something.

Scrambling after it, Diello found a stone. He dropped it and turned around to search the spot again. The hilt wasn't there. *But why did Sight show it to me if it's not here?*

A noise made him jump. It was Iones, stepping out from among the trees.

"What're you doing?" the servant asked. "Find something?"

Diello shook his head.

"Better hurry. Lord Owain's not patient."

"Then maybe he should help us," Diello muttered.

Iones vanished back into the brush. Diello found himself reluctant to leave.

He looked around once more, staring at a drift of fallen leaves. Something didn't seem right. . . . Crouching there, he swept away leaves and saw they'd been covering a tiny hutlike structure made of twigs.

Inside it lay the hilt, balanced on a base of stones!

Did the sprites make an altar for it? Diello didn't care. He put down his quarterstaff and turned the hilt over, brushing it clean. After he rubbed mud off the pommel jewel, he couldn't resist sliding his hand behind the guard and curling his fingers into position.

The hilt fit perfectly in his palm, better than ever.

Make me whole.

A vision of the entire sword, shining white and beautiful, flashed through his thoughts. For a moment he fell under its spell. If only he could keep the sword for himself . . .

But he hadn't forgotten the danger of Eirian's power or how seductive it could be.

He pried his fingers from around the hilt. It fell from his hands into the leaves. Carefully he bent and picked up the hilt by its crosspiece. Time to get out of there.

Diello heard a rustling nearby. "All right, Iones."

But the servant didn't answer. The rustling sound came again, closer.

Carrying the hilt in one hand and his quarterstaff in the other, Diello turned around, wondering if he were already surrounded.

Not again! he thought, and ran.

chapter twenty-four

there was someone in the trees ahead. Diello veered but was tackled from the right. He kicked and fought until a hand gripped his hair.

"Stop it!" Cynthe said. "Are you daft? You nearly took out my good eye."

It was Cynthe all right. Her hair was a tangle. She had an impressive black eye already from Owain's blow. And she was grinning.

"Did you think I was a sprite?" she asked.

He heaved her off and sat up. "Not funny. How did you get here?"

"You can thank Scree," she said, dusting off her hands.

The goblin-boy emerged from the brush, dragging a familiar, leather-wrapped object—Eirian's blade!

"I am very good now at sliding through the bars of my cage," Scree boasted. "I saw you last night when you were taken away into the sky. I went to help Cynthe. Was I not good help to you, Cynthe?"

She patted his shoulder. "Excellent help. Then Scree and I released Vassou. Well, Vassou figured out how to unlock the magic on his cage while I assisted and Scree kept a lookout, and—"

"But how did you get *here?*" Diello interrupted.

"Stole a chariot, of course," she said. She stood up, holding the hilt gingerly.

"You did *what?* But—but how? Don't tell me you caught a lion and handled it all by yourself."

"Well, I did. Mostly." Her coppery-green eyes danced with pride. "First, we made friends with one using food, then Vassou put a spell on it to keep it docile. Scree and I figured out how to hitch it to a chariot. I didn't harness the wagon and plow for Pa all those years for nothing. After that, simple."

Simple? Diello wasn't sure he'd have dared to fly a chariot on his own.

"So where's the chariot?" he asked. "Let's get out of here."

"Uh, we ran into a slight problem on landing."

"We crashed," Scree said solemnly. "There is a broken wheel, and the lion got away."

Cynthe nodded. "I guess it could've been worse."

"I have a scratch," Scree announced, pointing to a gash below his elbow. "I fell out of the chariot and landed in a prickly bush. Then Cynthe found your tracks, and we followed you here."

"Where's Vassou?" Diello asked.

"Keeping a lookout for sprites. So what about you?" Cynthe asked. "How did you get away from Owain?"

"I didn't. He probably saw you land."

"We used a *cymunffyl.*"

"Well, his servant is prowling nearby." Diello glanced around, wondering why Owain's voice wasn't in his thoughts. He pointed at the blade. "How?"

Cynthe smiled a bit smugly.

"I took it," Scree said.

"But you couldn't have," Diello protested. "Clevn must have had it locked up, or hidden inside a spell."

"It was not guarded, Diello," Scree said. "I was out of my cage and prowling. I like to prowl at night. It is something to do."

"But there are guards everywhere."

"They do not see me. I think like a mouse, and I stay low and scurry along the walls. They do not watch for one like me."

"But—but Eirian wouldn't have been lying just anywhere," Diello sputtered. "Clevn isn't stupid."

"It was in his room," Scree said. "I liked that room very much. It was warm and filled with rich things that I would like to have."

"Why were you there? How did you find his quarters?"

"I was not looking for them," Scree said. "I went inside because no one was there. I found many things to take and some good food. I like the food he eats, this important Fae you call Clevn. I like it very much. The cheese was—"

"Never mind the cheese. Are you saying the blade was just lying there, with no one watching over it?"

"It was hidden, but not with magic. I found it under some folded tunics."

"He hid it in his spare clothing," Cynthe said with glee. "The first place any thief searches."

"That's strange," Diello insisted. "Did he want it found?"

"I was not there to steal," Scree corrected Cynthe. "I was just looking."

"But you recognized the blade?" Diello asked.

The goblin-boy puffed out his scrawny chest. "It is like no other. As soon as I saw it, I knew what it was. You and Cynthe would never give it away. I thought you might wish it back."

Diello nodded, brushing his suspicions aside.

"I have made you happy? Then I am happy. It is a good thing I have done."

"Yes, you have done good, Scree," Diello said. "Now we can bargain for Amalina's release. I think if I call to Owain, he'll come back."

"He'll take the sword and cheat us," Cynthe said. "We've got to be smarter this time. We can't trust any of them."

A wolf howled close by.

"That's Vassou's signal!" Cynthe cried, tucking the wrapped blade in her quiver and tossing the hilt to Diello. "Run!"

Diello expected to see Iones, but instead he saw goblins coming toward them. He and Cynthe retreated to the clearing. They stood back to back, with Scree cringing against Diello's side. Diello knew his quarterstaff wasn't much of a match for goblin spears and clubs. Cynthe didn't even nock an arrow to her bowstring. They were completely outnumbered.

"Give me the blade," Diello said to Cynthe.

"No! You mustn't put it together."

"It's the only way to fight them. Please?"

She sighed and handed it over, but before he could unwrap it, a gor-goblin sprang forward, jabbing Diello's forearm with his spear. Crying out, Diello dropped the blade. Another goblin reached for it, but a shout rang out over the noise. All the goblins pulled back while a tall figure approached.

Diello pressed his fingers to his cut. Soon, the smell of his blood would make the goblins go crazy. *Hurry!* he told himself. Gritting his teeth, he reached for the blade again.

A skull-mace smashed down on the blade, pinning it to the ground and just missing Diello's outstretched fingers. Hammered gold gleamed at this goblin's throat and wrists. He wore a black cloak made of human and Faelin skin, and an empty, jeweled scabbard hung from the belt securing his loincloth.

Brezog!

"Touch the sword again, Faelin morsel, and I will cut off those fingers."

The gorlord grabbed both the hilt and the leather-wrapped blade, holding them aloft. All the goblins cheered, brandishing their weapons.

Why didn't I listen to Cynthe and leave Eirian where our parents hid it? Diello thought. *At least it was safe there. Why did I try to be a big hero? Now we've lost Amalina and the sword.*

Goblin drums began beating, and several small bloidy-goblins joined the victory dance while the gor-goblins chanted and clacked their weapons together.

"Let me see that arm," Cynthe said to Diello. Ripping a piece from her tunic hem, she bound his wound.

"What are we going to do?" she asked.

Owain! Diello called in his mind. *Where are you? If you don't hurry, it will be too late!*

The cry of an eagle made Diello look up. The large bird sailed by, and Diello saw more black flecks filling the sky. They weren't birds. They were chariots!

He forced his gaze down. Unaware, the goblins were still celebrating.

"Diello," Cynthe whispered. "I see them, but there are more goblins hiding in the woods."

"A trap?"

"Lord Rhodri told you he'd had reports of goblin maneuvers in this area. It looks like Brezog's got us here as bait."

"Not us," Diello said. "Eirian. With it, Brezog can't lose."

"Should we warn the Fae?" Cynthe asked.

The first of the chariots flew in low over the clearing, and balls of flame hurtled down at the goblins.

Screaming, goblins scattered in all directions. A few threw their spears at the chariots. *Thunk! Thunk! Thunk!* The spears bounced off as the chariots flew by.

Brezog had been struggling to assemble Eirian— hindered by his attempt to avoid touching the blade. Diello recalled the last time Brezog touched the sword and burned his hand. Now, as chunks of fire fell around the gorlord, he tossed down the sword pieces and grabbed Cynthe.

Diello rushed at the gorlord with his quarterstaff, but one of the goblins knocked him down. He saw that the Fae were preparing to make another pass.

"My Faelin shield," Brezog said as he lifted Cynthe above his head. "How loud can you scream?"

"We mean nothing to the Fae!" Diello yelled. "They won't stop for her sake."

"Then she will protect me from Fae fire. Better she burns than I do," the gorlord told him.

Cynthe screamed.

The chariots swooped down again, and more flames shot across the clearing. Ducking, Diello saw several goblins on fire, hopping around as they beat at themselves or rolling on the ground. Pine needles were dry tinder for any stray spark. The clearing filled with smoke.

Diello couldn't tell if Cynthe had been hurt.

Disoriented, he turned around and saw a chariot flying right at him. He flung himself to the ground. The wheels just grazed the top of his hair as the chariot landed. He realized that more chariots were landing on the other side of the clearing, away from the fire, their occupants yelling Fae battle cries. The rest of the army stayed aloft.

Can't they see it's a trap? Diello wondered.

A band of blue light encircled the clearing, forming into a *cloigwylie*. Now Diello understood what the Fae were doing. They'd trapped Brezog instead.

Diello's bones hummed. Looking around, he saw an elaborate chariot circling down in a smooth landing. It was drawn by two black lions. Clevn, clad in armor and a white cloak, handled the reins. The queen stood next to him.

Sheirae also wore armor. Hers was made of shining silver disks. She carried a full-sized bow, and a quiver of silver arrows hung at her waist. Her long hair was pulled back in a cluster of thick braids. Lord Rhodri's chariot landed on their right, and Owain's on their left.

The goblins huddled as far from the chariots as possible, and Brezog was not visible.

Owain jumped from his chariot and headed across the clearing. Meseiros roared.

"Owain!" Clevn commanded. "You're unarmed. Keep your position."

Diello saw his uncle looking at the pieces of Eirian lying where they'd been dropped.

No! Diello thought. *He mustn't get the sword.*

"Owain!" Clevn called again. He pointed at Owain's chariot with his staff.

Angrily, Owain strode back to it.

A hand gripped Diello from behind. He flinched, but it was only Scree.

"No, Diello," Scree said, hunched with fright. "Don't go out there."

"Where's Vassou?"

"Over there." Scree pointed, and Diello saw Vassou crouched near the edge of the clearing, snarling at the goblins. "What will you do for Cynthe?" Scree asked. "I will help you if I know what you plan to do. I am scared for her."

Diello couldn't see Cynthe or Brezog anywhere.

"Brezog!" Clevn called. "If you are hiding among your fighters, come forth."

The gorlord pushed his way into the open with a swagger. He clutched Cynthe in front of him. His dagger was pressed to her throat.

"It has been too long, Sheirae," Brezog said.

The queen's pale eyes flashed. "Release the girl. True warriors do not hide behind children."

The magic in her command seemed to have no effect on Brezog. "Shall I eat her heart for your entertainment?" he said. "It will taste bitter, I think. As bitter as Lwyneth's."

The Fae warriors swore oaths, setting off sparks in the air. Several lions bounded forward before they could be reined back. Even Owain scowled. Sheirae looked carved from stone, but her knuckles were white as she clutched her bow.

"Release the girl," Sheirae said again, and thunder rumbled around them. "This fight is between Fae and goblin. Faelin have no part in it."

"So you wish to think. But I know differently."

Brezog twisted Cynthe's arm behind her. Diello nearly jerked free of Scree's hold.

"Let me go," Diello said furiously.

"You must not," Scree pleaded. "He's trying to trick them. You must not help him."

Brezog turned in Diello's direction. "Come here."

For a moment, Diello thought Brezog was talking to him. Then Scree uttered a moan of despair.

"Son!" Brezog called. "Come to me."

Scree scuttled forward, casting one miserable glance at Diello before going to the gorlord. Diello had once seen Brezog brutally beat Scree and leave him for dead. They couldn't be father and son. They *couldn't* be.

Yet he remembered that Rhodri had said a half-goblin's allegiance is always to the goblins. And there went Scree, obeying Brezog's command.

Vassou howled.

Scree stood before the gorlord, hanging his head. When Brezog pointed, Scree cringed as though expecting a blow.

"Put the sword together," Brezog ordered.

"No!" Owain shouted. He flung a ball of blue flame at Scree, but Brezog's goblin fire hit the Fae magic with a dazzling explosion. Unharmed, Scree sank to his knees.

"Quickly, fool!" the gorlord snarled, giving Scree a kick.

With shaking hands, Scree pulled back a fold of the leather, revealing Eirian's milky-white blade. A gasp rose from the Fae. The goblins yelled with excitement, pressing forward to look.

"Scree, *don't*! " Diello yelled.

But the goblin-boy picked up the hilt and fitted it to the blade. Diello could actually feel the *click* as the pieces snapped together. It was as if Eirian were coming alive inside his mind. Diello saw white light flash around the sword and cried out again, fearing that Scree had been hurt by its power.

But the light faded, and there Scree stood with the sword lying across his palms.

"Give it to me," Brezog said.

Although Scree was whimpering, he held out the weapon to the gorlord.

Brezog shoved Cynthe, knocking her down, and reached for the sword.

"Stop him!" Cynthe gasped.

Diello was already running.

Brezog's claws closed on the sword. He hesitated, but Eirian's power did not strike him. He swung the weapon high. Diello flung himself at the gorlord as Brezog lifted the scabbard in his other hand.

"Sword and scabbard must not unite!" Clevn shouted. "Not for the goblin!"

I can't stop it! Diello thought.

Vassou had told Diello and Cynthe that whoever possessed both sword and scabbard could govern the world. They would all—Fae, human, and Faelin alike—have to serve Brezog.

Suddenly Scree sank his teeth into Brezog's hand. As the gorlord knocked Scree aside, Diello seized the chance. He jumped for Eirian and missed, but managed to rip the scabbard from Brezog's grasp.

The gorlord swung Eirian at Diello. He jumped to one side.

Fae fire streaked toward Brezog without hitting him. The gorlord attacked Diello again, and again Diello dodged the blow.

Another goblin shoved Diello back within Brezog's reach. A goblin spear was thrust between Diello's feet, tripping him. He landed hard on his knees in front of the gorlord.

Brezog loomed over him. "Give me that scabbard!"

Diello twisted around. "Cynthe, catch!"

He threw it with all his might, but his aim was wild. As Cynthe dived for the scabbard, an eagle came from nowhere and caught it in its enormous talons.

Diello felt the triumph of the bird's thoughts: *You are no longer supreme, Sheirae. Now Uruoc's people will know fortune and plenty, too.*

With a flap of its wings, the eagle flew away, and the scabbard was gone.

The Fae warriors were shouting. Diello stared at the sky.

Brezog turned to Diello and raised Eirian above his head. There was a whistling sound, and one of the queen's silver arrows thudded deep into the gorlord's heart.

chapter twenty-five

Brezog staggered. His red eyes stared at nothing.

Diello stumbled away from the dying gorlord. Cynthe put her arm around Diello's waist, hugging him close.

"It's over," she whispered.

But Brezog didn't fall. Still clutching Eirian, he let the sword sink until its tip rested on the ground. Leaning on it, he remained standing, breathing harshly.

Then he lifted the sword, peering at it. "Through its power, I live," he murmured.

"Strike him down, Lord Clevn!" one of the Fae called out. "Finish him!"

Queen Sheirae held up her hand. "Let the magic do its work."

The goblins watched their leader.

Brezog snapped off the arrow in his chest and flung it down.

Clevn pointed with his ivory staff, but the magic that shot from its tip was blocked by Eirian's blade.

"Stop," Sheirae commanded her brother. "Nothing can match its power."

"We can't let him live," Clevn argued.

"The sword keeps him alive," she said. "But the Wheel of Death is turning. If he still possessed the scabbard, my arrow could not have touched him."

"Your Majesty," Lord Rhodri said, "let me fight him. I will wrest Eirian from his hand."

"No. If we fight him now, we'll turn Eirian against us."

"Eirian belongs to the one who holds it," Brezog said to the queen. "One day soon, the last battle between us will come, and all the Fae will die."

"Eirian will poison you," Sheirae said. "You are unworthy of its power. The longer you hold it, the more it will destroy you. And if you let go of it for even a moment, you will die. That is your curse, Gorlord."

Brezog loosened his grip on the sword hilt, only to cry out in pain. At once he tightened his fingers, and a look of relief crossed his face.

"How long can you hold it?" Sheirae asked. "Your hand will grow tired. Will Eirian slip from your grasp while you sleep?"

"Better to be cursed and hold the sword than to wither without it. Eh, Sheirae? Why did you not bring your army down with you? Why did you not seek to destroy my horde? Because your mages are weak, weaker than the last time we met on the field of battle. Your army is weak. *You* are weak." He bared his sharp yellow teeth at her.

Lowering Eirian again, he struck the ground with its tip, and there was a flash of white light mingled with goblin fire. The Fae spell holding back the fire in the forest vanished, and the *cloigwylie* fell. The air filled with smoke.

Flames spread from tree to tree. Sparks and cinders swirled on the breeze, helping to spread the fire.

The chariots charged forward, but they could not maneuver among the trees. Even so, more chariots landed. The Fae warriors fought the goblins on foot until Brezog and the horde escaped.

Diello and Cynthe took cover with Vassou, trying to avoid flames and fighting. After the goblins were gone, the fires were put out with more Fae spells. Chariots flew low over the treetops, but Diello could tell the chase was futile.

Cynthe buried her face in Vassou's ruff. "Oh, Vassou, we failed," she said. "We tried so hard, and for *nothing*."

"Do not cry," Vassou said. "This wasn't your fault."

Leaving the wolf to comfort her, Diello walked over to Scree, who was crouched on the ground, rocking himself from side to side.

"Scree," he said quietly.

The goblin-boy went on rocking. Kneeling beside him, Diello touched his shoulder. Scree flinched.

Then Diello noticed Scree's hands. Both palms had angry red blisters, exactly the width of Eirian's blade. The sword had exacted its price for being mishandled—as it always did. Hunching over, Scree tucked his hands out of sight.

"You need help," Diello said.

Scree shook his head. "Do not bother," he muttered. "You hate me now. Do not pretend kindness."

"I don't hate you," Diello said. "I—I just feel terribly sorry for you. I'll go see if Lord Rhodri's aide has some salve."

"It won't help," Scree said. "Eirian . . ."

Diello located Ffoyd, but the aide showed no interest in assisting Scree. "Let him hurt. He should be put with the other prisoners."

"No. What happened wasn't his fault."

"A goblin's a goblin. Can't be trusted."

"He saved my life," Diello said.

"And lost us the sword!"

"I owe him. Please don't let him suffer so."

Ffoyd sighed. "There's not much that can be done, but I'll see he's treated."

"Thank you."

Finding Cynthe's bow, mercifully undamaged, Diello set about gathering what arrows he could. Most of them were broken or the fletchings crumpled. She had a lot of work ahead. Wondering why Cynthe wasn't searching for her weapon herself, he ran back to where he'd left her and Vassou. They weren't there. He roamed through the crowd of warriors and prisoners until finally he thought he heard her voice. He followed it deeper into the trees and found Vassou lying unconscious.

Diello touched the pup's fur briefly, his fingertips prickling as they brushed across the residue of magic. Cautiously, Diello hurried forward.

Past some bushes, he saw Cynthe sitting on the ground with a noose of blue magic encircling her throat.

Owain was standing over her.

Diello crouched out of sight. His hands balled into fists. He wanted to conjure fire and melt Owain where he stood, but, even if he could, Diello knew that wasn't the answer. He needed a plan before he took action.

"My Penrith will be the next queen," Owain said. "It doesn't matter that Chorl, the queen's samal wolf, refuses to go near her and none of the Auruu pack acknowledges her as the rightful heir. The samals like to think they're important because the queen listens to their counsel, but as soon as Sheirae is gone, I'll break any influence Chorl has. Penrith's been trained to rule since birth, and I won't have her eclipsed by a grubby Faelin girl. You are *not* chosen. You will not cheat her of her future."

"I'm no rival," Cynthe replied, gasping as he tightened the noose. "Please! I've no chance against—"

"As long as you live, as long as any Fae knows about your existence, you're a threat to her. The boy's different. I can make use of him. Can't I, Diello?"

Owain turned his head and stared right at Diello's hiding spot. "Come out."

Diello put down his quarterstaff and approached his uncle, holding an arrow nocked to Cynthe's bow. He was a competent archer, although not in Cynthe's league, but he doubted any arrow could pierce Owain's *cloigwylie*.

"You don't need to kill her," Diello said. "And how will you explain it?"

"The goblins can be blamed."

Owain tightened the noose. Cynthe clutched at her throat. Diello raised the bow, but Owain wrapped himself in a *cloigwylie*, as expected. Then his uncle channeled additional power through Diello, making his *cloigwylie* even stronger.

"Thank you, nephew. I used to have magic as potent as this when Lwyneth and I were as close as the two of you.

With Lwyneth's powers to bolster mine, I was almost as strong as Clevn. Without her, I've been weakened. But now I can defeat him when the time is right."

Cynthe's face was turning blue.

Diello didn't know how to block Owain. His uncle might call himself weak, but to Diello he was still a mage with dangerous powers far beyond an ordinary Fae's. Diello's fear for Cynthe was making it impossible to concentrate. *I can't use Sight as a weapon. Why couldn't I have Voice as a Gift?*

"How can you do this to us?" Diello yelled.

"How could your mother betray me? Better to lose Cynthe like this, boy, than to have her betray you later. A human knight arrived, escorting an envoy of visiting diplomats . . . and Lwyneth threw *everything* away."

Cynthe's struggles grew weaker. Diello loosed an arrow at his uncle, but it missed its mark and bounced harmlessly off a tree. Dropping the bow, Diello ran at Owain, swinging his quarterstaff like a club. The *cloigwylie* absorbed the blow, and Owain wrenched the weapon from Diello's hands.

"As long as you're useful to me, I'll spare you."

But Owain's concentration had slipped. Diello saw Cynthe gulp in a breath before their uncle's noose tightened again. Diello took hold of Owain's magic—the way he used to draw in Cynthe's stormy emotions when she was about to experience a tempest. He reached into Owain's powers and pulled them into himself.

The *cloigwylie* dissolved. Owain flung fire at Diello, but Diello dodged it and pulled again.

His uncle dropped to his knees, and the blue band

around Cynthe's throat disappeared. She lay there limply, her eyes fluttering. But she was breathing.

Diello tried to go to her. Owain jumped up to block him. He held Diello by the shoulders. "It's not over, boy. Amalina—"

"Please," Diello said. "If you ever loved your sister, have mercy on Amie."

Shoving Diello away, Owain hit him with blue fire, knocking him down. Diello's bones burned as he seized the magic, absorbing it. He pushed himself back on his feet, swaying. Another bolt struck him, and he absorbed that, too. A wind swirled around him now, whipping his hair and clothing. The magic he'd captured from Owain swelled inside him, and he flung it aside. The canopy of a nearby tree exploded. Branches and leaves came raining down, and part of the tree fell. It would have crushed Owain had he not jumped into the air, flying away.

The wind died, leaving silence. Owain's grasp on Diello was gone, along with Diello's hold on his uncle's powers. Diello brushed off twigs and dust, breathing hard as he tried to calm the tingling in his bones. *Someday*, he thought, *I'm going to learn how to command wind and lightning, too.*

"Lord Owain?" Rhodri called out, crashing through the brush. "Her Majesty wishes a word with you."

Diello rubbed his forehead and took an unsteady step toward Cynthe.

"Lord Owain?" Rhodri stopped. "Great Hand of Mobidryn! What happened here? Has Owain been fighting goblins with mage-fire?"

"I—I—"

Everything blurred around Diello, and he collapsed. He felt Rhodri lift him and tap his cheek.

"Wake up, my boy. Can you hear me?"

"Yes," Diello whispered. He opened his eyes while Rhodri steadied him on his feet. "I'm all right. But Cynthe!" Diello bent over her.

"Here now." Rhodri knelt beside him. "A battle site is no place for the pair of you. Has she been overcome by the smoke?" He took out a flask and held it to Cynthe's lips, coaxing a dribble of liquid into her.

She swallowed, then started coughing. They pounded her back until she twisted away from them, clutching her throat.

"What is that?" she asked.

"The finest Imjarian nectar. A special stock I always keep on hand." Rhodri nodded at her. "It can cure anything. Better now?"

"But you don't understand," Cynthe said hoarsely.

"Yes, I do, child. I understand everything."

chapter twenty-six

Wary of the general's unexpected kindness, Diello met his eyes. "But how can you? How do you know?"

Rhodri didn't answer. "Run along. Ffoyd has some food if you're hungry. Get that arm seen to properly. Then report to the queen. I have to find Owain."

The twins didn't move. *We've no reason to trust this man,* Diello thought, *so why do I want to?*

"Have you ever heard of a prophecy about Eirian?" Diello asked.

Rhodri shook his head. "I'm not a religious man. No time for prophecies and old legends."

"But there's something, isn't there?" Diello persisted. "Uncle Owain mentioned it, but he didn't explain."

"Well, ask him then, not me. Go and do as I've told you. I'm busy."

Not too busy to stop and check on us when you saw we needed help, Diello thought. *You don't dislike us as much as you pretend.*

Diello and Cynthe went back to look for Vassou, but the pup had gone.

"Owain ambushed us," Cynthe explained. "He knocked

out Vassou with magic, and then he was choking me. Where could Vassou be?"

"Come on," Diello said. "We'll look for him later."

Together they made their way back across the clearing. Cynthe was limping, and she kept touching her throat. Diello could see a bruised line around her neck.

Ffoyd looked harried as he strode here and there— checking on the injured, overseeing repairs to damaged chariots, soothing agitated lions, keeping the Fae from taunting the small number of goblin prisoners. Rather than bother him, Diello fetched food from a supply wagon that had landed. He also filched a damp cloth from one of the healers. He and Cynthe shared it, taking turns cleaning their faces and hands.

"Do you want to talk about it?" Cynthe asked Diello.

"Do you?"

She shook her head. "I can't sort out my feelings right now."

Vassou, his fur smudged with soot, joined them and flopped down tiredly. "I'm sorry," he said. "I failed to pro-tect you."

"You did your best," Cynthe said. "At least he didn't kill you."

"I have not served either of you well," Vassou went on. "I failed to detect Canthroy and the goblin shape-shifters, and I didn't know Scree would betray you. I am still young, with much to learn."

"None of us could have guessed about Scree," Diello told him. "You can't blame yourself. We couldn't have got-ten this far without you."

Vassou pressed his nose to Diello's hand.

"Look," Cynthe said. "There's Scree."

The goblin-boy sat on the ground a short distance away from the other prisoners. His hands and feet were bound, and his head was bowed. Someone had treated his burns.

"I wonder if he really is Brezog's son, or if Brezog was forcing him to obey," Diello said. "Maybe both are true."

"Don't defend him!" Cynthe replied. "He was supposed to be our friend."

An aide came for them. Wearily, Diello, Cynthe, and Vassou followed the man. Diello grew conscious of the warriors watching them, looking in particular at Cynthe, her bow, and the samal pup. *She's a younger version of the queen*, Diello thought with pride. *They all see it.*

The twins approached where the queen and Clevn stood talking. When their grandmother and great-uncle turned to face them, Clevn seemed to realize how the men were staring. His face puckered with annoyance, but Sheirae's gaze stayed on Diello and Cynthe. There was regret and longing in her eyes. *She saved our lives*, Diello thought. *She didn't have to.*

"That wolf is Kannae. He's forbidden to enter the queen's presence," Clevn said.

Vassou stopped at once. Diello stopped, too.

Cynthe put her hand on Vassou's head. "We belong together," she said.

The queen's black samal bristled and advanced stiff-legged to sniff the pup. Vassou calmly allowed it.

Ignoring the wolves, Sheirae said to Diello and Cynthe, "I am most seriously displeased with you both. Owain has explained the matter to me."

Cynthe said, "But he—"

Clevn lifted his staff. "Do not interrupt Her Majesty!"

"It's obvious you are not used to discipline," Sheirae said. "You've had no training. Your Gifts are evidently strong, but you lack proper knowledge in how to use them. Nor do you seem able to govern your rash impulses." She paused. "Were we so unkind to you that you felt you had to steal back the blade and run away? If Owain had not seen you sneaking out of the palace and followed, what might have become of you here?"

Diello and Cynthe exchanged looks.

"Were you that unhappy? I didn't expect you to jeopardize Eirian's safety just because you disliked us."

"That's not—" Diello began.

"Your Majesty," the black wolf interrupted. "This pup smells of mage-fire. May I examine the girl?"

"Is it necessary, Chorl?"

"May I?" the black wolf repeated.

The queen nodded, and the wolf approached Cynthe.

"I wish to put my muzzle to your throat," the wolf said to her. "Do not be frightened. I will not harm you."

"Vassou?" Cynthe asked.

"He is pack leader of the Auruu Clan," Vassou replied. "He is very wise, Cynthe."

Diello guessed what Vassou was trying to tell them. *Chorl will discover that Owain tried to hurt her.* "Let him," Diello said to his twin.

Cynthe bent over for Chorl to sniff her throat. The black wolf then stepped back. "Thank you," he said.

Diello was surprised when the wolf remained silent. *Is Chorl afraid to speak out against Owain?* But the black wolf didn't look as though he feared anyone. He lowered his front legs and bowed first to Cynthe and then to Diello before he retreated to the queen's side.

Diello didn't dare glance at his sister, but he saw Owain watching in the crowd.

Owain said that the queen's wolf won't go near Penrith, Diello thought, *but he just bowed to us. Maybe the queen will accept us now.*

But Sheirae ignored what Chorl had done.

"Are you so childish that you cannot understand the difference between what a queen wishes to do and what duty requires of her? The difficulties between your mother and myself involve larger issues than I think you realize."

"We weren't getting back at you, if that's what you think," Diello said.

"Heedless, foolish, careless. You've endangered many lives today and led my army into a near-fatal trap," Sheirae continued.

"That's not fair," Cynthe said. "Don't you care about our side of this?"

"I've heard it!" The queen's voice was sharp. "Owain has been your advocate, but no matter what he says, I blame you for what's happened. How shall we begin to count the cost of it?" She pointed at Scree. "This creature you brought among us—"

Diello squared his shoulders. "Your Majesty, I don't expect you to be pleased. We did our best, but—well, we're sorry."

"And a feeble apology is supposed to be sufficient? We're in worse danger than before."

"What can Brezog do?" Cynthe asked. "He's got the sword, but he can't use it. You said your curse will kill him."

"Not soon enough. And just the thought of Eirian in that creature's possession is unbearable."

"Diello stopped him from having its full power," Cynthe said. "The scabbard—"

"—is lost," the queen concluded.

"Can't some of your men fly after that eagle? If Diello could find the hilt in this clearing with his Faelin senses, why can't Fae hunt down the scabbard?"

"The 'eagle,'" Sheirae snapped, "was a Tescorsian shape-shifter, and Tescorsa is no ally of ours."

That eagle flying around the day the sprites attacked me, Diello thought, *was it after Eirian then?* "Who—or what— is Uruoc?"

"King of the Tescorsians," Clevn said. "How do you know of him?"

"Something I heard," Diello replied.

"Can't the Fae army invade Tescorsa and demand the scabbard's return?" Cynthe asked.

"It is not that simple," Sheirae said.

"You don't want the other realms to know Embarthi isn't as powerful as it used to be," Diello said.

"No one expects you to understand," Clevn broke in. "All you've done is share Eirian with our enemies."

"I had decided to keep you near me," the queen told them. "I thought we might achieve some sort of relationship.

But now I've reconsidered. It's too dangerous to have you in Embarthi. There are rumors enough, and what's been witnessed today will only fuel them."

Cynthe protested, "But we—"

"There will be no more discussion or excuses. You are banished from my realm. This is my will."

"Your will be done," the warriors around her declared.

We have Owain to thank for this. Diello took a step toward the queen, determined to reveal the truth. *But what about Amalina? The queen didn't listen when we mentioned Amie before. She won't help.* He faltered.

Clevn stepped between them, pushing Diello away. "Your audience is over," he said.

The queen watched without a word. *She doesn't want to know the truth*, Diello realized.

Orders rang out, and chariots lifted into the sky. As Sheirae walked to hers with Chorl at her heels, Diello turned to the mage-chancellor.

Look at me with Sight, Diello thought. *See what really happened!*

He felt something shiver through him and tried to open his mind to his great-uncle.

"Clevn!" Sheirae called.

The mage-chancellor hurried to step into her chariot. Gathering the reins, Sheirae sent her pair of lions soaring into the sky.

Diello watched them go. *She never really wanted us. She didn't want to like us. She never gave us a chance.*

More chariots lifted. Owain was among the few that lingered behind.

"Satisfied?" Diello called out.

Owain pulled Diello aside and lowered his voice. "I won't kill Amalina, but I'll make sure she forgets you. She will never know who you are. And if you or Cynthe ever dare set foot in Embarthi again, if either of you speak to Clevn or the queen about any of this, I'll sell Amalina to the goblins. Is that understood?"

"Yes," Diello said.

Owain strode away, brushing past Rhodri, and got into his chariot with his servant.

Tears glistened in Cynthe's eyes. She ducked her head, petting Vassou.

chapter twenty-seven

As soon as Owain left, Rhodri snapped his fingers, and his aide brought a bundle from the supply wagon. "Here's warm clothing and more food," the general said. "If I thought it could escape notice, I'd let you shelter through the winter in my mountain lodge. But I've no mind to be arrested for treason."

Diello took the bundle. "Did you overhear what Owain just said to me?"

"I didn't have to. I told you I understand the situation. And I'm not the only one who does."

"Who else?" Diello asked.

"I'm not at liberty to say." Rhodri pointed northeast. "If you go in that direction, you'll come to an Antrasin town. A squalid place, but maybe someone will take you in and give you work."

"Indenturing ourselves?" Cynthe asked.

"That might be too drastic a choice. But you have to winter somewhere. And the queen may soften."

Diello doubted it. "Which way is Tescorsa?" he asked.

"You can't go there," Rhodri told him. "It's a cold,

barbarous place, all mountains and precipices, fit only for Tescorsians . . . and a few goats. You'll find no settlements there. The people live in isolated houses. You'll freeze and starve before you ever reach the royal eyrie."

"The what? The royal nest?"

"Not quite. Eyrie is the word the Tescorsians use for their king's palace. It's perched high in the cliffs, on the tallest peak. Don't attempt that quest. You're not up to it."

"What about him?" Diello nodded toward Scree.

"His fate is up to you. Do you want him killed?"

Diello shook his head. Vassou pressed against him, putting a paw on his foot in agreement.

"Why should we have to deal with him?" Cynthe asked.

"You brought him here," Rhodri replied. "You are responsible for what happens to him."

"Set him free," Diello said.

"As you wish." Rhodri stepped into his chariot.

Ffoyd waved his hands, and Scree's shackles vanished.

The remaining chariots were lifting, one by one. In a moment, Rhodri would be gone. *I can't leave things this way*, Diello thought.

"Vassou, can you put a small *cloigwylie* around me and the general? So we can talk privately?"

"No, Diello!" Cynthe said. "Remember Owain's threat. Someone's bound to tell him about this."

Diello wouldn't look at his twin. "Just do it, Vassou. Please."

Diello went running after Rhodri with Cynthe at his

heels. "Wait!" Diello said, gripping the chariot's side. "I have to talk to you. I have to ask you something."

"I've done all I can," the general replied.

"I'm risking my sister's life to speak to you. Won't you just listen?"

Rhodri hesitated, then lowered his reins and nodded at his aide. As Ffoyd walked away, the *cloigwylie* shimmered around the twins and the general.

"Little fools," Rhodri growled. "Why not make a public announcement that we're conspiring together?"

"The queen won't listen to us, thanks to Owain's lies, but someone has to," Diello said.

"I told you once to take your troubles to Clevn. If you mean to accuse Owain of treason, you'd best have proof. Otherwise, he's untouchable."

Cynthe rubbed her throat. "Is this proof enough?"

"If I'd seen him harming you, it would be different. I didn't." Rhodri sighed. "I'm sorry. Political games are never pleasant. You're part of them now."

"Hear me out," Diello insisted. "Owain kidnapped our little sister to force us to bring Eirian to him. Now he's threatened to sell her to the goblins if we talk about what he's doing."

"Then you just sealed her fate."

"He's too angry. I think he means to hurt Amie whether we keep silent or not."

"You don't know that, Diello," Cynthe said. "You're risking her life, and for what? There's nothing Lord Rhodri can do for us."

"I'm not entirely without influence, child."

"Exactly," Diello said. "Lord Rhodri commands the army. The queen trusts you, doesn't she?"

"I doubt she will after she finds out I've talked to you like this."

"Will you help Amalina? Can you find her? Rescue her? Stop Owain from hurting her?"

Rhodri was looking uncomfortable. "Do you know what you're asking? Owain is the queen's son. If I meddle in his affairs, I stand to lose—"

"He betrayed our mother to the goblins so they'd kill her," Diello said. "He admitted it."

"He *boasted* about it," Cynthe added.

The color left Rhodri's face. "My poor Lwyneth," he whispered.

"You warned us about Owain from the first, and you were right," Diello went on. "He's a monster. And Amalina's only a small child."

"For your mother's sake, I'll do what I can."

"Thank you!"

"I promise no results, mind you." But the grim determination in the general's voice satisfied Diello that at least he would try.

"I have to ask you something else," Diello said. "What really happened with our parents? Why did they take Eirian?"

"Great Guardian, boy! It's forbidden to talk about that."

"We want to know. We deserve the truth."

"I suppose you do. But you won't like it."

"Tell us," Cynthe said.

Rhodri sighed again. "You think your grandmother's harsh, but she has to be. She's ruled a long time. Lwyneth was her favorite. It nearly killed Sheirae when your mother decided to balance power among the realms by giving Eirian to the Antrasins."

"Is that why she and Pa took it?" Diello asked.

"You were asking earlier about the prophecy. Well, you're right. There's an old one that says Eirian belongs in Antrasia. The Afon Heyrn has tried to suppress it for years, of course."

"But—but why there? Why with them? Antrasins can't work magic."

"I don't know or care. The reason's lost in antiquity. Most Fae—myself included—believe that if our ancestors were smart enough to seize possession of the sword and gain prosperity for Embarthi, we should leave well enough alone."

"Eirian must be returned," Diello whispered. *Returned to Antrasia? I completely misunderstood Pa.*

Cynthe looked bewildered. "Why didn't our parents give it to the Antrasin king?"

"Afraid to, probably," Rhodri said.

"Pa wasn't afraid of anything!"

"Your father was badly wounded coming out of Embarthi. Your mother worked a powerful spell to throw off her Fae pursuers."

"Were you one of them?" Diello asked.

"I was. They made it through the border *cloigwylie* and disappeared. We couldn't trace her magic after that."

"She gave up her magic to keep Eirian safe," Diello said.

"That much we guessed. We couldn't go into Antrasia after them." Rhodri paused. "The humans are touchy about invading armies on their soil. I was certain that Stephel would hole up in his home shire, but the baron governing there shielded him and wouldn't give him up."

"Lord Malques," Diello said. "They used to be friends."

"Well, Clevn complained to the Antrasin king and threatened war. Of course, he couldn't say a word about Eirian, but he got his point across. To appease us, the king stripped your father of his rank and expelled him from his order. Since then, no Carnethie Knight has ever again been sent to the Liedhe Court as an Antrasin diplomat."

So Pa wasn't a thief, Diello thought. *He was trying to do the right thing, like always. And so was Mamee.*

"Eirian belongs here," Rhodri said, watching them both. "The Fae have guarded it and never misused it. You need to understand that what your parents did was wrong. And look who has Eirian now."

"I hope Brezog dies soon," Cynthe said.

"I don't," Rhodri replied. "May it be a long, lingering, nasty death."

"Either way, we don't deserve to be banished," Diello said. "Owain and Brezog are to blame for what happened today."

"Her banishing you may have saved both your lives if it puts you out of Owain's reach. After all, this makes two attempts against you that you've survived."

"Then she knows?" Cynthe asked.

"Don't look so surprised," Rhodri said. "The queen's no fool."

"She should punish Owain instead of us," Cynthe declared.

A small smile came from the general. He said nothing.

"It's not a punishment, is it?" Diello said. "Not really. She can't take her army across Antrasia to go after Brezog, but we can go wherever we like."

"You mean she *wants* us to go after him?" Cynthe asked, frowning.

"Maybe she does. Am I right, Lord Rhodri?"

"I do not speculate about the queen."

"We need your help," Diello said.

"Ask no more from me. I've granted one favor and answered far too many questions. As long as you're under an order of banishment, it's treason to assist you."

"Aren't you doing that now?" Diello asked. "Giving us supplies? Advising us?"

"A simple courtesy, that's all. Children should not be thrown out into the cold without a few comforts."

"What if we return with Eirian? All of it, next time?" Cynthe asked. "Will she unbanish us?"

"Unbanish?"

"Whatever the proper term is."

Rhodri kept his gaze above her head. "I do not speculate about the queen," he repeated. "Now I must part ways with you."

At Diello's signal, Vassou dropped the *cloigwylie*. Rhodri shouted to Ffoyd to join him.

"Farewell, children," Rhodri said. "Good luck to you all."

Diello and Cynthe watched his chariot soaring into the afternoon sky. The woods seemed very quiet.

Vassou nudged Diello's ankle. "Scree is sneaking away. Do you wish him to go?"

Diello saw Scree creeping into the woods. "Scree!" he called. "Stop him, will you, Vassou?"

Vassou trotted after the goblin-boy.

"We can't keep him with us," Cynthe said. "We can't trust him."

"Until Scree mends, he's helpless out here," Diello said. "It's not his fault if Brezog is his father. Besides, we need a guide if we're to track down Brezog."

"Then you're determined to do it, to get the sword back?"

"Of course I am," Diello said.

"If we catch up with Brezog, what will stop Scree from betraying us again?" Cynthe asked.

"Maybe nothing," Diello admitted. "But I know what it's like to have someone take over my thoughts, trying to force my obedience. We owe Scree a second chance."

"I suppose you're right," Cynthe said. "So where do we head first? Tescorsa or back across Antrasia to Brezog's territory?"

Diello turned toward the far mountains, in the direction the eagle had flown. "The scabbard first, and then the sword."

"Remember what Rhodri said. That we'll freeze and starve if we travel through Tescorsa in the winter."

"And then he gave us special clothing and food," Diello reminded her. "No matter what he says, it can't be impossible. Now that Brezog's not on our trail, we can use as much of our magic as we want."

Cynthe nodded. "We owe it to Mamee and Pa, don't we?"

"And Amalina."

As Vassou and Scree joined them, Diello held out his hand, and Cynthe clasped it in a hard shake.

"We're making a new pact to continue the quest," Diello announced. "Are you with us, Vassou?"

The wolf pup placed his paw atop their hands. "Yes."

"Are you with us, Scree?"

The goblin-boy's eyes filled with gratitude. "You can forgive me?" he whispered. "You can let me stay with you after—after—"

"Are you with us?" Diello repeated, but gently.

Scree put his injured hand very lightly atop theirs. "I am with you."

Coming in Spring 2013

the faelin chronicles

Book Three